I, RODION

ALEXANDRA PUGACHEVSKY

ISBN:979-8-9923881-4-5 (Paperback)
979-8-9905465-8-5 (eBook)
Author: Alexandra Pugachevsky
Cover Design: Damonza and Diego Catto Val
Editor: Mark Swift

- Website: sashkina.com
- Instagram: @sashkina_author
- Facebook: @sashkina.author
- Email: sasha@sashkina.com

CHAPTER 1

PAPA

'd been waiting for this day all my life. All almost five years of it.

"Go have something to eat, Rodion. Auntie Lena is here. She'll make you a sandwich." Mama waved toward the kitchen, where I heard the clanking of cutlery. I walked in and saw our tiny kitchen table completely covered in dirty dishes. It reeked of alcohol. Several empty bottles of vodka stood by the wall.

"Rodion, here is a cheese sandwich. You gotta hurry and eat. The taxi will be here in twenty minutes." Auntie Lena handed me a plate and disappeared. Auntie Lena was Mama's best friend, and like family.

"Hey, dork," I heard Sergei's voice. My older brother walked into the kitchen, ruffled up my hair, and gave me a rueful smile. "Ready for the big day?" He winked at me, and, without waiting for an answer, left. I sat down at the kitchen table, pushing the dirty dishes to the side, and chewed on my sandwich.

America! I thought dreamily. From the corridor, I heard the sound that had become familiar in the last few days. A suitcase being opened and closed, followed by Mama's sigh.

Mama had been trying to pack our most important possessions into the six suitcases we would take with us to America. Two for each one of us. Mama, Sergei, and me.

My whole life, it was always the three of us. Mama, Sergei, and me. And I liked it that way. Papa was a fairy tale character. Mama told me stories about him right before I went to sleep, shortly after reading me a story. So, it was the three little pigs, and then Papa. Or Cinderella, and then Papa.

"One day, Papa will bring us to America. And then, we'll live in a big house, on a pretty street, in a city called Pittsburgh." This was the story I heard right before falling asleep, night after night. "Papa works very hard, and soon we'll all move there. Very soon, Rodion." The fairy tale had lots of details, like how big and strong Papa was, how handsome, how hard he worked, how much he loved me, and how badly he wanted to see me. "Papa can't wait to meet you, Rodion. He loves you very much."

Sometimes, when Mama wasn't too tired, she told me the story of how she and Papa met at The Lab. The Lab was part of some secret Research Institute, and Mama worked there as a technician. The story of how Mama and Papa met was part of family lore, just as much as the fairy tale of how Papa waited for us in America.

"Sergei had just started second grade, and I was late for work one day. I had to drop your brother off, you see. So, I was rushing, not paying attention to where I was going, and a handsome guy bumped into me in the corridor."

"And that was Papa?" I'd ask, eyes wide, staring at Mama in excitement. The story never got old.

"Yes! That was Papa! He was just like a prince. He came to The Lab and swept me off my feet!" Mama would stare into the distance, lost in thought.

"And then what happened?"

"And then Papa and I went to see a movie. And then he

got me flowers. And a few months later, I learned that I'd have a little boy."

"Me?" I'd ask. Fortunately for Mama, back then, I wasn't very concerned with the exact mechanics of how watching a movie or getting flowers led to a baby.

"Yes, sweetheart, that was you. And then you were born. And I named you after your grandfather. Rodion."

"Your papa?"

"Yes, sweetheart, my own papa. It's a very special name. It means heroic and brave. And you're my little hero."

Then Mama would usually get very quiet. All I knew about my grandfather was that he died when Mama was young and that she barely knew him. The only thing remaining from my grandfather was a two-tome edition of *The Count of Monte Cristo* published in 1946, and a hunting knife engraved with my grandfather's name.

Rodion Likharev.

And that was my name, too.

Mama, Sergei, and I all had her maiden name, and it was to honor her papa, Grandpa Rodion.

"One day, sweetheart, when you're older, you'll inherit your grandfather's knife. It's already got your name written right here."

Mama would take out the hunting knife and show me, allowing me to feel the steel, its cool blade, and run my finger on it. Then, she'd put it away and open up *The Count of Monte Cristo*.

I don't remember the first time Mama read it to me, but by the time I was five, I knew the story of the Count and his miraculous escape from Château d'If by heart. Mercédès was the prettiest name any woman could have, and Edmond Dantès was a courageous man, whose pursuit of taking justice into his own hands was the moral of the story.

And now, the knife, and the two-volume edition of *The*

Count of Monte Cristo, were safely packed in our suitcases and coming with us to America.

To Papa.

———

July 14, 1995

We landed in Pittsburgh in the middle of a historic heat wave. It was the first time flying for all of us, even Mama. Too nervous to sleep on the plane, we were exhausted by the time we landed. As soon as we got out of the plane, we saw him standing right at the gate. Papa.

I recognized him right away, though he didn't look quite like the superhero I'd imagined. Papa's height was average, and so was his build. He had a receding hairline, and his eyes were small and shifty. And when he reached to kiss Mama, I noticed he had a paunch.

"Rodion," Papa said gravely. I'd imagined this moment so many times, and now it was happening in real life. I immediately hid behind Mama's back.

"He's just shy." Mama kissed me on the cheek. "He needs a bit of time."

"Of course, of course." Papa's voice was a deep baritone.

"Sergei, say hi," Mama said, and turned to my older brother. Sergei grunted something akin to a greeting.

"Hey there, sport!" Papa slapped Sergei's hand.

"My boys. All of you together," Mama mouthed, teary-eyed.

"Welcome to America!" Papa led us to the baggage carousel. "In America, you have to think of everything. If you don't, life gets expensive. Boris lent me his car, because I knew you'd have lots of luggage." Papa wiped beads of sweat off his forehead, pushing the cart loaded with our belongings.

Outside, the heat slapped us. It was nothing like I'd ever experienced before. The air felt thick and moist.

"Do you wanna see your new house?" Papa turned to me. I was still too shy to speak, but nodded in agreement, peeking out from behind Mama.

On the drive from the airport, I fell asleep and didn't wake up until the following morning in a strange bed.

———

On our first morning in America, Papa took us grocery shopping.

"An American supermarket is like nothing you've seen in Russia," Papa gushed, as we walked out of the house and turned the corner onto Greenfield Avenue. We approached a large, gray building that occupied an entire block. As we entered, I felt a blast of cold air and shivered.

"This is incredible! So many options!" Mama gasped.

"Welcome to the land of plenty," Papa chuckled. "But in America, people save. This store has coupons, so every week, you gotta check what's on sale first. You don't just buy things, you check for the coupons." He took a bright paper with colorful photos of packages and stuck it under Mama's nose. "See? That's how shopping is done in America. You gotta be careful with spending, Lydia." He gave Mama a careful stare.

"Of course, honey." Mama's cheeks turned pink.

"I'm not a rich man, you see. I'm just getting settled here," Papa said, looking around the supermarket as if seeking approval from the other customers. "Of course, we could have waited a few more years, but you were in a rush because of Sergei. And I understand, he's fifteen, and you don't want him to deal with the army."

Papa picked up an onion and placed it in our cart. "I know, I know the Russian army is scary, but if he had shown more academic promise, that wouldn't have been an issue. So, here we are. I'm just two years into my job, and in America they can fire you like that." He snapped his fingers. "It's not like back home, not like that at all. It's cutthroat here." Papa moved his hand across his neck and I noticed it had loose skin. I'd never looked closely at a man's neck before and kept staring in fascination. Papa took my expression for admiration and his eyes lit up. "Good, good, I can see at least my son is paying attention."

"Of course he is, honey. Rodion is very bright." Mama took me by the hand. We were now in the dairy aisle.

"Oh, so, what's important is the type of food that you buy. Coupons, of course, but also, here is some cheese, for example." Papa took a package with bright orange slices and handed it to Mama.

"What's this, honey?" she asked, flipping it in her hands.

"That's cheese. Special American cheese. It's not what we're used to, but that's what Americans eat. So, I want the kids to get used to it. I don't want them being like all those immigrants, hanging on to what's familiar. We gotta get the kids Americanized, and quickly."

"Of course, honey." Mama nodded and gave me a doubtful look.

I clutched her hand as she obediently put the cheese in the cart.

CHAPTER 2
VLADA

Just a few weeks later, on August 8, I turned five years old, and Papa announced I was old enough to go to kindergarten.

"It's free and there is an elementary school down the street."

"But he's only five. Maybe we can keep Rodion at home for one year? It's a big adjustment," Mama fussed.

"It's better that it happens right away. Otherwise, what's he going to do, sitting at home all day long?" Papa furrowed his brow. The implication, of course, was that she was sitting at home all day long.

"And you? You want to learn how to speak English?" Papa turned to me now. I wasn't afraid of him anymore and responded with confidence.

"Yes."

"Good boy!"

Before I knew it, the first day of kindergarten arrived. Mama packed my lunch, and we walked together to the bus stop, while I clutched her hand for safety. The yellow bus came, rumbling down the street. I got in and ended up in a seat next to two little girls, right in the front.

One of them spoke to me. She had light brown pigtails and big brown eyes. She was smiling, opening and closing her mouth, and I understood absolutely nothing. It took all my willpower not to break into tears.

We pulled up to an enormous building, and I followed the crowd inside. Before I knew it, I was in a classroom, shriveling in terror. The day passed in a blur. I understood nothing.

At the end of the day, after getting off the bus, as soon as I saw Mama waiting for me at the stop, I ran outside, my lower lip trembling.

"How's my little guy?" she asked.

I started crying. I wept so hard, as I've never cried in my whole life. Mama squatted next to me, hugged me, kissed my tear-streaked face, trying to console me.

"I don't wanna go back! I don't wanna!" I cried and cried, and then, when I couldn't anymore, I hiccuped.

"Oh, my sweet little boy, come on, let's go home and have a snack." Mama led me up Greenfield Avenue to our house.

That's when I noticed a woman standing on top of the hill, hands on her hips. To my horror, she was staring directly at us, and, from the concerned expression on her face, it was evident she'd witnessed my meltdown. Mama must have noticed the woman, too, for she squeezed my hand and we continued to climb up the steep hill.

"What's she doing there?" Mama mumbled under her breath. We were the only Russians on our street and no one understood us. I looked down at the ground and quickened my pace.

"Good day," the woman said in perfectly accented Russian, and I gasped. She was dressed like an American: practical beige pants, matching sandals, and a short-sleeved pink top with a collar. She looked older, her short hair streaked with gray. "What's your name, little guy?" The woman leaned over. "Why the tears?" She continued speaking in Russian, leaving no doubt as to her origins.

"My name is Vlada." She extended her hand to me. I didn't take it.

"This is Rodion," Mama responded, putting her hand over me in a protective gesture.

"What a beautiful name. Traditional, Russian." The woman nodded in approval. Her voice was unusually deep, almost like a man's.

"I am Lydia," Mama said. "You're Russian!" she added unnecessarily.

"Oh, yes, we moved here five years ago, from Novosibirsk." Vlada flashed a victorious smile. Five years was my entire lifetime.

"How nice. We are from Moscow. Moved here last month."

"Oh? I can't tell from your accent."

"I was born in Kolomna," Mama said. I looked up at her with surprise. This part of her biography had never been mentioned before.

"That's good. Muscovites are so snobby. Dreadful people," Vlada said, without missing a beat. "And you seem like a nice lady. A month is nothing. How are you adjusting to America?"

"Oh, just fine. We came here to join my husband. And he's settled in Pittsburgh." There was pride in Mama's voice. Her words sounded just like the fairy tales she'd told me when I was little, about my strong papa welcoming us with open arms in America, and I also straightened up.

"What's going on with the little guy? I have three boys of my own. If you ever need help, or some advice, come by. I'm happy to be of assistance."

"Oh, thank you. But we're fine. We're just going home. First day of school." Mama started moving uphill suddenly, as if regretting taking this stranger into her confidence, and pulled me along.

"Well, don't let me keep you," Vlada said, panting slightly, but following us. "I live right down the street. Right on top of this hill." She pointed into the distance.

"Alright." Mama turned around, still gripping my hand tightly. Forced to come to an abrupt stop, I tripped and fell. Immediately, I started crying again. "What now?!" Mama yelped, then, noticing my knee, turned to Vlada in exasperation: "Listen, it's not a good time."

"I've been through it all," Vlada spoke over my cries of agony. "Listen, let me help you."

"I don't need any help!" Mama screamed, and the next moment she, too, was weeping. Red blotches appeared on her cheeks, and she sniffled. "I just can't take it anymore." Mama smudged her mascara. "You're the first person who's been kind to me here."

"Oh, my dear." Vlada shook her head. "America is a tough place, initially, but you'll get used to it. I'm so glad I ran into you two. It was like God told me to go for a walk at exactly this time, so I can help you."

"I just don't know what to do," Mama admitted, completely ignoring me and my scraped knee. "I really am about to give up."

"Oh, dear, dear, let me walk the two of you back," Vlada fussed. "Come on, Rodion, let's help your mama out."

Vlada turned to me and, gently but firmly, ordered: "You lead the way!"

I clenched my jaw, and, proud of this responsibility, walked uphill toward our house. It was only a short walk, up the hill and then to the right, but I felt like a general leading an army. I could hear Mama speaking to Vlada, their muffled voices behind me, but I didn't turn around. Not even once. Five minutes later, we were standing on our porch, Mama fumbling for the keys.

"And here we are."

"Oh! So, you're Philip's wife? I should have guessed!"

Vlada exclaimed when Mama opened the front door. "But I've known him since he first moved here."

"You have?" Mama took her shoes off. "Please, here are some slippers."

She offered a pair to Vlada, who had already taken off her sensible beige sandals.

"Oh, yes, of course, we were the first Russians to buy homes in this neighborhood. Philip and us, we bought houses just a month apart. And used the same real estate agent, Tatiana. She introduced us. Tatiana's clients all know each other."

"I had no idea." Mama led Vlada to the kitchen. "Have a seat, please, and let me make you a cup of tea."

"I'm not a fan of tea. Though I do like strong beverages." Vlada let out a giggle that sounded like a horse's neigh. "If you catch my drift."

"Of course, yes. But I'm not sure if I have anything to offer you right now." Mama turned her head frantically around the kitchen, then rushed to the freezer. "Vodka maybe?" Mama held out a large bottle.

"Oh, don't worry about it. I prefer cognac. It does wonders for my high blood pressure." Vlada said. "And your boy is just adorable."

"Rodion!" Mama remembered me.

I'd been standing in the doorway, still wearing my back-pack. The blood on my scraped knee had now dried. I must have been a sad sight, because immediately Mama let out a squeal.

She rushed to me and gave me a hug.

"Your knee! How is it?" She squatted next to me, then, noticing my bag, fussed. "Oh, sweetheart, take your bag off. Oh, my poor baby." She led me to the chair, and I sat down. Mama then changed her mind, made me get up, and walked me to the kitchen sink, where she proceeded to wash my scraped knee, mumbling to herself. Once Mama was done, she told me to go be a good boy and wait for her in the living room.

I was getting hungry. I hadn't eaten since that morning and had been too shy to have lunch at school, but I found our new acquaintance to be extremely intimidating, so I sat on the couch and waited. I heard the clanking of glasses and Vlada announce in her low voice, "Na zdorovye!"

I am not sure how much time had passed by, because, when at last the front door opened and Sergei walked in, I had drifted off to sleep. I jerked up and stared at my brother. I'd completely forgotten that it was the first day of school for him, too, and evidently, so had Mama. She ran up to the front door, bypassing where I'd been sitting.

"Sergei, hi, sweetheart."

Sergei threw off his black leather jacket that he'd insisted on wearing to school regardless of the warm September weather.

"Sergei, we have a new friend. Meet Auntie Vlada." Mama pointed to the kitchen.

"A new friend?" Sergei narrowed his eyes, then, glancing in my direction, said: "I'm tired. Going to take a nap upstairs."

"Don't you wanna tell me about your day?" Mama asked, but Sergei was already halfway up the steps.

"No, thanks," he said, and, seconds later, the door to his room slammed shut.

"Yes, Sergei is my oldest. He's fifteen, going on thirty." Mama laughed.

"They grow up fast, don't they!"

"They sure do."

My stomach rumbled, and I expected Mama to tell her new friend that it was time for her to feed me, but Mama proceeded back to the kitchen and took her position at the kitchen table.

I turned on the TV.

CHAPTER 3

RYDER

By November, my English was good enough for me to understand almost everything at school. One of those things was that my name was useless. No one could pronounce "Rodion" correctly, and it was quickly shortened to Rod. I hated it with a passion and complained about it at home.

"You know, some kids pick new names when they come to America," Papa announced one evening. We were in the kitchen, Mama, Papa, and I, and I'd just finished my plate of mac and cheese, a dish Papa assured us was what American kids ate. Papa was eating soup. He put his spoon down and looked at me critically.

"Maybe Rodion can change his name? I'm sick of hearing his complaints."

"What?" A loud clank followed. Mama had been collecting silverware from the table, and some of the pieces dropped to the floor.

"It's not such a big deal. If my name weren't universal, I would have changed it a long time ago. We all need to adapt." Papa rolled his eyes. "Is there any soup left?" He looked at the stove.

"But Rodion was named after his grandfather." Mama walked over to me and kissed the top of my head.

"Rodion, do you want a new name?" Papa turned to me. "Why don't you think of a nice new name for yourself? It can start with an R."

"Yes, Papa," I said. I was a good boy. "Ronald?" I said tentatively. "Like Ronald McDonald?"

"Oh, no. People will immediately think of Reagan." Papa shook his head. "Is there another name you would like?"

"Philip, it's too much to ask of Rodion. Let's talk about this later. Rodion, go spend time with your brother." Mama gently pushed me out of the kitchen.

I went upstairs, where Sergei, as usual, was sitting on his bed, playing guitar. Back in Moscow, Sergei always played songs by the band Kino. He adored its lead singer, Viktor Tsoi, and dressed all in black, just like Tsoi did. The song Sergei favored was 'A Star Called the Sun,' and I knew the words by heart. But now Sergei was playing a song I didn't recognize, and it was beautiful.

"Hey! Listen to this." Sergei was unusually friendly.

> Riders on the storm.
> Into this house we're born.
> Into this world we're thrown.
> Like a dog without a bone.

Sergei's English was the best in the family. He'd studied it in school in Russia, and he pronounced each word carefully.

"It's this band called The Doors. 'Riders on the Storm'!" My brother smiled.

"It's the last song Jim Morrison ever recorded before he died. He was the lead singer. He was real young, only twenty-seven. Just like Tsoi. It's kinda amazing. But Jim Morrison was deep. So, this song, it's about philosophy. Heidegger. He's got the answers. You see, our lives, they've got no meaning. That's what Morrison meant. We're just thrown into this world and we don't have answers. You get me, Rodion?"

I was quiet. What could I say?

"This is what everything is about. Random. Throwing us into the world. Like, what's the point? Is there a point? We're all riders on the storm. You get me?"

I nodded.

"Papa told me I could change my name," I said after a pause. "So I can be more American."

Sergei shook his head in indignation and sighed. We heard a noise of a car pulling up outside. I ran to the window, grateful for the distraction. A truck had stopped in front of our neighbor's home. It was a yellow truck with huge black letters.

R-Y-D-E-R

I read out the letters. I had just finished learning the alphabet at school and was learning to read.

R-Y-D-E-R

"Ryder!" I yelped in excitement. "Look! Ryder!"

"What are you talking about?" Sergei put the guitar down and walked up to stand next to me.

"Ryders on the storm! I wanna be called Ryder!" I jumped up and down. "My name!"

Without waiting for Sergei's reaction, I ran downstairs and announced my decision.

"Mama! Papa! I wanna be called Ryder. Like the truck."

"What truck?" Mama opened her eyes wide.

"Nice! Ryder has a nice ring to it." Papa smiled at me with approval.

"Yes, come look!" I pulled Mama by the sleeve to the window and pointed at the truck. "See?"

"Rodion, we'll let the school know tomorrow." Papa gave me a high five.

"Philip, you can't let him be named after a truck! That's his whole identity. This is a serious decision…"

Mama was speaking, but Papa and I weren't listening.

Papa picked me up and spun me around, as we both chanted: "Ry-der! Ry-der! Ry-der!"

From that day onwards, I would be known as Ryder Likharev.

CHAPTER 4

BABUSHKA

At school, we were getting ready for Thanksgiving. We drew turkeys, talked about the Pilgrims and got an assignment to ask our parents what they were thankful for and to report the next day at school.

"What are you thankful for?" I asked Mama, as soon as I stepped off the bus.

"Oh, my little guy!" She leaned close and I could smell her breath. It was unfamiliar, pungent, and fruity. "I'm grateful for you, Rodion!" Mama took my hand in hers. She refused to call me Ryder, and so did Sergei. "And you know what? You're going to meet your grandmother soon."

"My grandmother? Babushka?" My mouth gaped open. Babushka was Mama's mother, and she was dead.

"Well, you have two babushkas. My mom and Papa's mom." Mama clutched my hand. "Papa's mother is coming to visit us. For Thanksgiving."

"Where is she now?" I asked, immediately picturing a fairy tale granny, like in "Little Red Riding Hood", somewhere in the forest.

"She lives right here, in Pittsburgh, but she was busy and couldn't come meet you before." Mama averted her eyes.

Ahead of the visit, Mama acted strangely, rushing around the house with a rag, wiping nonexistent specks of dust from all surfaces. She sent Sergei to the store to get mayo, then forgot about it and sent him again, tearing up when he confronted her. Then Mama set out two china sets on the kitchen table, staring at them for hours, trying to pick the right one for the dinner. All of her conversations focused on the menu for Thanksgiving. She'd speak to no one in particular, not expecting an answer. "I should make the Olivier salad, and then piroshki? With meat or potatoes. Or both? Or borscht? That could be a nice touch."

The biggest challenge was the turkey. Mama had never cooked it before. For advice, she called Vlada, and they spent over an hour going over what needed to be done to adapt the Thanksgiving classic to Russian taste. That required substituting the bread stuffing with fruit, which, Vlada assured Mama, would make it edible.

That afternoon, Papa came home early, carrying a bouquet of orange roses.

"Put these in water, please." He handed the flowers to Mama. She moved her finger across the petals, her eyes sparkling.

"Thank you, Philip. You shouldn't have."

"It's for Mother," Papa said curtly. "I am about to go pick her up now."

"Okay." Mama bit her lip, and I noticed she rolled her eyes.

———

Grandma Oxana was a short, stout woman, her hair dyed jet-black. Her beady, assessing eyes took in our place and settled on me. She hummed and raised her eyebrows, then announced, "I gotta take my boots off."

"Mother, one moment," Papa fussed, arms flailing. He let

out a yelp and ran to the kitchen, appearing a moment later with a chair. He positioned it by the front door and led Grandma Oxana to it. "Please, have a seat."

"Thank you." Grandma sat down and Papa kneeled next to her, looking like a knight about to receive an accolade. Papa unzipped her long boots that went all the way up her shins.

"Ooh, that feels good." Grandma let out a breath and wiggled her feet. Through her stockings, I could see the curved nail of her right big toe and it made me gag.

"The slippers! Where are Mother's slippers?" Papa turned his head widely. "The furry ones." When no one answered, Papa grunted, rising, and reached for the shoe rack.

"Here you go, Mother, I've got them right here!" A radiant smile crossed his face as he put the slippers on Grandma's feet.

"I'm just like Cinderella." The old woman giggled. "My prince!" She threw an adoring look at her son. "Well, show me what you've been up to." Grandma rose from the chair and put her hands on her hips.

"This is Lydia, Mother." Papa pointed to Mama, who came out from the kitchen, an aloof look on her face. Mama was wearing her best sweater, the one Auntie Lena had given her before we left for America. It was beige with sparkles sewn onto it, and Auntie Lena told Mama it made her hair stand out and was "tasteful."

"I heard a lot about you," Grandma said, walking over to Mama. "And this is the boy?" Grandma fixed her gaze on me again and I had no choice but to leave my hiding spot from behind the couch. "Rodion?" Grandma squinted at me. "Well, hello there, boy."

I didn't respond, so petrified was I with fear. I even forgot to say my new name. Ryder.

"Is the boy mute?" Grandma raised her eyebrows.

"No, no, he's just shy." Papa stepped in to defend me. "Let's have lunch, Mother."

"I'd like to wash my hands first," Grandma Oxana said, and retreated to the bathroom.

As soon as the door closed behind her, Papa slapped his forehead so hard that a red mark appeared.

"I can't believe I forgot!" He ran to the kitchen and grabbed the roses from the vase, still dripping water. Papa wiped the stems on his shirt and took a position by the bathroom door like a soldier standing guard.

"Mother, I'm sorry; I forgot to give these to you sooner. My fault. But we got you this bouquet," he said solemnly, as soon as Grandma walked out of the bathroom.

"Thank you, Philip, my boy." Grandma Oxana took the bouquet, then paused and started counting. "One, two, three, four," she began, her face turning pale. "Twelve? Did you get me twelve roses?"

"Yes, I suppose it's a dozen," Philip mumbled, scratching his forehead, the red mark fading slightly.

"Did you do this on purpose? Do you want me dead?" Grandma pushed the flowers at Papa with such force that he stumbled back. Several petals fell to the floor.

"Mother, that's how they sell them here. It's a dozen roses."

"You know we get even numbers for the dead! Why did you get me these flowers? Is it her?" She narrowed her eyes and looked at Mama. "It was her? Tell me! I know it was! I should never have agreed to meet her."

Grandmother huffed and rushed out of the house, slamming the front door.

"Mother, please, it's just a misunderstanding." Papa ran after her. From the outside, we could hear shouting, the sound of the car door slamming shut.

"Mama, is Grandma coming back?" I asked.

"No, Rodion, I don't think so. Let's sit down and eat."

"Lydia, you'll need to apologize to Mother," Papa said when he came back that evening, looking haggard.

"Apologize for what?" Mama threw her hands up in protest.

"For the flowers."

"I wasn't the one who got her the flowers." Mama's voice sounded screechy. "You got them, you apologize."

"I already did." Papa shook his head. "Mother is very sensitive. Why didn't you count the roses? Now she doesn't want to come back. And it took me months to convince her to meet you."

"Good riddance," Mama mumbled quietly, so Papa wouldn't hear.

But I did.

CHAPTER 5
THE CONSOLE

Growing up in Russia, I was used to snow. It was on the ground for six months out of the year. Snow in Russia was gradual and fell slowly, with snow piles accumulating over a few weeks, growing tall. So, when Papa got home from work one day and announced—panic in his voice—that it was about to snow, Mama, Sergei, and I were amused.

"So what?" Mama opened her eyes wide. "Snow isn't a big deal!"

"Get ready. We need to spread salt on the steps." Papa placed a large bag right by the door, expression on his face serious. "We're about to get snowed in."

"Why would you need salt if it's about to snow?" Mama frowned.

"To melt the ice." Papa turned to Sergei. "Hey, sport, help me out here."

Sergei followed Papa outside, and the two of them spread ice on the steps and the driveway. When they came back inside, there was a light dusting of snow on their coats, their hair moist from precipitation. I ran outside and, before Mama could stop me, stuck my tongue out, catching the snowflakes. It was almost like being home, in Russia.

———

That weekend was the best one I'd had in America. Snow fell for two days straight, blanketing our neighborhood. I watched TV and slept. Mama and Papa were unusually nice to each other, and Sergei was in his room, playing guitar, and I would hear him singing songs by The Doors over and over.

In the evenings, we made plans for the future. Papa promised to take us to Lake Erie in the summer.

"As soon as it gets warm, we'll go there for the weekend. Rent a house. And we'll go swimming. Water is very clear, beautiful. And we can picnic outside. It's budget friendly," Papa promised, then furrowed his brow. "Maybe we can even rent a camper."

"A camper? What's that?" I asked, staring at Papa.

"One of those cars; you sleep in it and you can drive around, see different places."

"Like a house on wheels?" I sat up straight. It sounded like a dream I didn't know I had.

"Exactly, Ryder." Papa ruffled my hair. "That's my guy."

Sergei had been sitting with a detached expression on his face, but even he perked up at the mention of a trip to Lake Erie.

On the third day of the blizzard, after the snow had stopped falling and Papa and Sergei had ventured outside to clear it from the steps and the driveway, we had a visitor.

It was Vlada. She came dressed in a thick winter jacket with the Penguins' logo on it. I'd seen a few high school kids wear those, but never a woman. She was wearing sturdy winter boots, and when she took them off, snow fell out of them, as if she'd stuffed them with it on purpose.

"Love this weather!" Vlada exclaimed, pulling off her hat. It was a pink knitted beanie, the color of it contrasting with the rest of her black outfit. "I've been walking in the snow for two days straight. Can't get enough," Vlada exclaimed. "I should have told you I was going to come over, but I wanted it to be a surprise!" Vlada let out a laugh. "So, here it is!" She produced a rectangular package, tightly wrapped in newspaper.

I immediately recognized the lettering of *New Russian Word*, a Russian immigrant newspaper. Philip subscribed to it and Mama read it regularly.

"You shouldn't have. Please, come in, sit down!" Mama fussed, taking Vlada's jacket.

"I wanted to say hi to Rodion." Vlada winked at me.

"Ryder," I breathed out, and Mama sighed.

"He only wants to be called Ryder."

"That's fine. Nothing wrong with experimenting with different names." Vlada's face softened. "I wish I'd changed my name when I first came to America. It's a great opportunity to start a new life."

I fidgeted, my eyes fixed on the package. I suspected it was for me but wasn't entirely sure. I could feel something important was about to happen. A transformation.

"So, little guy, I hear you've been a good boy at school." Vlada looked directly at me. "So, I decided I'd give you this. The boys are grown. It's just sitting there, collecting dust. But I know they sure loved this thing." She handed me the package. "Go ahead, unwrap it."

I accepted the gift and took the paper off. The newsprint stained my fingers, and by the time I put it aside, they were gray.

I was holding a game console.

"Thank you!" I gasped. I'd seen the console at Vlada's house. Sergei and I even played it one evening when we were over there with Mama.

"Vlada, this is so generous of you! You shouldn't have!" Mama leaned in to give Vlada a hug.

"I'd like for Rodion to use it." Vlada game me an encouraging smile, and I immediately rushed to plug in the console, connecting the cables and deftly inserting the game cartridge.

"See, he knows what to do. It's meant for little Rodion," Vlada noted.

Mama took Vlada to the kitchen, and by the time I smelled the coffee brewing, I'd already connected the console, gotten the right channel, and was staring at Stewart the Fox's adorable face. With the console, Vlada brought a treasure trove of games her sons had played. The tune of the Stewart game played loudly, and I was enthralled, moving the little fox on the screen. He was spinning into a ball, baring his teeth, his red spiky hair ready to defend him, to prickle and attack.

"Hey, what's this?" I heard Sergei's voice. It came out of another dimension and pulled me back to reality.

"Ha?" I turned, with some difficulty tearing myself from the screen.

"Where did you get this?" Sergei brushed the snow from his jacket and walked up to me. His boots left wet footprints on the carpet. I hadn't even noticed he'd been outside. "Is that a game console?"

"Yes." I turned back and Stewart flashed me a smile. I rocked back and forth, and Stewart and I both knew we'd found each other.

The next moment, Stewart spoke to me.

"Ryder." A wink followed. Hand on the hip. "Let's play!"

"Alright!" I yelped, and edged closer to the screen. I wanted it to possess me. I wanted to be there, with Stewart, inside of the game, running and spinning on the purple bricks with him. I wanted to flip just like him, to be as fast.

"Rodion, what are you doing?" Sergei shook me.

"What?" I looked up at my brother.

"When did you set this up?"

"Just now. Vlada brought it over." I put the game aside and snapped back to reality. Adrenaline was rushing through my veins. I jumped up and down, just like I'd seen Stewart do, then I did a flip.

"Easy now, easy." Sergei shook his head in mock admonishment.

———

My life changed that day in more ways than one. I started to wear all red. Like Stewart. I had one shirt that color and I wore it every day, refusing to wear anything else until Mama got the clue and took me shopping to Gabe's. We took two buses to get there, because Papa needed to go swimming. He went to the gym every Sunday because it was important for his health.

At Gabe's, Mama let me pick out new T-shirts for myself. We found several shirts with Stewart the fox on them, and I immediately started wearing them.

"My little fox," Mama cooed, watching me as I paraded my new outfits.

I loved the game. Stewart took over my life. There were other games, but I didn't care for them. I identified with him. I was him. We were one. I could trust him.

Stewart listened to me and he appeared to me in my dreams. More than once, I woke up to find Stewart sitting on my pillow, speaking to me. It wasn't Russian or English, but our own language. What Stewart wanted me to know percolated into my brain through sounds. Stewart would stay, but only if I didn't move. If I tried to reach for him, he'd move away and disappear. I figured it out after some tries, and once I did, I'd lay motionless, in a sort of paralysis, waiting for Stewart to transmit messages.

What did he tell me? Everything. Mostly, the revelations

were about getting to the next level in the game. But some were about the ways of the world. Stewart told me about my true mission in life. It was to be his mouthpiece. I was to help him communicate with the world, to let the true Stewart be seen. I didn't know what that meant, not entirely, but he would smile coyly and tell me that "all would reveal itself in due course" if I pressed him for more information.

CHAPTER 6
THE THREE MUSKETEERS

The summer came and so did my kindergarten graduation ceremony. To celebrate my achievement, Grandma Oxana agreed to come over. I didn't care for her visit, and neither did Mama. Sergei took the upcoming nuisance in stride. He had turned into somewhat of a philosopher and was reading Heidegger in German. This was all related to his exploration of the futility of human existence and the connection to Jim Morrison. Sergei would sit in his room, peering into the English-German dictionary, then into a tome of Heidegger's works, underlining several words, then writing them out. The process was incredibly time-consuming, but, Sergei noted, "he wasn't in a rush."

But I was.

I was in a rush because I was just like Stewart the Fox. Our goal was to run. To move, to sprint. We were runners, not walkers. Our feet were our wings. And really, Stewart and I could practically fly, if you thought about it. I sure did. If I could be a creature of the forest, I'd be invincible. I could defeat just about anyone. Those were my thoughts when I was standing in a green gown, graduating from kindergarten.

Mama ran up to me and handed me the flowers. I checked the number. There were six roses.

"Mama, why are you giving me half a dozen roses?" I asked. "Isn't it supposed to be for the dead?"

"Rodion, sweetheart, don't be ridiculous. Don't listen to Grandma!" Mama laughed. "When did you become so superstitious?" I took the flowers in one hand and extended my other hand to her. We walked up to Grandma Oxana and Papa. Sergei was standing to the side, observing us. He liked to be on his own.

"Congratulations," Grandma said. She was scrutinizing me with her small, beady eyes. I noticed her glancing at my bouquet and expected her to say something about the number of flowers, but she didn't.

For the ride from the graduation ceremony, we all piled into one car. Grandmother Oxana sat in the front seat, next to Papa, and I caught her surveying me in the rearview mirror. Mama, Sergei, and I were in the back of the car. After a few minutes, Grandmother Oxana, directing her question at Mama, said: "You know, your little one looks a lot like you, Lydia."

"Yes, I think so." Mama nodded.

"Both of your boys do," Grandma Oxana added graciously.

Sergei gave me a side-eye and elbowed me in the ribs. This was an expression of affection.

"I guess so," Mama agreed, her cheeks turning pink. "Rodion, please, can you move a little to the side?" Mama shifted in her seat and moved her purse that had been squeezed by my booster seat.

"So, does your older one look like his father?" Grandma continued her query. Mama tensed. I could feel her arm freeze in place.

"I couldn't say." Mama swallowed hard.

"You don't have any photos of your first husband?" The

question was like a bomb exploding. Papa gripped the wheel tightly, and Mama gulped. Sergei rolled his eyes. I stared bravely straight ahead and my eyes caught Grandma's cold stare. Her eyes were like those of the Ice Queen. Light blue. Unforgiving.

"Mother, perhaps we can discuss this later." Papa cleared his throat.

"I am just curious. I'd like to know as much as possible about my grandsons. Both of them." Grandma rounded her eyes.

Mama's anxiety was palpable. She breathed hard, her hands were shaking, and she fidgeted in her seat, as if she wanted to catapult right out of the car. She opened her mouth as if to speak, but no sound came. At that moment, we pulled up to our house. Mama opened the passenger door and got out. Making her way to the steps, she leaned on the railing, her mouth wide-open as she struggled to breathe.

"Mama! Are you alright?" I unbuckled myself and moved to help her.

"Yes, yes. It's okay." Mama wiped beads of sweat on her forehead. "Let's go inside."

Grandma followed us, head up high, a sly smile on her face.

———

I'd been looking forward to my first summer vacation in America. We'd go to Lake Erie with Papa in a "house on wheels" and I'd get to practice swimming. I was a little nervous about that part, not entirely sure I still remembered how to swim, but Sergei assured me he'd remind me what to do. And of course, the summer meant unlimited time with Stewart the Fox.

Sergei got a summer job, so most of the time it was Mama and me at home. She'd been taking English lessons at a community center in Squirrel Hill, but they had ended for the summer. And so Mama and I stayed together with little to occupy our time.

All day long, I played Stewart the Fox. And Mama gossiped. As soon as Papa left for work, she would pick up the phone and call Vlada, inviting her to come over. And immediately after that, Mama called Zhanna. Zhanna was another woman from the neighborhood, a recent immigrant whom Vlada had introduced to Mama sometime in the spring.

Those three were now inseparable and called themselves the three musketeers. Vlada always showed up first, at around ten in the morning. Without fail, she would bring with her a bottle of Armenian cognac and set it on the kitchen table.

The smell of freshly brewed coffee spread through the house, as Mama brewed coffee for the two of them in a special copper pot, then served it in her favorite porcelain cups. She'd add "just a dash" of cognac, and they chatted.

Busy with Stewart, I paid them little mind. He and I were progressing, and my dreams about him were getting more and more vivid. At one point, I think it was right around July 4, I finally made it. I'd become Stewart. I got to run around the purple brick wall and spun myself into a tight little ball. I could even feel the red pointy hair sticking out of my head. It was the best dream ever, and I punched and sneered at the audience. Yes, I even had an audience. I was inside of the game!

Zhanna, the third musketeer, would pop in a bit later, usually closer to noon, on account of her husband being a "late riser." He painted houses, and Zhanna complained he drank too much, was a cheater, and was "way too lazy." Zhanna cut hair for a living and operated an illegal hair salon from her home, where she offered five-dollar haircuts to both men and women, and also colored women's hair for a reasonable fee. Zhanna preferred consistency, as she admitted herself, and mostly dyed her clients' hair black. I wondered if Grandma also went to Zhanna to get her hair done, or whether there was some unwritten code where all immigrant women of a certain age had agreed to have the same hairstyle.

Once Zhanna joined them, Mama and Vlada would have another round of cognac-laced coffee.

"This one is for the blood pressure," Vlada announced. "Just a teeny bit, to get it down. Down-down," she sang in her deep voice, not the least bit ashamed of how tone-deaf she sounded.

"Here, in America, I also am starting to get high blood pressure," Mama admitted. "I'm glad Vlada came up with this natural cure. I'm getting headaches. All the time."

"You are?" Zhanna shook her head, a look of concern on her face.

"Yes, it's unbelievable. You know what this hag said to me the other day?" Mama's voice was now a hoarse whisper, but I could hear her just fine. I'd lowered the volume of my game so I could pay attention.

"What?" Zhanna and Vlada asked in unison.

"She was hinting that Rodion isn't Philip's son!"

"No!" I heard the two friends yell out.

"How dare she?" Zhanna gasped.

"What a piece of work!" Vlada added in her near-baritone.

"I know!" Mama cried out.

A clinking of cups followed, and I guessed that the three women were still tending to their respective high blood pressures.

"Is he?" Vlada asked after a pause. "You'd tell us, wouldn't you?"

"Of course he is Philip's son!" Mama was indignant. "I don't get where she gets these ideas. It's like she sits there scheming, trying to find ways to make my life impossible. It's difficult as it is!"

"That's America for ya," Zhanna said. "Everyone suffers here. It's a dog-eat-dog place."

"But I'm her daughter-in-law! Doesn't she want Philip to be happy?"

"No. She's one of those mothers. You know…" Zhanna's voice trailed off. "Monster-in-law type. Her kind hates anyone their son marries. They want their boy to themselves. You can't win."

"But Philip isn't a mama's boy!" Mama said. Bouts of laughter followed. Zhanna, Vlada, and Mama guffawed hearty belly laughs.

"That's a good one, Lydia! By the way, where's your boy? He's been awfully quiet for a five-year-old," Vlada said, and I immediately turned the volume up.

Stewart did another flip, and I hummed the tune of the game loud enough for the women to hear.

CHAPTER 7
THE COUSIN

It was late July when Papa made it clear that we wouldn't be going to Lake Erie for a camping trip.

"I'm sorry. I didn't get my leave sorted out in time, and now all the good cabins are rented out," Papa was saying.

"But what about the camper?" I asked, turning on the console. It was early on a Sunday morning and I'd just woken up, but I'd been dreaming about Stewart and needed my fix. The cute fox appeared on the screen and right away got my full attention.

My parents were sitting in the kitchen, Papa drinking his coffee. Mama was flipping through the *New Russian Word*, presumably looking at classified ads. The ads were for jobs in either Philadelphia or New York City, where most Russian immigrants lived, but that did not stop Mama from looking at these regularly.

"I hear Brooklyn is quite nice. A lot like Moscow," Mama noted, ignoring my question and Papa's announcement.

"Lydia, don't be ridiculous. No one wants to live in Brooklyn. People are trying to leave, not move there."

"It's just that Pittsburgh is so small. And nothing goes on

here. I've been stuck in Greenfield for a full year now!" Mama pouted. "And now we can't even go to Erie."

"Next year." Papa sighed. "But you know what? We can throw a nice, big party for Ryder. What do you say?" Papa turned to me. "I know you've been looking forward to going to the lake. So, how about a party to celebrate your sixth birthday?"

I didn't react. I was trying to get Stewart to the next level.

"Ryder!" Papa called, louder now. I looked up at him in confusion. "How about a birthday party?"

"A birthday party?" I jumped up. "Thank you, Papa!" I rushed over and put my arms around him. "Thank you!"

I'd never had a birthday party before. Back in Russia, Mama, Sergei, and I would have some cake, and that was it. But in my year in America, I'd learned that kid birthday parties turned into huge celebrations, with lots of guests, elaborate cakes, and presents. Lots of presents. So many that the kids didn't know what to do with them and were forced to write thank you cards to the gift bearers.

"Thank you, Philip. What a wonderful idea!" Mama smiled.

On my actual birthday, which fell on a Thursday, Mama baked the traditional Russian honey cake, Medovik. Mama, Papa, Sergei, and I ate the cake together after lighting candles and singing the Happy Birthday song.

The party took place the following Saturday. Mama and Papa invited their friends to the festivities. Papa's friends, Boris and Rita, Vlada and her husband, also named Boris— who would miss the party on the account of his ill health and general misanthropy, according to Vlada—as well as Zhanna and her husband, Anton. Sergei brought over his friends, Jimmy and Nate. Like him, they loved The Doors and wore all black: black leather jackets, black Dr. Martens boots, black T-shirts and jeans. Thick chains connected to their belts. Mama called the three of them "the undertakers."

There was one problem: my friends. I couldn't invite anyone, because Mama didn't speak English and hadn't exchanged numbers with any parents of my kindergarten classmates. Not even the parents of the two girls from the school bus.

"Next year, we can prepare better, and we'll invite lots of children. Alright, sweetheart?" Mama kissed me on the forehead after telling me the guest list did not include anyone my age.

"Yes, Mama."

I didn't care whether there would be other kids at my party. Not one bit. I had Stewart. I asked for more Stewart-themed gifts. And maybe an actual, real-life fox that could be named Stewart? I pictured chasing him around the house and smiled. But Mama put an end to that idea fairly quickly.

"Rodion, sweetheart, don't be silly. Foxes are wild animals. They aren't meant to be living indoors."

"But Mama, what about Stewart?" I protested, pointing at the console. "He's just fine indoors."

"That's just a game. He isn't real!" Mama pecked me on the cheek and ran into the kitchen. She'd been washing fruit to prepare for the party.

Papa, like a real American dad, went to the supermarket, Giant Eagle, and got large balloons with "Happy Birthday" written on them. We borrowed plastic chairs from Vlada, and Papa set them in our tiny backyard. We didn't have a grill, but Mama made sausages and hamburgers on the stove that tasted delicious. And then Papa brought in the cake. It was a huge, white sheet cake with a picture of a truck on it.

"Happy Birthday, Ryder!" was written in the middle of this beauty in large blue letters. There was a smudge next to the name, but the frosting had been fixed and sculpted back to correct the letter, so the "R" looked giant. As if my name was larger than life itself.

"Here you go, big guy!" Papa placed the cake in the

middle of the kitchen table. As if by magic, he produced a package of six candles and stuck them into the cake. Everyone cheered when he lit the candles. And then they all sang, half of them in their accented English, the other in Russian.

"Happy Birthday, dear Ryder!"

"Happy Birthday, dear Rodion."

It was as if there were two kids celebrating. Rodion and Ryder. I felt incredible. I blew out the candles with one large breath.

Everyone clapped.

"Did you make a wish?" Papa asked. I nodded. "Well, don't tell anyone, or it won't come true!"

Everyone laughed.

I had made a wish. It was to have Stewart the Fox become real. I edged toward the console so I could play my game, but then Grandma Oxana walked in.

"Surprise!" She held a package in her hands, which later turned out to be a sweater.

"Mother!" Papa let out a scream. "How did you get here?"

"Marina brought me." A victorious smile appeared on Grandma's face.

"Marina?" Papa stammered.

Confused expressions. A rustle of voices. No one knew anyone by that name.

"Come here, dear girl. Say hello." Grandma, with a gesture of pulling a rabbit out of a hat, pushed forward a slouching woman about Papa's age, maybe a little younger. Her face was sickly white, with the pallor of someone who rarely went outside. Watery eyes scanned the room for danger and settled on my mother.

"This is Marina," Grandma murmured. "Your cousin," she added after a pause.

The newcomer nodded vigorously and scratched her face. I noticed several deep marks peppering her cheeks. A scab on her chin.

"Nice to meet you." Zhanna sauntered over to Marina. "Would you like some cake?"

"Thank you. I prefer natural sugars," Marina responded. "I'd like an apple, please."

"Lydia, have you got any apples?" Zhanna asked. "Marina here wants one."

"Oh, yes, of course." Mama walked up to them. "Nice to meet you. I didn't know Philip had other family in America." Mama extended her hand to the newcomer.

"Men aren't good at these things." Marina turned red. "Keeping track of blood relations." She scratched her cheek.

"Of course. How very true." Mama nodded.

While this conversation was unfolding, Vlada was getting to know Grandma. It was an incredible match. They were like two gladiators in the arena, throwing punches at each other, going for the kill.

Grandmother and the new cousin were the first to leave. Then, Boris and Rita. Sergei and his two friends went upstairs, and Papa went to "clear his head." Soon it was Mama and her two friends, who stayed behind to help her clean up.

"Did you see what she was wearing?" I recognized Zhanna's voice. "Who dresses like that for a kid's birthday party?"

"I didn't notice. Was too stressed out," Mama responded.

"Those tiny shorts? And with her legs, you'd think she was fifteen."

"I bet the men noticed," Vlada added with consternation.

"I swear I saw Philip checking her out." Zhanna raised her eyebrows for effect.

"Philip? But they're related." Mama shrugged.

"Kissing cousins, Lydia. That's what they're called. And who knows if she's actually a cousin? The old witch may have brought her over just to muddy the waters."

"That's true. Philip never mentioned any relatives living here." Mama frowned.

"You see? You'd better watch out. Men will go for anything easily available. And this woman seems desperate."

"Desperate? What makes you say that? She just seemed a little awkward." Mama shrugged.

"Don't be so naïve, Lydia. Didn't you see how she was scanning the room? She's hungry for a guy."

"Well, thank you for the warning." Mama sighed. "As if I didn't have enough to deal about with my mother-in-law. Now, I got this cousin, too."

"You'll be alright."

————

When I hear the expression "the wife always knows," I can't help but think of Mama. I wonder if she knew.

Vlada was the one who broke the news of the affair. It was the Sunday before Thanksgiving, our second one in America, and I was sitting in the living room, playing Stewart the Fox. I heard a loud knock on the door and went to open it.

"Is your mother at home?"

Vlada was on the threshold, out of breath. Her face was grim. Without waiting for an answer, she rushed into the house. She didn't bother taking off her shoes or her jacket.

"Lydia!" Vlada screamed, opening the kitchen door.

"What's happened?" I heard Mama's voice.

"It's Philip."

"Philip?"

"Yes. Sit down."

"What is it?" Mama yelped. I hit pause and perked my ears.

"We were at Ikea, Boris and I," Vlada's voice cracked. "I wanted a new china cabinet, you remember, Lydia? So, we were over there. That place is a maze. Going from one room to the next, on and on. And I heard someone speaking Russian. And you know how Boris never speaks, but I told him to be quiet, and I saw them!"

"Who?" Mama's voice was faint.

"Philip and that woman. From the birthday party."

"What? That can't be. Philip is at the gym. Swimming."

"No, Lydia, he's with her. They were acting like a proper couple. Holding hands, kissing. They didn't see us. Thank God Boris is like a mute. So, I rushed out of there with Boris, and we drove straight back. So I can tell you in person."

"Philip is with Marina? But that's his cousin."

"No, Lydia, she's his mistress. I've called Zhanna to come over. She's on her way now."

"Zhanna? Why?"

At this point, I'd stopped the game completely and was standing by the kitchen door, listening, but hearing that Zhanna was about to come over, I ran back to my spot in the living room. And just in time. A minute later, there was a knock on the front door and Zhanna waltzed in.

"Lydia! I am so sorry!" She rushed to the kitchen, paying me no mind. I crouched in the corner, listening.

"It all makes sense now, doesn't it?" Vlada's low voice said.

"So, it's true? Philip...oh, how could I have been so stupid?!" Mama yelped.

I wanted to tell Mama it was a bad word, but didn't dare go into the kitchen.

"I think Lydia needs to hire a lawyer," Vlada said. "I have a friend. She filed for divorce, and she got alimony. Lots of money. Do you know how much Philip makes?"

"I don't know anything," Mama wailed. "I can't believe this. Oh! God!"

"Lydia, calm down. Better you know the truth."

Mama started crying.

"What do you expect? He's just a man!" Vlada jumped to

Papa's defense. "You didn't think he'd spend five years alone, did you?"

"I did!" Mama said through the tears.

"You poor thing. You were busy raising his kid all on your own, waiting!" That was Zhanna.

I guessed she was speaking about me, and I wondered why raising me was such a big deal. I was practically raising myself. I shrugged and turned the game back on.

"But now you gotta plan. You can't leave the guy until you get your papers. You have your green card, and now you gotta get your citizenship," Zhanna continued.

"That's another two years." More tears.

"So, just wait the two years. Whatever it takes. And then you file for divorce."

"So, I just pretend like nothing happened? Like I don't know he's been cheating?"

"I say sleep on it. Wait until a few days have passed. Don't do anything rash," Vlada boomed.

"But I don't think I can control myself."

"Here, have a drink. Calm your nerves. Your blood pressure is probably sky high."

I could hear a liquid being poured, Mama drinking, then coughing, then drinking again.

"That's my girl. Relax, it's just life. You're in America; you're the one who's married to the guy. He brought you and the two kids over here. He chose you. You get it?"

"Yes," Mama said, her voice calmer now, "he did."

I could just imagine her staring into the distance.

"Think of the children," Zhanna noted, pleased that she'd managed to calm Mama down. "Little Ryder will thank you later."

"Philip's mother is a real piece of work," Mama said.

"That she is. That she is. But they all are. Never met a mother-in-law who wasn't a total disaster," Zhanna said. "The stories my clients tell me."

"But this one, she brought the mistress to her grandson's birthday party! What kind of monster does that?" Vlada chimed in.

After that, I tuned them out and focused on the game entirely. There was more drinking, crying, toasting, talking. It wasn't until an hour later, just when Papa was due to come home, that Vlada and Zhanna shuffled out of the kitchen. Mama followed her girlfriends out.

"I'm so lucky to have you by my side," she said, closing the door behind them.

CHAPTER 8
THE EXPERIMENT

Mama said nothing to Papa, and I quickly forgot about the strange conversation she'd had with her friends, plus the tears. Life went on as before. I went to school and spent all my free time with Stewart the Fox. A new version of the game came out during Christmas and I was thrilled. I am not sure whether Mama had a plan or whether this was a way of burying her head in the sand. Hoping Papa's affair would just go away. Disappear, like a bad dream.

But it didn't.

———

The summer before second grade was remarkably similar to the previous one, minus the birthday celebration. To mark the occasion, Mama baked the honey cake and invited Vlada and Zhanna. The three of them drank to my health and toasted while I played Stewart.

Several days after my birthday, Papa sat me down and took my hands in his.

"Son," he said. "I love you. You realize I love you. You're

my little boy." Then Papa started crying. I'd never seen him cry before. He'd whined before, he'd complained, but he'd never shed a tear. But this time I saw huge tears rolling down his face. I stared at Papa in utter shock and confusion.

Mama came over and kissed my head.

"How would you like to visit Papa at work? It'll be a special day, just the two of you. Your birthday treat."

The prospect was so exciting, I could barely keep still. I'd never imagined I could visit Papa at work, let alone spend a whole day together, and thought of the wonderful things we would do, and of how I'd tell Mama and Sergei about it later. I didn't even mind not being able to play Stewart.

Papa and I left home early the following morning. I was dressed in my favorite Stewart T-shirt. We drove through Schenley Park and pulled up to a two-story building. Papa led me inside.

Laboratory the sign on the door read.

"Is this where you work, Papa? Is it like The Lab in Moscow where you and Mama met?" I asked.

"The Lab? No." He shook his head. "We're just going to do a quick experiment, and then I'll take you to my real job."

"What's The Laboratory? What kind of experiment?"

"Ryder, hold on, please."

Papa approached the front desk.

"Philip Begunov." He cleared his throat. "I have an appointment."

"Of course. Just a moment." The receptionist, a woman with a bright red manicure, flashed a smile. "I've got you checked in, Mr. Begunov. Please wait right there." She pointed to the plush chairs.

Papa and I did as told, and Papa picked up an issue of *People* magazine. I noticed his hands were shaking. I fidgeted in the seat.

"Maybe it's not a good idea," Papa mumbled to himself

and rose to leave, but at that moment the receptionist called: "Mr. Begunov. They're ready for you."

Papa glanced over at me and took me by the hand.

"Let's do this, Ryder."

"You'll be in Room 4," the receptionist added, and Papa and I walked down the long corridor. We saw another woman, wearing a white waistcoat, standing by the door.

"Mr. Begunov." She was holding a printout and read off the details to Papa, which Papa dutifully confirmed and signed. "Please come in," she gestured.

"Have a seat right there, on the cot," the woman told me, and I obliged. Papa continued standing by the door, watching. The woman walked to the counter, washed her hands, put on latex gloves.

"Now, just open your mouth." She approached, her eyes narrowed. The woman was holding what looked like a giant Q-tip. "I gotta take a quick swab."

"Is that the experiment, Papa?" I turned to my father.

"Yes, that's the experiment." He nodded, and I opened my mouth. The Q-tip scraped my mouth, and I jerked back.

"That's it. Good boy. We're all done." The woman cleared her throat and, turning to Papa, said,

"You'll have the results in five to seven business days."

"Papa, what results?" I asked.

"Just something. I'll show you later." Papa averted his eyes.

———

My world unraveled shortly after. On a Friday before Labor Day, Papa came home early. Instead of greeting us, he walked up to Mama, shaking a piece of paper. His face was pale, brow furrowed.

"You lied to me!" he hissed.

I immediately paused the game, though that morning I'd

just reached a new level, where Stewart got to a magical forest.

"What's this?" Mama put her hands on her hips.

"Proof that you brought a bastard into my home. Two of them, in fact, but I knew about one."

"How dare you!"

"Is Ryder my son? Look at me!" Papa was screaming now, his eyes bulging. "You lied to me! You made me pay for you and the two bastards to move to America. I sacrificed every-thing for you! Everything!"

"Philip, what are you talking about?" Mama blinked fast.

"I'm not falling for your lies!" Papa shook the paper again. "I tested him and he's not my son!" Papa threw a look full of disdain in my direction.

"What?" Mama stepped back.

"I guess you didn't expect this?!" Papa pointed at the paper. "This is proof Ryder is not my son. DNA testing doesn't lie."

"Of course he is your son. You love each other." Mother shook her head in protest.

"Out! I want all of you out of my house. And you have to pay me back. Every single penny I spent on you."

Mama stared at him, wide-eyed.

"Out of my house! Now!" Papa punched the wall. "Out!" He stomped his feet and moved at her, as if about to strike her, too.

"No," Mama said quietly. "I have rights."

"What?" Papa cackled. "What rights? You are only here because you lied to me. I will squash you like a bug. Go back to Russia, where you belong. And take your bastards with you."

"No." Mama raised her head up high. "I know about the affair."

Papa's face turned ashen.

"Vlada saw you two together. You and your cousin."

Mama swallowed hard. "I followed you to one of your swims and I know where you've been going every Sunday. I have proof."

"You are lying," Papa mumbled, his voice weak. Beads of sweat formed on his forehead.

"I am not. Please leave now or I will call the police," Mama said.

Papa stepped back and ran out of the house. The second he left, Mama collapsed on the couch.

"Mama, what's wrong?" I asked.

"Nothing, Rodion, go play."

"Mama, what happened? Is Papa coming back?"

"I don't know."

"Mama, maybe you need to drink something for your blood pressure," I offered the solution I'd heard so many times before.

"Oh, yes. Good idea." Mama got up and walked to the kitchen cabinet. She poured a shot of cognac and downed it. No coffee this time.

———

As well as I remember my first year in America, my third year was a blur. All I recall is Stewart the Fox and the many hours I spent in front of my console. Stewart became my best friend. Vlada got me a toy fox, and he was with me at all times. Naturally, I named him Stewart. I took him to school and hid him in my backpack during the day. Each night, I would confide in him before falling asleep.

"Stewart, I think it's my fault Papa went away," I told him one night.

"Don't worry, Ryder." Stewart winked. "I'll help you. And Papa will come back soon."

"When?" I shook the fox's paw. "Mama cries whenever I ask her about Papa. What do I do?"

"Just keep playing. Things will be fine."

Stewart yawned and fell asleep, indicating that it was time for me to go to sleep, too.

Mama started keeping strange hours. She constantly complained of insomnia and stayed up late into the night, sitting in the kitchen all alone. Sometimes she called Auntie Lena. Some mornings, Sergei and I would find Mama still awake at six in the morning, and she would yawn and go to bed while we got ready for school. Sergei walked me to the bus stop, then went to Allderdice.

I never saw Papa again. He never came to say goodbye.

I was his son for two years and then I wasn't. I don't know if he ever cried, if he ever missed me. I know I missed him. I cried my eyes out. That was another memory of that year. I ached to see Papa again. My seven-year-old mind could not grasp what had happened. I connected Papa's disappearance to The Lab, but I couldn't quite understand why. All I knew was that it was my fault. I was the reason for Papa's departure, and for Mama's ill health. I had done something terrible.

I loved Papa. Every day, right around the time Papa would come home from work, I'd sit by the door and wait. I'd stop the game, put the toy fox next to me, and the two of us listened for the sound of Papa's car. I expected Papa to walk through the door, to give me a hug, sit down next to me on the couch, and ask me about my day. And when, day after day, he didn't, I wept.

And then, one day, I heard the sound of a motor outside. I leaped to my feet, expecting to see Papa, but instead I saw Grandma Oxana climb up the steps, breathing hard.

"Is your mother at home?" She fixed her gaze on me. I let out a yelp and ran to the kitchen to warn Mama. But Mama was already standing in the living room, her face stern.

"Why did you destroy my boy's life?!" Grandma Oxana yelled out.

"Get out of here!" Red blotches appeared on Mama's face.

"Leave the house. It's Philip's. Get out of my boy's home. You don't deserve to be here. Aren't you ashamed of yourself? Being a squatter!" Grandma Oxana screeched. She balled her hands into fists and approached Mama. "Freeloader! You don't deserve to be in America!"

"And you do? What makes you so special?" Mama hissed. "Leave, or I will call the police."

"You'll pay for this! One day you will!" Grandma Oxana puffed.

She turned around and left.

As soon as the door closed behind Grandma, Mama broke down. She clasped her heart and leaned on the table, as if about to collapse. I was about to suggest for her to drink some cognac, but Mama did it all on her own. She poured a shot and downed it.

CHAPTER 9

THE MELTDOWN

F all '98

That summer, the divorce was finalized, its terms generous, I later learned. Mama, Sergei, and I got to stay in the house for two more years, and Papa would pay Mama alimony during that time. After the divorce ruling, Mama, Vlada, and Zhanna got together to celebrate.

"I'll start those English classes," Mama mused, pouring the three of them coffee, then adding the cognac.

"Great idea." Vlada nodded.

"Maybe you can meet someone else?" Zhanna opened her eyes wide. "After you learn English. You could meet a nice American guy."

In response, Mama giggled. I could tell she was pleased. By then, I'd stopped asking her about Papa, though I still ached to see him. I started the third grade that year, and Sergei was a senior in high school. He surprised everyone by doing well on his SATs, and was applying to colleges. Or, rather, to just one college. To Pitt. Sergei decided to major in Philosophy there, so he could focus on his favorite German philosopher, Heidegger.

The three of us, Mama, Sergei, and I, were now happily

settled in Pittsburgh. At least for the next two years, until the alimony ran out, and we'd have to move.

———

It was a beautiful October day. Crisp, sunny weather. The leaves had turned yellow and orange, and, unusually for Pittsburgh, there wasn't a cloud in the sky. I snuck out of my first period class and left the school building through the back door. I'd never cut school before, had only seen it in movies. But Stewart had come to me in a dream the night before and told me to go to Schenley Park. He told me there was a surprise waiting for me there.

Carefully, I made my way through the alleys to the Greenfield Bridge. It was a short walk, and, once there, I ran across it and walked down in the direction of Panther Hollow Road, just as Stewart had instructed me to do. I knew the road well. Sergei and I had walked to the pool over the summer that way. I turned on to the trail to the left and walked down the path, looking left and right. Stewart hadn't told me what the surprise was, and I hoped it was a fox. I'd been wanting a pet for some time and decided a pet fox would be the perfect addition to our family.

And that's when I heard it. It was Papa's voice. He spoke Russian. I froze in place. That's what Mama and I always did if we heard anyone speak Russian in public. His voice was faint, with the sounds of the trail, the birds, and the noise of I-376 drowning it out.

"No need," Papa said. "Ne nado." It was definitely him. Papa. I dashed toward the sound. Papa had come back for me! He was in the park. He wanted to see me.

I moved fast, turned the corner, and saw Papa. He was pushing a stroller. Next to him was Marina. She looked fatter, her belly protruding, and was dressed in a long, flowing dress. She leaned to the stroller and tucked the swaddling cloth, cooing. Papa put his hand on the small of her back and said something to her. She giggled. Papa pushed the stroller forward, and they disappeared from view.

I stood, unable to move. Papa had a new family. A son. I was sure the baby in the stroller was a boy. A real son, not like me. I turned back and ran. I ran all the way back home, out of the park, across the Greenfield Bridge and up the hill to our house.

I made it home, panting, sweating.

I opened the front door and walked in. I was struck by the smell. Or rather, the absence of the smell of coffee. With Mama drinking four or five cups of coffee all morning long, our house smelled perpetually of coffee. But not that day.

"Mama?" I called. There was no answer. I sighed and went to the kitchen. The dishes from our breakfast, the left-over cereal, the half-eaten eggs, were sitting in the sink, unwashed.

"Mama!" I called out, louder now, and went upstairs. The door to Mama's bedroom was closed. My hand trembled as I pushed down on the lever and walked in. The air in the room was stale, unmoving. I gulped. I saw her face. It wasn't hers. It was a mask. Mama's eyes were staring into nothingness. Her face was yellow.

"Mama?" I stepped closer and touched her hand. It was heavy and stiff. And very cold.

I pulled back and screamed and ran downstairs, out of the house and all the way to Vlada's.

"Help!!!" I yelled, rushing into Vlada's home. "Help!"

"What is it? What's wrong?" Vlada took one look at me and put her coat on. "Come on." We ran back together, Vlada breathing hard behind me. As soon as we got there, Vlada ordered, "Stay here."

I said nothing, but waited for her, standing guard by the front door. A few moments later, I heard a wail.

That's the last thing I remember. When I came to, I was in

an unfamiliar bedroom. It was dark, with black sheets and dark curtains. The smell was musty, like the bedroom hadn't been used in a long time. Vlada was standing over me, holding Stewart.

"Thank God!" She touched my face, then reached to feel my forehead. "No fever," she mumbled to herself and handed me the toy. I hugged the fox and put him next to me on the pillow.

"Mama," I called softly.

"Mama isn't here," Vlada responded. Her voice cracked. "You are going to stay with me now. Boris and I agreed. You and Sergei."

"Where is Mama?" I insisted. "I want to see her." Lifting myself up, I perched on my elbow and looked around the room.

"Sweetheart, I'm sorry." Vlada brushed her hand against my cheek. Tears streamed down her face.

I clutched at the fox, willing the vision to go away. I wanted to be back in my living room, a controller in my hands. To see Stewart moving on the screen, jumping and running, obeying my commands. To hear Mama call me to dinner.

But that was in the past. I was about to enter a new phase of my life.

———

"Can you believe it? He never even returned my phone calls!" Vlada was sitting in her own kitchen, drinking coffee. Zhanna sat in front of her, hand under her chin, listening intently.

I was in Vlada's living room, playing Stewart. The one constant in my life.

"You're an angel for taking the kids in. You really are, Vlada."

"Come on, it's the right thing to do. Poor children. I just

can't believe he didn't even come to the funeral. Nothing! Didn't offer to help with the arrangements, as if he wasn't ever married to Lydia."

"Some people are just cruel."

"He is a monster. Didn't return my calls. Just pretended like he never even knew the kids."

"So sad."

"Sergei will start college next year, and it'll just be Rodion," Vlada's low voice boomed. I'd been hearing some variation of this conversation regularly ever since Mama's funeral, and usually didn't pay it much mind. But this time I perked my ears.

"They're lucky to have you."

"Poor Lydia. She must have been in so much pain, but never showed it," Vlada said.

"Acute liver failure!" Zhanna noted. "Poor soul."

"She couldn't afford to go to the ER, was afraid of the medical bills. No insurance."

"Philip as good as killed her."

"That he did. As good as killed her. Poor Lydia."

I sat, my mouth gaping open.

Papa as good as killed Mama. The words reverberated in my ears.

Papa killed Mama.

He was to blame.

CHAPTER 10

APRIL

Fall '06

Sergei and I had finally moved to our own place. It was a tiny two-bedroom duplex in Greenfield, just a few blocks away from Vlada's house. Vlada insisted we stay close to her, and though initially Sergei wanted to leave Greenfield, he couldn't say no to her. After staying with Vlada for seven years, it was strange to have our own place. It felt empty and quiet.

Having graduated from law school the year prior, Sergei was working as a junior attorney at a family law firm down-town. He picked family law because of what happened to Mama.

"I want to help people in these kinds of situations. Especially women," Sergei announced when he was applying for law schools.

"Your mother would have been so proud," Vlada noted, wiping away a tear.

My older brother was winning at life, and I was far from it. Unlike Sergei, I didn't like school. I hated doing homework because it took time away from my two favorite activities, gaming and reading. After Mama's death, I started reading a lot. At first, I read because it reminded me of being little and reading together with her. And then I got into it. My favorite book was *The Count of Monte Cristo*.

The two-tome edition we'd brought with us from Russia was still there, but I couldn't read it because my Russian was rudimentary. So, I had invested in my own English-language edition of Dumas' classic. The parts of the book I loved were when Edmond Dantès exacted justice on those who had done him wrong. The meticulously planned revenge, the unsuspecting villains. Settling the score, I reveled in the descriptions of how the Count took justice into his own hands. I admired the Count and dreamed of one day becoming just like him. I would avenge Mama's death and exact justice on Philip.

I had stopped calling him Papa after Mama's death. He was now Philip. Phil. The Groundhog. I called him that after Punxsutawney Phil.

In Mama's memory, I changed my own name back to Rodion. Ryder was in the past. It was the name Phil had helped me pick out, and so I couldn't keep it.

I suffered through school, though I'd managed to get decent grades. The only subject I tolerated was Art, and it was because of the teacher, Dr. Clark. He appeared gruff and unassuming, but was caring and kind. I was initially afraid of him, until, a few months into my freshman year, I came to his class soaking wet after walking to school in the pouring rain. Dr. Clark took one look at me and gave me dry clothes. And that expression of care and concern for my well-being changed my opinion of the teacher.

After that day, I loved going to Dr. Clark's class. He never asked me about my parents, but he must have known I was an orphan, because he always gave me inspirational talks. He'd ask me to stay after class and mention his ancestors, tough Irish immigrants who, despite all odds, made it in America.

"Rodion, the key to America is working hard and having no fear," he would tell me. "That's how my grandparents made it. Get your education, Rodion. It's free, at least for now." He'd give me a pointed stare. "And Allderdice is a great school."

"Yes, Dr. Clark." I'd nod. I didn't mind his speeches; I knew he meant well.

"You'll be alright, kid," Dr. Clark would note, twisting his mustache, and I'd be free to go. Usually, after his speeches, I would consider doing better at school and would even apply myself for a few days. But that effect didn't last very long. I had other priorities: my revenge.

———

On the first day of school my junior year, I got to class early to claim my favorite spot at the large table in the corner of Dr. Clark's classroom. We sat, four to each table, and I'd had the same spot for two years in a row. My intention was to continue this tradition. The room was filling with other students, but the seat across from me was still empty. The bell rang, and Dr. Clark cleared his throat, about to greet us. I held my breath, my heart leaping at the thought there wouldn't be anyone sitting across from me for an entire semester. And then a girl walked in.

"Sorry I'm late," she breathed hard. "It's my first day."

"Have a seat." Dr. Clark pointed at the seat right across from me.

The girl sat down and smiled at me. I averted my eyes.

She was pretty. Very pretty. Light brown hair and large brown eyes. There was a wholesome look to her, like she believed everything in the world would be alright. I immediately regretted my outfit. I had on Sergei's old T-shirt with Jim Morrison's face on it. I almost always wore my brother's old clothes to school. Black jeans and T-shirts. They felt like armor, as if my older brother was with me at all times, helping me deal with the world. But that day I wished I was dressed in newer clothes.

Dr. Clark did roll call.

"Rodion Likharev."

"Present," I responded.

"Welcome back." He gave me an approving nod.

"April McPherson," he continued.

The girl said: "Present."

April.

Until then, I never understood why women got named after months. Maya. Julia. Augusta. Especially not Augusta. But April's name suited her. It was pretty. Just like her. I gaped at her and didn't realize it until after she lifted her eyes at me. I saw her cheeks turn slightly pink. *Does she like me?* I looked away.

Dr. Clark had placed several objects in the middle of the table. Animal skulls. It was how we usually started the year in Art class. That day, the one I'd picked out was a fox skull, and I took it as a good omen. Though I no longer slept with the fox lovey, and almost never played Stewart the Fox, I still loved foxes.

The hours I'd spent, the levels achieved, the dreams I'd had featuring Stewart, all that was important to me. I sat there, staring at the fox skull, preparing to draw, when the girl spoke to me.

"Hey," April whispered.

I looked up at her and felt myself blush. She was so pretty; it was hard to look at her.

"Do you remember me?" Her eyes were incredible.

I looked down at the skull, pretending like I couldn't hear her.

"You're Rodion!" she insisted. I was forced to look up at her again. April was looking directly at me and smiling. A nice, open smile, as if I was a long-lost friend she had found at last. I almost rolled my eyes, but then I remembered. The smile! Only the last time I'd seen it, she was missing a front tooth.

"The school bus!" She smiled. "Do you remember?"

"Excuse the interruption, folks, but how about we focus on drawing?" Dr. Clark walked up to our table and narrowed his eyes. I could almost see a smirk on his face. I looked back to the skull and drew, counting the time until class ended.

April was the girl from the school bus. The very one who sat right next to me when I first went to kindergarten without speaking a word of English. The class dragged on forever, and I couldn't wait for it to end. When, at last, the bell rang, April spoke first.

"Rodion! I can't believe it's you. I barely recognized you. What a coincidence. It's my first day here."

"I know," I said, and immediately regretted how gruff I sounded.

"You speak English now."

"Oh. Yeah." I shrugged. "So, where have you been all this time?" I asked, and my face flushed red. I sounded so corny.

April grabbed her bag, and we walked out of the classroom together.

"In Singapore."

"Wait, for real?" My mouth gaped open.

"Yes, we moved there right after kindergarten. Because of my dad's job." She sighed.

"What does your dad do?"

"It's some Artificial Intelligence stuff. We barely see him. Cutting-edge research." Another sigh.

"Artificial Intelligence? Isn't that dangerous?" I tried to keep the conversation going as long as I could.

"No, of course not." She waved her hand to dismiss the idea.

"Haven't you seen *Resident Evil*?" I gave April an incredulous look. "The Red Queen? You know, the destroyer?"

"That's just a movie. I mean, I've never seen it myself. But my dad wouldn't do stuff like that. But anyway, we moved back here, so I could apply to colleges. You know what they say, junior year is the most important year of high school." She rolled her eyes.

"Yeah." I didn't know what else to say. April suddenly seemed so out of reach, with her global travels and plans for college. I was just a loser, an orphan with a dubious future. I'd be lucky to graduate from high school.

"And what about you?" She ran her hand through her hair.

"My mother died when I was eight. And I never had a father," I heard myself say.

"I'm sorry." She gave me a look full of compassion. I felt tears well up in my eyes and, to avoid crying in front of her, I turned around and scurried off.

"Rodion," I heard her call after me through the noise of the corridor, and clenched my fists in anger as I turned the corner and went to my next period.

Stupid girl. Stupid idiot. What am I even doing talking to her?

I tried not to think about the encounter but couldn't. This had never happened to me before. Usually, the second I got home, I was in my zone. I attached myself to the console, and I was gone. Closed to the world.

But not that day. The second I turned on the screen, it was April's face I saw in front of me. Her beautiful eyes. The compassionate look on her face when I told her my parents were dead. I wanted to kick myself for being vulnerable in front of a stranger.

Tomorrow, it'll be different. I won't talk to her, I promised myself, and tried to play. But I couldn't. "I'm sorry," I heard her voice and wanted to wail in pain. To shriek.

CHAPTER 11

TIME BRANCH

The next day, I walked into Art class, determined to avoid April at all costs. I decided I'd sit in a different place, but the second I walked in, April waved at me. She was already sitting in the seat across from my usual spot.

"Hey, Rodion!" The expression on her face was so open and sincere that I had no choice but to wave back.

"Hi, April," I responded, and to my horror, felt myself grinning as I walked over to sit across from her.

"How are you?" She scanned my face for a reaction, then continued, "Listen, my mom wants to meet you."

"What? Why?" I almost choked on a piece of gum I was chewing.

"I told her we met on the school bus back in kindergarten, so she wanted me to bring you over. To say hello."

"Okay." I nodded, despite myself. I couldn't believe I'd just been invited to April's house. It was like being invited to the moon.

"So, how about this Saturday? Maybe you can come over for lunch? We live over by Wilkins and Murray."

"Yes." I nodded with such eagerness I was sure I looked like a total loser.

"I'll give you my address after class." She promised.

The bell rang and Dr. Clark started roll call. I couldn't focus. Here I was, Pip from *Great Expectations*, about to go to April's house and meet her mother. I pictured April's mother as a Miss Havisham grilling me until I was broken.

———

I hadn't planned on telling Sergei about the visit, but he was home before I left for April's and forced me to dress up.

"You're going to meet someone's parents. You gotta make an effort, look nice. You wanna make a good impression, don't you?"

"No."

"Of course you do. Is she cute? The girl?"

"No."

"Alright, listen, if you want to go dressed in rags, fine, but you'll regret it later."

"I won't. I couldn't care less," I said, then remembered how I'd regretted wearing the black jeans and the Jim Morrison T-shirt at school and sighed. "Alright, fine, give me the clothes."

"And you'll need different shoes," Sergei said, but I stopped him.

"Not the shoes. I'm wearing sneakers."

"Alright, alright." He chuckled.

So, there I was that Saturday at 12pm, standing in front of a three-storied brick mansion on Woodmont Street, dressed in beige pants and a sweater. I adjusted my belt, looked down at my sneakers, drew in my breath, and knocked. April opened the door.

"Hi!" She smiled. "Come in."

I took in the spacious hallway, the fluffy carpet on the floor of the living room that lay to the right. A large gray cat appeared and positioned itself next to the bannister, blocking my passage. Its green eyes inspected me.

"This is Oliver!" April giggled. "He's very friendly. You can say hello if you want."

I approached the cat. I had no idea how one said hello to a cat, so I simply stared at the animal. The cat meowed and turned its back to me, wiggling its tail.

"He wants you to pet him," April translated. I squatted next to Oliver and petted him between his ears. Immediately, he purred loudly.

"He likes you!" April clapped. "That's great. It means you're a good person," she announced. "Animals pick up on things like that."

She led me to the kitchen.

"Mama is waiting for us in the kitchen," April said, and pointed to the back of the house. The way she said, not Mom or Mother, but Mama, for a second I thought it was my mama waiting for us. My brain short-circuited, and I could see my mother's face right in front of me. I could almost feel her hands comforting me. My eyes welled up with tears and I let out a deep breath. I needed to run away from this place, to disappear before I had a meltdown. I dug my nails into the palms of my hands to prevent myself from unraveling and followed April into the kitchen.

A tall, energetic-looking woman with bright blue eyes rose to greet me. Her hair was pulled back in a ponytail, and she was wearing jeans and a black T-shirt.

"Rodion! Nice to meet you. I am Mrs. McPherson. Elizabeth." She flashed a smile. "April tells me you met all the way back in kindergarten."

"Yes." I nodded.

"Your name. Rodion. It's very unusual."

"I guess so. I was named after my grandfather," I responded. I hadn't thought of this in years.

"How interesting. I guess you've read *Crime and Punishment*?"

"No, not yet." I averted my eyes. I had tried reading the book, but each time I started, I grew bored and confused by all the different nicknames and storylines and gave up.

"You know, there is a character with your name in the book. Rodion Raskolnikov." Mrs. McPherson looked very pleased with herself, carefully pronouncing the difficult Russian name.

I nodded.

"I hope you read it and let me know what you think. April is about to read it, too." Mrs. McPherson gave her daughter a pointed stare. "We're having lasagna for lunch, Rodion," Mrs. McPherson turned to me. "Do you like lasagna?"

"I've never had it before," I admitted, then added, "But I've always wanted to try it. Because of Garfield."

"That's the cutest thing. So, you learned about lasagna from watching *Garfield*?" Mrs. McPherson clapped her hands in excitement.

"Yes. Well. The video games, mostly."

"Ah, I see."

April's mom placed a huge slice of lasagna in front of me. We ate in silence.

"So, how do you like it? Do you get Garfield now?" Mrs. McPherson asked, smiling, as she watched me take several bites of the dish.

"Yes! I really like lasagna. A lot. Thank you."

"Well, I am glad I got to introduce you to this dish."

I took the last bite of the lasagna and got up to help clean up the dishes.

"Thank you, Rodion." Mrs. McPherson smiled. "Not many friends of April's are so polite."

"Mom!" April raised her eyebrows.

"It's true. Not one of your friends ever offered to help me clean up after eating." Her mother shrugged.

"I'm used to cleaning. It's just me and my brother, that's why. If I don't do it, he has to, and he doesn't have time."

I put the dishes into the sink.

"I see." Mrs. McPherson bit her lip. "Listen, Rodion, how would you like to come here, visit us, from time to time?"

"Thank you. Yes, I'd love to."

———

After that day, I started going over to April's. At first, it was once a week, but then my visits became more frequent. After a while, her mother started leaving us alone. I never met April's father. It was almost like he didn't exist at all, though April mentioned his job took him to California, to Silicon Valley.

We usually walked to April's house together after school. Our unusual pair attracted some attention at first, but then people got used to our spending time together. April and I spoke about everything. In the beginning, she spoke more while I listened, but then I started sharing things with her as well. April told me about her favorite books and songs. April's world consumed me. She confided in me, told me things I never thought I would learn about anyone.

"You know, Rodion, my aunt, she does this thing. It's kind of like time travel."

"What? For real?"

"Yes, past life regression therapy. She helps people connect with their true self and live out different life scenarios."

"That doesn't exist in real life. That's like a video game." I shook my head.

"It does! She has a lot of clients. Some of them are famous."

"No way! Have you ever done it?"

An idea popped into my head. I would go to a life scenario where Mama was still alive.

"Not yet. I want to try it out, though. But my aunt said I have to wait till I'm eighteen."

"Why is that?"

"So my brain is formed. She says I'm still too young."

"Oh. I guess I'm too young to try it, too?"

"Yes, she won't do it until you're eighteen. But we can maybe try it together? When we're older?"

I felt a knot form in my stomach. *Was April talking about a future together?* I felt the tips of my fingers grow cold. *Did I want a future with her?* Immediately, I brought up a topic that was sure to get me into a grim state of mind.

"You know, I haven't told you how I came to America. My mom married this dude. He was kind of like my stepfather, and then he dumped us." I omitted the part where Phil believed he was my biological father and how he'd learned the truth.

"What?" She stared at me. "You never told me about him."

"No. He's awful. I don't like to think about him."

"I'm sorry. Where is he now?"

"Around." I shrugged. "He's got a new family now."

"So, he didn't help when your mom died?"

"No." I shook my head. I was on the verge of bursting into tears, but there was another emotion rising in me. Revenge. "But I want to punish him for what he did."

"What are you gonna do to him?"

"I dunno yet." I clenched my fists. "But I'm gonna wait until I'm older, like the Count of Monte Cristo. And then I'll find a way."

CHAPTER 12
THE FIGHT

all' 07

I don't know at what point I realized I was in love with April. It happened gradually, and I eased into this feeling in such small increments that by the time it happened, I couldn't stop it even if I wanted to. I woke up thinking about April and went to bed wanting to be with her.

We spoke on the phone every day, and I felt like the only times I truly lived were when I was with her. The rest of the time, I waited to see her. I did my usual stuff, survived in school so I could graduate, played video games, read some books. I had no plans for what I would do after graduation, but with the end of my senior year still over six months away, I wasn't too worried. Meanwhile, April was busy applying to colleges and spoke nonstop about what she would do after graduation.

"Rodion," she brought up the topic casually one day. We were sitting in her kitchen, having just finished eating turkey sandwiches. Mrs. McPherson had instructed me to eat anything I wanted, and I was grateful. I was growing and hungry all the time. "I'm applying to Penn early decision,"

April said. She had mentioned Penn before. Her parents had met at Penn their freshman year.

"They'll let me know by December if I got in, and then I'll have to decide right away," she went on, her voice chipper.

"Wait, isn't Penn in Philly?" I asked, stuffing a bite of a sandwich into my mouth.

"Yes."

"So, that means you'll leave Pittsburgh?" The possibility of parting with April hit me for the first time, and I stopped chewing.

"If I get in," her voice trailed off.

"What about Carnegie Mellon?" I stared at her, clutching on the last bit of hope. April had mentioned applying there, and it was the best school in Pittsburgh, one of the top universities in the country.

"It's a good school if you want to do Engineering. Sciences, Math, stuff like that. But not for Humanities."

"Oh, okay," I mumbled. "So, you don't wanna stay in Pittsburgh then?"

"Rodion, it's not that, I do. But Penn is an Ivy League university. My parents went there. Both of them. It will open doors for me."

"Doors." I chuckled. "The Doors of Perception."

"What?"

"Oh, nothing." I got up, leaving an unfinished sandwich sitting on the table. "I gotta go."

"You're leaving already?" April stared at me, her mouth gaping open.

"Yeah. Sergei wants me home early tonight." I dashed out of her house. I knew April would immediately understand I was lying, because she knew very well that Sergei never wanted me home early, rarely checked on me, and I had unlimited freedom, at least for a high school kid.

As soon as I got home, I threw myself on the couch. I was about to turn on the console, but then I noticed the two-tome edition of *The Count of Monte Cristo,* and I reached for the book.

Mama. I missed her so much. My mamochka. She could have made everything alright. I started thinking about reading this book together, the injustice of everything Dantès went through. And then, sweet, sweet revenge. The Count's methodical revenge, where he defeated his enemies one by one. In my case, it was an easier task. I only had one person to punish. *Phil, the groundhog.*

I closed the book with a sigh and went to bed.

———

April and I didn't speak after that encounter for several days. I didn't know how to deal with the prospect of losing her, so I avoided her. And April, as she later told me, expected an apology. I'd never apologized for anything in my life, and so our friendship came to a stalemate. We went from being the closest people to each other to nothing.

Cutting April out was easy for me. I was used to the people I loved disappearing from my life by then. First, Phil. Then, Mama. So, I figured, it made sense that it was only a matter of time before April would also disappear, and this proved me right. *Perhaps I have the magic touch. All I have to do is love someone, and then they go away,* I thought, bile forming in my throat.

"What are you doing, moping around all day? Did your girlfriend dump you?" Sergei asked, seeing me at home for the fifth day in a row, glued to the console.

"I'm not moping."

"Did she actually?"

"No one dumped me. We were just friends."

"Yeah, right." Sergei chuckled. "What did you do?"

"Nothing."

That afternoon, we went to Vlada's house. We were

invited to some family gathering. She had them a lot, huge parties with dancing, drinking, toasts, and lots of speeches. Vlada called us her "bonus sons" and told everyone she had five boys.

"My boys!" Vlada exclaimed, as soon as Sergei and I walked through the door. She rushed to embrace us, Sergei first, then me. "Let me look at you!" She stepped back and immediately shook her head. "What's going on with this one?" Vlada pointed at me as she turned to Sergei. She had this manner with me, speaking about me in the third person, as if I weren't there.

"His girlfriend dumped him," Sergei noted nonchalantly.

"Girlfriend? Little Rodion had a girlfriend? Who is it?" Vlada pulled me aside and started asking questions. Or, rather, grilling me. I knew she wouldn't stop until she knew everything. It was easier to fess up than to keep lying, so I did.

"Rodion, you need to apologize to this girl," Vlada concluded, after hearing my story. "You can't act like that with women."

"We're just friends," I countered.

"Or with friends. Get her some flowers. Go over there and tell her you're sorry. And that you don't want to lose her."

I felt my stomach churn at the idea. I shook my head vigorously.

"If you don't do it on your own, I'll take you over there myself," Vlada threatened, and I knew she meant it. Vlada didn't make empty promises. I pictured her going with me to April's, having to introduce her to April's mother, their conversation in the kitchen, details of my childhood being dragged out into the open.

"Alright," I said. "But can I do it without the flowers?"

"How many days has it been?"

"I dunno," I lied. I knew exactly how many. It had been five days since we last spoke. I'd counted every single one.

"Well, if it's less than two, you might get away with no flowers. Otherwise." She sighed. "Suit yourself."

"Vlada, there you are!" One of the guests appeared and pulled her away.

I went over to the table, set with the traditional Russian fare. The sight of the food made me nauseous. I knew if I didn't leave right there and then, I'd be stuck at the party until after the meal, which could, with all the toasts, chatting, and several courses served, easily take over three hours.

My eyes darted to the antique clock, Vlada's pride and joy, that stood in the corner. It was 4pm. I backed out of the living room, bumped into a guest, turned around, and dashed into the street. I ran all the way to Giant Eagle, remembering to check for my wallet only when I was already inside of the supermarket.

The bucket with the flowers that stood by the door put me into a stupor. I stared at them, then hesitantly picked up a bouquet of orange roses. A moment later, I remembered Grandma Oxana and the fight over the flowers the first time we met her and dropped the bouquet into the bucket. I swallowed hard, my heart beating fast. Ready to bolt, I stepped back and bumped into a guy. He was tall, broad-shouldered, dressed in a T-shirt with the Carnegie Mellon logo on it.

"First time?" he asked, giving me a sympathetic smile. I knew right away what he meant.

"Yes."

"Take these." He handed me a bouquet of pink roses, picking them up from the bucket. "It's a nice color, not overly romantic. But could be, if you wanted it to be. You don't want to get red or white."

"Thank you," I mumbled.

"Any time." The man extended his hand. "Christopher."

"Rodion." I shook it. His hand was warm, and the handshake felt reassuring. Immediately, I felt better.

"Good luck to you," he said.

I took the pink roses and was about to say something else to the man, but Christopher vanished, as if he had never existed.

On the way to April's, I went over several scenarios in my head. Each one was worse than the other. They ranged from April not being at home, to April slamming the door in my face, to April inviting me in, then telling me she never wanted to see me again. I got to her house, barely able to breathe. My hands trembling, I knocked on the door. It opened immediately, as if April had been expecting me.

"Rodion!" April exclaimed and stepped towards me. Her eyes looked red, purple bags under them. "What are you doing here?" her voice cracked.

"I came back," I extracted, sounding like a moron. None of the scenarios I'd rehearsed in my head involved April looking the way she did.

"Come in." She stepped back, opening the door to allow me inside. As I walked in, she noticed the flowers and gave me a questioning look.

"These are for you." I followed her eyes.

"Thank you." She started crying. Tears streamed down her face, and she wiped them away, but they kept on coming. I went to help her, to help wipe them, but she pushed me away. "No." She shook her head. "You can't do this. I was just getting used to being without you."

I gulped and said nothing. I reached for her hand, and she let me take it.

"Don't you have anything to say?" April looked at me through the tears.

I couldn't do it. I couldn't say the words. I stood there in silence, staring at her, holding her hand.

"Is that all?" She pulled her hand away. "Why did you even come here?"

I still couldn't answer. I stared at her, feeling faint.

"Rodion?" April looked at me, wide-eyed. Her face was

suddenly spinning over my head. The pink roses merged into a cupola and it pulled me inside.

When I came to, I was on the floor, Oliver purring on my chest. I slowly opened my eyes and saw April. She was sitting on the floor next to me.

"Hey!" I said. "I'm sorry." The words came so easily now. She sighed.

"Let me help you get up." April extended her hand to me. "Are you okay?"

"I guess so." In reality, I was petrified. I had blacked out, and it came from nowhere.

"It might be because you're growing quickly. I read it can happen."

"Oh, yeah? It was weird."

"Listen, Rodion, do you promise to never disappear like that again?"

"I'll try."

"Because even if I go away to college, it doesn't mean that we won't be friends. Right?" April attempted a smile, as if simply continuing a conversation we had started before I'd run out of her house.

"I don't want you to leave," I said, and it took all of my willpower to say those words. I stared at her, feeling my fingertips grow cold from the tension. We'd never spoken about the nature of our relationship before.

"I don't want to leave, either." April stared at me.

Then she leaned in and kissed me. And I kissed her back. We held hands and kissed each other, and I felt as if my whole life, my whole world, was complete.

"April, I love you," I said.

"I love you, too."

That day, we became boyfriend and girlfriend.

When April told her friends about it, they gave her incredulous looks, because everyone had assumed that we'd been dating all that time. But it took us over a year to admit to having feelings for each other.

"You're my best friend, Rodion," April told me, and I told her the same. Except she was my only friend, too. I had a few acquaintances, but there was no one I'd call a real friend. Only her.

April sent her application to Penn, and by late December, she would know whether she got in. It was a little over a month away, and that month had filled me with hope. I was happy. I barely thought of Mama, of my own lackluster prospects in life, and of my revenge against the Groundhog. And because I was now spending more time with April, I barely played video games.

We'd gotten into a routine, and I would go over to April's twice a week, right after school. The other days I had my part-time job at a pizza place on Murray Avenue, and April was busy with after-school activities.

On the last day of school for the year, we got to April's, when, having just walked up to the porch, she suddenly yelped, pointing at the mailbox: "The envelope!"

My eyes followed her gaze, and I saw the corner of an envelope sticking out. A blue and red logo on it. My heart sank. I could just make out the outlines of the letters "Pennsylvania" on the seal.

"Rodion, feel it, please. I'm too nervous to do it myself." April closed her eyes and turned away.

It was childish and I would have laughed, had I not felt terror at the prospect of April leaving Pittsburgh. With trembling hands, I reached into the mailbox and pulled out the envelope. The mailbox clanked, and April asked, "Is it big? Or small? If it's big, then I got in." I swallowed hard, twisting the large envelope in my hands.

"It's big," I said after a pause.

"It is?" April turned to face me and ripped the envelope out of my hands. She examined it, turning it left and right, then shook it and finally ripped the top open, exclaiming: "Alright, here I go!"

"Congratulations!" she read. "You have been admitted to join the class of 2012…" April stopped and looked at me. "I got in! Rodion! I got in!" She jumped up and down. "Oh, my God! I'm going to Penn! I gotta call my mom. And Daddy. Wow! They're gonna be so excited."

I swallowed hard. I knew April wanted this, but until that moment, I didn't realize just how much. A few more months, and she would leave. Just like everyone whom I loved did.

I stood there, staring at her, trying to stay calm. And remembered my plan. I had important business to finish. I had to avenge Mama's death.

CHAPTER 13
THE GRADUATE

High school graduation came and went. I found the whole thing ridiculous. Happy, teary-eyed parents, the flowers, the smiling seniors. I didn't want to go, but Vlada made me. She attended with her silent husband, and Sergei, of course. I wore Sergei's old cap and gown that had miraculously survived our move out of Vlada's. She invited us over for dinner after and there we spoke of my future.

"Rodion, what will you be doing now?" Vlada asked, serving me a huge slab of meat jelly. Holodets was her signature dish, made of congealed boiled meat bones. Vlada assured us it worked miracles for the immune system, and we'd gotten used to it.

"I dunno." I shrugged and looked at my plate. Other than dedicating myself full time to gaming and to putting together a plan of revenge, I had no other ideas, though I figured a plan would emerge on its own. Eventually, without my active role in it.

"You're good at that tech stuff, Rodion." Vlada was smiling proudly, kind wrinkles forming around her eyes. I blushed. Ever since I helped her install a wireless router, she considered me a demigod.

"Umm-umm." I took a bite of the holodets.

"He is great at that stuff." Sergei chuckled. I couldn't tell if he was being serious.

"Zhanna told me," Vlada announced, pausing for effect. "Vista Communications is hiring technicians." Sergei and I both looked up. "Zhanna's nephew just got a job there. The pay is good, and they give you all the training you need."

Vista was the biggest telecoms company in Pittsburgh, and it had a good reputation. I'd seen their white trucks with the red logo around, and pretty much everyone in the city used their fiber-optic cable network.

"What a great idea." Sergei nodded. "Thank you, Vlada. This is perfect. How does he apply?"

I pulled back from the table and put my fork down. A brilliant idea just hit me.

What if I got access to Phil's house? Driving around in a van with the Vista logo would give me enough credibility to do what I wanted. Revenge. I could get in unnoticed, exact my revenge, and disappear.

"I'm in," I said immediately.

"You are?" Vlada gave me a quizzical stare. "I didn't expect you to agree so quickly."

"Yes." I flashed her a reassuring smile. I was picturing Phil, his face contorted in pain, me standing over him, triumphant.

———

Two days later, April and I were sitting on Flagstaff Hill, on the edge of Schenley Park. It overlooked the city, with the perfect view of Downtown Pittsburgh.

Every Sunday and Wednesday night in the summer, there were movie screenings after dark. We went there, like clockwork, and sat together, at the top of the hill, looking over the city, mostly ignoring the movie, talking, holding hands, kissing. Families would set up their blankets around us, complete with picnic baskets, kids would run around and frolic, while April and I were in our separate little universe.

That night, there was yet another wholesome family movie showing. It was always something "the whole family could watch," like *Shrek* or *The Little Mermaid*.

"I love you," April whispered.

"Love you, too," I said back. I leaned in to kiss her, when I suddenly heard someone speaking Russian. I tensed. A woman's voice cut through the darkness.

"Over here! Syuda."

I froze inside, struck by the vision. It was a woman dressed in pastels, shorts, and a tank top, a white flowing tunic. She'd gotten fatter, but I recognized her. It was Marina.

She pulled along a gaunt boy of about eight or nine. And closing the procession was Philip. I felt as if I'd been punched in the stomach and nearly gagged. Time stood still.

My nemesis was moving downhill, a foldable chair hanging on one shoulder, a cooler bag in the other. He was maneuvering through the crowd, looking for an empty spot, turning his head left and right. A true family man. I gulped, anger rising in me. It was the life he took away from me.

Oblivious to me, Phil and his new family passed us and continued down the hill. I sat there, mouth gaping open, panting like a dog.

"Rodion, what's wrong?" April took my hand. "Your hand feels so cold. Rodion?"

"I'm okay." I swallowed hard. "Just saw someone I used to know."

"Who is it?" April turned her head left and right. Suddenly, she screamed. "Look! A fox!"

"What?" I followed April's line of sight and there it was. A fox. Running on the edge of the hill, ignoring the crowd. It waved its tail and disappeared into the woods.

"It must have gotten lost." I stared after the animal, not sure whether the vision had been real.

"Are you okay?" April took my hand in hers.

April was real, and I loved her. I turned to face her.

"I am." I nodded.

"Rodion, I am worried about you," April said.

"Why? I'll be fine. I'll work at Vista."

"Listen, my dad's lab is hiring. I've been meaning to tell you, but I had to check with him first."

"Isn't that like top secret AI stuff?"

"Yes, that's the thing. They are looking for a tester. And I think you'll be perfect. Get this, they want a young male, aged between eighteen and twenty-two, with experience in gaming. So, I thought, since you're turning eighteen in August…" April's voice trailed off.

"But that's like, half of Pittsburgh. Guys like me are a dime a dozen." I chuckled.

"I know. It'll be competitive, and they got lots of applicants. But I asked him, and you can still apply."

"Alright, I'll do it. For you." I kissed her.

"Great. It might actually be kinda fun. And I think they pay way more than Vista," April added.

The following day, April and I were sitting in her kitchen.

"Here, Daddy said you gotta fill this out." April produced a thick folder and handed it to me. I opened it and took out a stack of papers. It was a ten-page form, double-sided, followed by several pages of disclosures, all written in tiny print.

"You gotta fill out everything and then initial," April said, pointing to the bottom of the first page. "Everywhere where it's highlighted."

I frowned, staring at the documents.

"Listen, maybe it's not such a good idea."

"Come on, this could be such a good opportunity. It's just the stuff their lawyers make them put because of confidentiality."

For a moment, I thought of taking the papers home and asking Sergei to review, but April was looking at me expectantly. So, I nodded in agreement.

"Alright." I sighed and sat down, chewing on the tip of the pen. "Let me just get it over with."

"You're welcome, by the way." April said.

It took me nearly thirty minutes to go over the questionnaire. It asked me about my health history, my family health history, place of birth, linguistic abilities, favorite hobbies and foods. Height, weight, birth date, movies and books I liked. Without hesitation, I put *The Count of Monte Cristo* as my favorite book. For music, I put The Doors. Favorite movie—*The Matrix*.

I was almost enjoying it until I got to the last page. There, I saw the following text:

"Dear friend, thank you for applying for the tester position at The Lab. We'd like to get to know you as a person to ensure that we're the right fit for you. Please let us know about a social cause you care about, something you think is important in 500 words or less."

"April, hey, look at this thing." I showed the blank page to April. "They're asking for an essay."

"They are?"

"Yeah, can you just do this for me?"

"No, Rodion, I can't. You gotta do this yourself. It's just a short essay. Just write something."

"But I don't care about any causes. This is ridiculous."

"Sure you do. You care about justice, don't you? You talk about it all the time."

"Umm, I guess so. Justice? But is that a social cause? I thought they'd want me to write about baby seals or stuff like that."

"No, just write about social justice. Or the criminal justice system?"

"Alright."

I forced myself to sit down and write. I remember writing about the concept of blind justice and how it wasn't entirely true. And that it was up to the private citizens and individuals to exact justice in the world, because the judiciary system wasn't balanced, blind, or even fair. I wrote about cases where the justice system couldn't persecute a criminal for reasons of lack of proof, and in some cases it was up to private citizens to take justice into their own hands. Once I started going, I was on a roll. I thought of the Count and the fact that Mama's death was unfair. And how the legal system didn't consider Phil a criminal. In fact, in the eyes of the law, he was a good citizen. And yet, he killed Mama. His actions had destroyed multiple lives. At least three, as far as I knew. But possibly, many others.

CHAPTER 14
THE LION'S GATE

My eighteenth birthday was approaching. I thought little of it, but April was ecstatic.

"Rodion! This is amazing. You're going to be eighteen, and the date this year. It's the Lion's Gate, but even more amazing than usual. 08/08/08!" She clapped.

"Who cares?" I shrugged.

"That's special. Even the Olympics in China, just think about it. The entire country of China thinks the date is special. They picked this special date for the big event. We have to celebrate."

"How?" I gave April a kiss. "It's just a number."

"But it's your number." April's eyes sparkled. "So, you don't wanna celebrate at all?" The expression on April's face was gentle, and I could tell she was about to ask about my mom and talk about feelings. I couldn't have that, so I agreed.

"I guess we could do something. Just the two of us?"

"Remember, we talked about visiting my aunt? The one who does past life regressions?"

"The weird aunt?"

"Yes. That's the one. She said she can do the regression if you're eighteen. So, that might be a cool thing to do for your birthday. What do you think?" April reached for my hand. "It could be our special time, right before I leave town."

"Okay." I nodded. I was trying to avoid speaking about April's imminent departure, and the way it made me feel. Powerless and weak. Like I would lose her forever.

"Alright, I'll tell Aunt Molly we're coming."

———

April had her driver's license and her parents let her drive their old car, an old Volvo station wagon. I found it pretty ugly, but April was immensely proud of it.

"Don't you think it looks like a refrigerator?" I'd tease her.

"No, it's cute. It's their signature shape, and it's very safe!"

April pet the car, as if the Volvo could understand her. Maybe it did, because that Volvo, despite being at least twenty years old, worked like clockwork. Its motor purred and when April pulled up to pick me up on the morning of my birthday, I could have sworn the car winked at me.

"Ready?" April asked, as I opened the door and got in. "I brought us some snacks." She pointed to the back seat, where I saw bottles of water and a cooler.

"Thank you! You are amazing."

"Happy Birthday!" April said. "Listen, I thought we'd take the scenic route. Not the turnpike," she noted, as we drove out of the city.

"Sure." I nodded.

I did my best to show an understanding, though I'd only been out of Pittsburgh a handful of times since moving there from Moscow. *Thirteen years,* I thought, suddenly remembering the anniversary of my arrival in Pittsburgh had passed almost unnoticed. April put her hand on my knee, and I put my hand over hers. Holding her hand in mine settled me, as it usually did.

We got on Route 30 and, just a few minutes after leaving the city, the scenery changed completely. Gone were the strip malls, the houses, the streets of the city. Instead, the road took us along green hills, with the occasional farms.

"This is so nice," April murmured.

"It is. Look! Cows!" I exclaimed, fidgeting in my seat. It was the first time I'd seen cows in America.

"Oh, yeah. I guess we're entering farmland."

April turned to me for a second and I squeezed her hand. A feeling of love overwhelmed me. April was the closest person I had in the whole world.

With determination, April turned off Route 30 onto a country road. We drove in silence, the shared magic between us, and then the road got narrower. April pulled her hand away from mine and scratched her head.

"It's gotta be right around here," she said under her breath. "We're almost there, Rodion."

Immediately, I felt a knot form in my stomach. Until that point, April and I had been in a magical universe, just the two of us, and now I was thrown back to reality.

"I see it!" April braked hard, and my seatbelt tightened. We came to a stop. "Right there!" April pointed to a tree, and I saw where she was pointing. It was a sign, and it read *Molly's Organic Farm*.

The writing looked old, paint peeling, but at some point, someone had cared enough to decorate the sign with cherries and leaves.

"We're here," April said unnecessarily.

"Yeah," I mumbled.

April steered the car, and we turned onto a gravel road right behind the sign. We pulled up and stopped at a yellow arm barrier blocking the way.

"I forgot about this thing." April shook her head. "I think we better leave the car here. I'm not sure how to move this thing. What do you think?"

"Here's what I think." I turned to her and gave her a kiss. I knew it was corny, but it was the only thing I could think of doing at that moment.

April kissed me back, then leaned to me and looked me in the eye. "I love you," April mouthed.

"Love you, too." We sat like this, staring ahead of us, not moving. I wished the moment would last forever.

"Shall we?" April asked after a pause.

We walked around the barrier, leaving the car sitting on the side of the road. The gravel road climbed steeply uphill. It got darker and darker, as the tops of the trees grew dense above us. And then we came to a clearing and saw a house.

It was painted dark brown, its color blending with the surrounding forest. A tall birch tree grew by the entrance, the leaves rustling. A path curved around the house, and I saw a meadow covered in flowers.

"It looks so pretty. Every time I come here, I feel so peaceful." April noted, and at that very moment the door of the house opened and a woman appeared on the threshold.

She looked to be in her fifties and was dressed all in black, with a long skirt, a long-sleeve shirt, and a black apron over it. Her hair was slicked back and was also black with streaks of gray.

"April! Come here, sweetheart." The woman smiled brightly and extended her hands.

"Aunt Molly!" April exclaimed and hugged her. "This is Rodion." April turned to me.

"Nice to meet you," the woman said and smiled. It was a genuine, kind smile, and I felt welcome.

"Great that you made it out here. And where's your car?"

"We left it by the arm barrier."

"I should have moved it out of the way. Mike!" the woman yelled into the house.

"Yes, honey," we heard a low voice.

"You forgot to lift the arm barrier. April is here!" Aunt Molly yelled. Then, turning to us, said: "Come in, come in!"

Aunt Molly was about to say something else, but a large man materialized by her side. Everything about him was oversized: he was tall, over six feet, broad-shouldered, had a large protruding belly, huge hands, and even his beard was long.

"Hello there!" He smiled at April, then, turning to me, rumbled, "I'm Mike."

He extended his enormous hand to me, and I shook it.

"You two must be tired. Driving always tires me out. Have a seat. Let me feed you."

Aunt Molly fussed, leading us into a cluttered kitchen. There was a round table, several chairs, a buffet, and a book-shelf. On the ceiling hung ropes with drying mushrooms and berries. On the stove that was in the corner of this strange-looking kitchen was a huge pot of water, boiling over, steam rising.

"Honey, I was just preparing the brine," Mike noted, and, grunting, took a seat at the table.

"Yes, alright." Molly turned the pot off. "Mike is a taxider-mist," she said, as if that explained anything.

Only then did I notice the animals. Two huge deer heads hung on the walls above the kitchen entrance. Several taxi-dermy rabbits were on the windowsill. A squirrel stood on the kitchen table. And in the corner of the kitchen stood a life-sized taxidermy bear.

"Did April tell you?" Aunt Molly asked, turning to me.

"No," I said, staring at the animals in awe.

"I always say our house is like a zoo. Only the animals are dead." Mike chuckled.

"Oh, honey." Aunt Molly shook her head, as if at an adorable child.

"Do you hunt?" I asked.

"Occasionally," Michael noted. "But mostly I work on animals clients bring to me."

"You made all of these?"

"Yes, of course. Have been doing this for over fifty years." The man surveyed the room proudly. "Started when I was thirteen."

"Mike, tell them how you got started, honey. It's a great story." Molly gave her husband an adoring look.

"Killed my first eagle when I was thirteen, and my uncle told me to stuff that sucker up. So, I learned. Back then, I did it through a subscription catalogue. And never stopped. Been going strong all these years."

"That's amazing." April stared at the man. "I've never heard that story, Uncle Mike."

Molly brought out a plate of cured meat.

"This is bear meat. We prepared it last night," Michael noted, and took a slice off the plate. "You can really taste how fresh it is. Bears are tricky." He took a bite and nodded in approval. "If a bear eats trash, like those city bears do, the meat won't smell as good. But this guy came from the mountains. Fresh-smelling meat."

"Excellent, honey." Aunt Molly gave her husband a smile of approval. "So, let me show you around the farm."

"Thank you." April rose from her seat and started after Aunt Molly. As they were nearing the door, April turned to me. "Aren't you coming?"

I was enjoying sitting at the table and listening to Mike, but I rose and followed April out. Molly led us through the meadow to a garden that had been concealed from view. It was partly shaded and meticulously maintained.

"This is my farm. I do everything here myself. Everything." She walked, showing us the plants, tomatoes, cucumbers, squash. "Getting ready for Halloween," she noted, showing us the pumpkins. "And a little to the side is my orchard, remember it?" The woman turned to April. April nodded.

"And this is our water tower." She pointed to a large structure. "We're very careful with water here."

We spent over an hour touring the farm, and by the time we got back to the house, I felt exhausted. April, on the other hand, appeared to have been invigorated by the walk. She gave me a radiant smile and squeezed my hand.

We found Mike still sitting at the table, pieces of leather cuttings and a pocket knife spread out in front of him.

"Ah, here you are. While you were out, I prepared you a surprise." He handed us a small package wrapped in cloth. "I made one for each of you."

"Thank you." April accepted the gift on our behalf. She unwrapped the cloth, and we saw two large claws. "These are real bear claws. Fresh from the brine. Made just for you." Michael smiled. "You can wear it for good luck. Native Americans used the claws to protect themselves from harm. It's a symbol of bravery."

"Thank you so much!" April said again, and I also thanked our host for his generosity.

"Thank you!" I ran my finger over the claw. Pointing to the pocket knife, I added: "You know, my grandfather left me a knife. A hunting knife."

Now, it wasn't entirely true. My grandfather didn't leave me the knife. He died long before I was born, but it didn't matter. I had the knife, and I'd been named after my grandfather, Rodion Likharev. So, it made sense for me to continue his legacy.

"That's interesting."

"Yes. It's a Soviet hunting knife."

"I'd love to see it. Come back and bring it here some time," Mike offered.

"Sure." I nodded.

"And April tells me you're interested in doing a session?"

Aunt Molly asked. She was sitting quietly, and I assumed April hadn't told her about my interest in past life regression.

"Oh, yes." I nodded. "But maybe next time?"

"It's alright; since you're here already, why don't we go ahead?" Aunt Molly gave me a reassuring smile.

"So, I'll get to time travel anywhere I want?" I opened my eyes wide.

"Yes. More or less. It's whatever your higher self wants to show you," Aunt Molly responded. April and Mike were observing in silence.

"So, I can see the future?" I drummed my fingers on the table, picturing a scene where I avenged Mama's death, and where Phil had paid for his betrayal.

"Some people can, absolutely. But sometimes you'll see the past. Even past lives that are relevant to you now. Ready to go ahead and try?" Aunt Molly pushed back her chair.

CHAPTER 15
TIME TRAVEL

Molly led me to the back of the house, into one of the bedrooms. "Don't worry," I heard Mike tell April, and then the door closed behind us.

It was a narrow space, with two twin beds on each side, each pushed against the wall. The narrow passage between them was just enough for one person. Thick curtains covered the window, submerging the room into near darkness.

"This is where I do all my work," Molly said.

"Work?" I asked, my voice raspy. A knot had formed in my stomach.

"Yes. I know it's unusual." Molly fluffed up the pillow on the bed by the left side of the room while I remained standing by the door, cognizant that if I moved, I'd bump into her. "I have regular clients. Help them through things when they need answers."

"So, how much do you charge? I can pay." I had no idea how much something like that would cost, and hoped the price Molly named would be so outrageous that I would not be able to afford it. A part of me wanted to get out of that room and forget the whole idea.

"Oh, don't worry about that," Molly said. "I feel it in my heart that I need to help you."

"Alright. Thank you."

Her answer was strange, but what did I expect from someone who helped clients travel in time? I shrugged, sure she couldn't see my reaction in the dark.

"Have a seat right here." I heard Molly pat the bed with the fluffed-up pillow. "We're gonna have you prop up on the pillows, so you don't fall asleep."

She maneuvered out of the way, and I inched to the bed and sat down as instructed. The bed was firm, comfortable, but not overly so.

"Alright." Molly sat across from me. "Now, don't cross your arms or legs, just take a few deep breaths. Close your eyes, but not to go to sleep."

I did as told.

"There you go. Just follow my voice."

Molly fell completely silent, and I wondered whether she'd fallen asleep. But then her voice broke through the darkness. It sounded melodious and lulled me into a dream state.

I saw myself floating through a yellow space, illuminated by sunlight. It was bright and warm, and a star shone up above. It was "A Star Called the Sun." I recognized the song by Kino Sergei loved in Moscow. I heard it loud and clear. And then I saw my brother. He looked younger than he did now, not older than twenty, despite looking disheveled. He had deep red circles under his eyes, like he hadn't slept in several days.

"Hey!" I ran up to him and started singing along. I knew all the words by heart, and it came easily to me. I remembered every single word.

And where we were was familiar. It was our old apartment in Moscow, where we'd lived before leaving for America. The wallpaper was the familiar green and the old furniture was there. I was so happy. I was back! I turned to look outside and noticed a large crack in the window.

"Sergei, why is the window broken?" I walked over to inspect it.

"Oh. Stop asking me that. You're so annoying. It was the hurricane, alright?" Sergei threw an indignant look at me.

"What hurricane? There are no hurricanes in Moscow," I protested.

"Well, we have them now. There was one last summer." He rolled his eyes.

"Really?" I asked, frowning.

"Are you alright, little man? June 1998. Did you forget or something?"

"No." I shook my head. Outside, it looked to be wintertime. "June was a long time ago," I noted.

"Yes, Rodion. It was." Sergei shook his head.

"I'm gonna ask Mama." I walked to the couch.

"What the hell?" Sergei stood up and threw his guitar on the floor. "What the hell?" he repeated. Without looking at me, he stormed out of the room. I followed him, eyes open wide, blinking away tears that were welling up in my eyes.

"Sergei? What's wrong?"

"What's wrong? Go away, idiot."

"Why?"

"Because I got enough problems to deal with. Like finding enough money to keep this apartment. Like figuring out all the inheritance paperwork."

"What?" I had a sinking feeling in my stomach.

"What? Why?" Sergei's face contorted in anger as he mocked me. "You know what, Lena is coming over soon, you talk to her, alright?"

"Auntie Lena?" My mouth gaped open as I saw my brother go into Mama's bedroom and slam the door shut.

I stood, staring at the closed door, then walked to the

kitchen. I wanted to weep, but the stench was so strong I immediately stopped crying.

The kitchen was a mess. Dirty dishes were everywhere. Breadcrumbs, old chewed-up salami, pieces of cheese stuck to plates. A bowl with a stale Russian salad stood in the middle of the table, reeking of spoiled mayonnaise. I felt nauseous. I ran out of the kitchen and into the bathroom. I was about to throw up when I heard the doorbell. It took all of my strength to stop the wave of sickness, but I forced myself to go to the front door. I opened it, only then remembering I should have asked who it was first.

Auntie Lena stood on the threshold. She looked just like I remembered her, only her hair was longer and dyed platinum blonde.

"Hi, Rodion." She didn't smile. The corners of her mouth drooped. "How's your brother? Fighting again?"

"No." I shook my head, blinking fast to fight the tears that were about to betray me.

"It's alright. I know it's hard for you guys. Don't worry, I will figure it all out. There is someone coming to fix the window tomorrow."

"Okay."

"And we will say goodbye to your mama today."

"Where is she?"

"Oh, sweetheart. Baby Rodion." Auntie Lena dabbed her eyes. "Come here." She reached for me, but I pulled back, shriveling into the corner.

"Where is Mama?"

"Mama. Your Mama passed." She squatted next to me and grabbed my hand.

"Passed?" I stared at her in confusion. The word was so unclear. *Passed where? How? Passed a test?* I tried to free myself, but her grasp was strong.

"It was a hard year for her. The crisis of '98. Oh, God."

Auntie Lena looked up, as if searching for a higher power there. "My poor little guy. And your brother. Poor babies."

"Mama died?"

"Yes, Rodion. You found her when you came home from school last week. And you did the right thing. You called me to come over."

"No." I shook my head. "That didn't happen. We're in Moscow. Mama is alive."

"It's the shock. Of course. So much happening all in a few months. And your mother. I told her to stop drinking. But of course, losing all her savings in August. No one could survive that."

Auntie Lena was speaking fast, shaking her head. All the while gripping me by the hand as if to stop me from vanishing.

"Come here, let's go get your brother. We gotta go to the cemetery today. Alright? Let's go, but dress warmly. It's cold out. We gotta find your winter coat, okay, Rodion?"

She threw a look full of resentment at the cracked window.

"And that window. Unbelievable. Six months with this crack. I should have fixed it for you earlier. But Lydia told me she would do it. I should have paid more attention." And then she let go of my hand and collapsed on the couch, sobbing. "Oh, God. Oh, God."

I stared at her for a few moments and then screamed.

"No! No! No!"

The next minute I was back, propped up on the twin bed in the bedroom, submerged in semi-darkness. "No!" I sat up and saw the outlines of Molly's figure on the bed across from me. She was sitting bolt upright.

"What was that?" I yelped.

"It was an alternative scenario of how your life would have turned out if you'd stayed in Russia," Aunt Molly said.

"No, Mama was alive in Russia!"

"Your higher self showed you that your mother would have died in 1998 in Moscow."

"What higher self? There is no such thing!"

"There is, Rodion. It's your soul, but connected to the higher powers. It has the ability to communicate with your guardian angels," Molly explained, her voice steady, but I was having none of it.

"No! Mama died in America because of Philip. Because he left us. She would have been alive if we stayed in Moscow." I yelled. This was the story I'd told myself for ten years. "Moscow would have kept Mama alive."

"It doesn't look like that to me. Your mother would have died, regardless. You saw it with your own eyes."

"I don't believe it!"

"It's hard to accept. I know. I can only guess that sometimes our parents leave us and that's a contract our souls make with each other. To grow stronger, to learn certain lessons..." Molly's voice trailed off.

"But I thought you were going to show me the future," I yelped.

"It all depends on where you are. And what is the most important question for you today."

"So, it was important for me to see my mother dying? Again?" I felt a lump in my throat. "That doesn't seem very helpful."

"Yes, Rodion. I think your guardian angels and your higher self want you to accept your mother's death."

"How am I supposed to accept her death? Mama wasn't meant to die. That's some sick game you're playing." I jumped up and stormed out of the room.

April and Mike were sitting at the table, and Mike was holding what looked like a claw of a large animal and showing it to April.

"Rodion, what's wrong?" April rose towards me.

"I gotta go clear my head." I ran to the front door and put on my shoes.

"Rodion, wait," April called after me.

"Let him go," I heard Molly's voice as I bolted out.

Mama was meant to die.

The thought crushed me. I wanted to rescue her, to make her come back, to have her talk to me. I let out a blood-curdling scream and ran into the woods. I ran, not knowing where I was going, and stopped only when I realized I was surrounded by a thick forest. *Mama would have died anyway.* The thought cut like a knife. "No! No!" I screamed into the woods. *This was just a weird dream. There's no way any of this was real*, I decided and turned back.

"There you are." April was standing by the front door of Aunt Molly's house. "Are you alright?"

"Yeah." I nodded and sighed.

"Let's say goodbye to Aunt Molly and Mike, alright?" April gave me a questioning look.

"Of course."

We walked back into the house. I half expected Aunt Molly to fuss over me, but she was perfectly calm.

"Rodion," she noted, shaking my hand, "I know what you saw wasn't easy. But it means you've got a very strong channel."

"Channel? What kind of channel?" I stared at her in amazement.

"An ability to see things. Clairvoyant capabilities," Aunt Molly noted. "It's a gift, and you can make it grow stronger. And what you were shown today is important. I am certain of that."

"Aunt Molly, does it mean Rodion can see the future on his own?" April asked.

"We can all see the future, April. But some of us refuse to accept it. That's the only difference."

"Molly, you're going to confuse the kids." Mike chuckled. "I'll go ahead and walk them to their car," he said, and we stepped outside.

CHAPTER 16
THE OFFER

The day of April's departure for Philadelphia came. We said goodbye the evening prior. I couldn't imagine how I'd survive without having her at my side. After finishing high school, she'd become my lifeline. And now I had nothing. It was like stepping into a void, with no reason to go on. No classes, no job, and no April. I'd applied for a job at Vista but hadn't gotten a response.

I got home that evening and found Sergei waiting for me.

"Bro, you got this thing right here. Delivered by DHL." He handed me a package and gave me a curious stare.

"What is that?" I accepted the package and flipped it over in my hands. There was no return address, only something that looked like a seal with two snakes intertwining.

"Open it," Sergei urged. I'd considered going to my room to do so, but my brother was hovering over my shoulder, so I ripped the package open, taking care to not damage the seal. It looked interesting, like something I'd like to cut out and put on my wall.

A folder fell out.

"That's it?" Sergei exclaimed. We were both staring at a

black, fancy-looking folder. The same seal was on its cover, but this one was emblazoned in gold.

"Wow, it looks like something out of Batman." My mouth gaped open. Hands trembling, I opened the folder and took out the cover letter.

> *Dear Mr. Likharev,*
>
> *We're pleased to offer you the position of tester at The AI Experimental Laboratory, 'The Lab.' Should you accept this offer of employment, pease notify us immediately by dropping a signed copy of the enclosed paperwork at our HQ at 5252 Forbes Avenue, Pittsburgh PA. Your monthly salary will be $5500 per month, net of taxes.*

"What's this?"

"I guess I got a job." I jumped up. "Not so useless after all."

"Tester? What are you gonna be testing for that kinda money? Illegal weapons?"

"I'm not really sure." I shrugged. "I guess they liked my essay."

"Essay? What the hell? Bro, is this even legal?"

"Of course it is. April's dad hooked me up," I said, glowing on the inside. "I gotta tell her."

"Wait, Rodion, what's going on?" Sergei narrowed his eyes. "Are you sure this is legit? Like, are you 100% sure there's nothing weird going on?"

"What, you think I'm not good enough for something cool to happen to me? Maybe this is my big break." I pulled my arm out of his grip and reached for my phone.

I texted April in all CAPs, not caring if my message looked crazy.

> I GOT THE JOB!!!! THANKS!

The very next day, I went to hand in my paperwork.

The place was nothing like I expected. What I imagined was something straight out of the future. Like a research lab from the movies. White walls, bright lights, a futuristic-looking building with white lines and clean, open spaces. I expected professorial-looking types running around in white coats, test tubes in and programmers with focused expressions on their faces, slouching in front of computers. Maybe a couple of robots standing in the hallway. How I'd fit in with that crowd didn't bother me, but it remained a question.

Instead, The Lab was located in a mansion on Forbes Avenue, right across from Carnegie Mellon University campus. I'd passed it lots of times on my way to Oakland, and it looked like just another house.

I'd found the building right away, but then circled the block several times to make sure I hadn't made a mistake. I opened the folder, re-read the offer letter, verified the address, and then finally approached.

The mansion was painted burgundy and had a cobblestone driveway, characteristics that made it look even more residential. I climbed up the five steps and stood on the porch, about to knock. Unexpectedly, the door flew open and a guy with fiery red hair appeared.

"Hi, can I help you?" he asked.

"Hey, I'm here to drop off this." I handed him the folder.

Immediately, his eyes lit up.

"You must be Rodion Likharev. Come in!" He opened the door wide, revealing a living room set up. I followed him in and he turned, extending his hand. "I'm Ben. I work here. One of the researchers. Nice to meet you."

He sat down on the couch and offered me a seat on an armchair across from him. The furniture was off-white leather and reminded me of Vlada's living room. She considered it the epitome of good taste and got a white leather set from Ikea, often mentioning her dream of replacing it with high-end white leather couches one day. I was no expert, but the couches in The Lab looked expensive. The leather felt buttery, and I brushed my fingers on it, feeling the surface of the couch.

Ben was absorbed in reviewing my paperwork, and I surreptitiously examined him. He was wearing a gray T-shirt with the Carnegie Mellon logo on it and I noticed his bulging muscles. Red freckles populated his face. Ben did not look like a geeky programmer who led a sedentary lifestyle.

"Alright, we're all set." Ben flashed me a smile. "Thanks for accepting our offer." The tone of his voice sounded like he was saying it as a mere formality, and I nodded in silent agreement. He rose and walked to the door, inviting me to follow him.

"See you next week. The day after Labor Day. Oh, by the way, our hours are from noon to 8pm. It's mostly because of California time. We start later, when it's morning over there. Three-hour difference, you know."

I didn't, but nodded again.

I wanted Ben to like me.

———

The rest of the week passed in a blur as I waited for my first day at The Lab. I thought of the wonderful turn of events in my life, the cool job, the amazing offer, and the money. The incredible salary I was about to earn, all thanks to April. She was the real guardian angel in my life, not some weird entity that projected nightmares. My heart filled with gratitude each time I thought of April and what she had done for me.

On the first day of my job, I woke up early. Though I didn't have to report to The Lab until noon, I was too wired to stay in bed and jumped out of bed at six that morning. Sergei was still asleep, and I made my way downstairs, trying to make as little noise as possible. I paused in the living room. Submerged in semi-darkness, our tiny place looked even smaller than normal. *My life is about to change,* I thought, plopping down on the couch. I looked to my left and saw Mama's urn on the shelf, in the usual spot. Next to it was the hunting knife. It always sat there in its sheath, and that morning I picked it up, took it out, and stared at the cool steel blade, running my finger along the sharp edge. *Rodion Likharev,* I read the engraving. It was in Russian, but I could read it. My grandfather's name, which was also mine.

"Mama, I'll make you proud," I mouthed, and flicked on the console, deciding gaming was the best way to spend the next few hours. I picked the Stewart game, since playing it always calmed me down.

Even after playing the game and having breakfast with Sergei, I had ample time, so I walked through Schenley Park to get to the office. It was a sunny September morning, and, unusually for Pittsburgh, it hadn't rained in over a week. Walking on the streets of Greenfield, I thought of the first time I walked them. With Mama by my side. I remembered taking the school bus and cutting school.

Melancholy hit me as I thought of my life in America, the strange turn of events that had brought us there. *Could it be true that Mama would have died in Russia?* I remembered the vision at Aunt Molly's and discarded it right away. *No. It was all Phil's fault.* Anger at Phil felt familiar, and I easily slipped into the familiar emotion. I clenched my fists. *Just a little longer and I'll avenge Mama.* Suddenly, I remembered Aunt Molly's words about my ability to predict the future and see things. *Maybe this job will bring me closer to avenging Mama's death? This is my purpose in life. The only thing that matters.*

At exactly 12pm, I knocked on the front door of The Lab, expecting Ben to answer. I'd prepared to greet him with a high five and even plastered an eager grin on my face in anticipation. But instead, a young woman answered the door. She had a blonde bob haircut, small blue eyes, a button nose. Her arched eyebrows gave her face a look of perpetual condescension. As soon as she opened the door, she checked her watch and nodded in satisfaction.

"Great, you're on time," she muttered.

I cleared my throat and, dignified, said, "Rodion Likharev. It's my first day."

"And I'm Kate." She didn't give a last name, as if that didn't matter one bit.

"Nice to meet you."

I was about to extend my hand, but she didn't offer hers. Instead, she scrunched up her face and deep lines crossed her forehead.

"Let me show you around."

She led me into the same space I'd already seen on my first visit, and once more I was surprised by the setup. This was nothing like a research space in my understanding. I followed her, gaping, taking everything in. The white leather couch, the matching armchairs, the table with the magazines. I followed Kate into the dining room—where a large oak table sat, complete with eight dining room chairs—and then into the kitchen. On the kitchen counter sat a plastic tray with sandwiches from Cost Right that I recognized right away, having eaten them at Vlada's house.

Kate turned to me.

"Here, we have snacks, meals, whatever you need. So, just help yourself whenever." She shrugged.

"Aha."

My mouth started salivating right away. The prospect of free meals sounded great, especially since I was always hungry. I started calculating how much money I'd be saving by eating at The Lab, but Kate interrupted my thoughts.

"And of course, the way to where you'll be spending your day is right through here." She pointed to a white painted door that had a lock code. "You'll need a code to open it. It's important the door stays locked at all times."

I swallowed hard. Suddenly, the space didn't seem so cute and harmless. My heart beat fast and I bit my lip to stay calm. Kate deftly punched in the code, not even trying to hide it, and I wondered whether she did it on purpose or out of carelessness. I noted the numbers. It was *0808*. My birthday. *Is it a coincidence or did they do it on purpose? Easy to remember regardless.*

"Got it," I responded, keeping the tone of my voice casual, and followed her down the steps. We descended into a large basement, and that was what looked like an actual lab.

A long white desk stood in the middle of the space, with three huge computer screens sitting next to each other. In front of each, there was a chair, and the screen in the middle was connected to what seemed like a myriad of other machines, all buzzing, clicking, and beeping. I stared at this setup in awe. I was about to be a tester at this high-tech establishment! My heart leaped at the idea. All my doubts were washed away in a matter of seconds. I wanted to run up to the screen and start right away, but Kate, as if sensing my eagerness, stopped me.

"Now, we've got to get you hooked up first. Make sure the setup is correct."

"Yeah."

"This is where you'll be working," Kate said, pointing to the chairs in front of the middle computer screen, the largest one there. "Have a seat and we'll test out the equipment."

I did as told, and she proceeded to adjust the chair and the desk, maneuvering them up and down and asking me to bend my arms and legs. She then took a few of my measurements and ordered, "Alright, try it out now. Comfortable?"

I fidgeted in the chair and nodded. I wasn't sure what level of comfort was expected because I'd never sat in front of a computer screen at a desk. I usually either gamed from my couch or sitting on the floor. But Kate furrowed her brow, inspecting me.

"We've got a few more things to do, alright?" She didn't wait for me to answer, and produced a camera. "I'm just gonna take a few photos of you, just like that. Here, go stand over there." She pointed to the white wall, and I rose and walked to stand against it. Kate took several photos of me, mumbling to herself as she did so.

"Very good, very good. Now, I think you can get started. Have a seat."

I sat back down, expecting Kate to give me instructions, but she bit her lip, flipping through a pile of papers.

"Listen, umm, Rodion, you dropped off your paperwork, right?" She furrowed her brow, a look of concern on her face.

"Yeah." I nodded. "I brought it over last week."

"This is kinda strange. I don't see the full packet here. There are several consent forms. And the non-disclosure agreement," Kate mumbled. "Hey, let's just go upstairs for a second. I can't leave you alone here if you haven't signed them."

She turned and walked to the steps.

I rose, and, with a feeling of regret, followed her. I wanted to stay downstairs. It was clean, modern, well-organized, and had a pull on me. Whatever was about to happen there, I could tell, whatever testing I was about to do, would be nothing like anyone had ever done before.

Kate's heels clicked on the steps. My sneakers made no noise. To open the door, Kate punched in the code again, *0808*.

Why didn't she tell me what the code was? How would I get out if I didn't have it? The uncomfortable thought flashed through my mind and disappeared.

"Wait right here," Kate ordered curtly, showing me to a stool in the kitchen.

I sat next to the tray of sandwiches. Salivating, I waited for Kate to reappear, not sure whether I could have the sandwiches already given the incomplete paperwork. *What if they tell me I can't work here?* I thought. *What if my paperwork was wrong?*

My stomach rumbled. *Maybe I can quickly eat a sandwich and no one will notice?* Glancing at the tray, I almost reached for it, but then noticed a blinking dot of a camera on the ceiling. It reminded me of the cameras in *Resident Evil* and I shuddered. For a second, my mind wandered, and I pictured the paralyzing gas being released. I chuckled at the thought.

Steeling myself, I stretched, settling in for a long wait, but a few moments later Kate reappeared, followed by Ben. At the sight of him, I felt relief, as if I had just met an old friend.

"Hey!" Ben extended his hand and grinned at me. He was wearing the same Carnegie Mellon T-shirt, and I wondered whether he ever changed clothes or if he had a whole set.

Kate watched our interaction with narrowed eyes, then, turning to Ben, asked, "What's going on? Why didn't you follow the protocol?"

"It was my first day back after vacation. Gimme a break," Ben huffed. "I have his stuff right here."

He shoved a folder to Kate, who gave him a side-eye.

"The consent forms should have been in the file. And I don't see the NDA. And did you even scan these?"

"Scan these?" Ben threw his hands up in protest.

"Yes! Everything has to be in electronic format!" Kate shrieked. "I don't get why I'm doing all the secretarial work around here."

"Relax, it's gonna be fine." Ben rolled his eyes. "Didn't the Doc say 'it was all hands on deck?'"

"Yes, all hands, not just mine!" Kate yelped.

Who is the Doc? I wondered, staring at the two of them in fascination. It was like watching a ping-pong match.

"Why didn't you go over this with him last week? I thought you'd done the orientation! And he needs to get a copy of the contract." Kate glanced in my direction.

They continued to bicker like that for several minutes, seemingly forgetting about my existence, until Kate turned to me.

"Rodion, listen. Can you come back tomorrow? We'll get everything set up by then." She threw an indignant look at Ben.

"No! Just wait. I'll get everything done." Ben shook his head. "Just chill. I'll scan this thing."

He threw a look full of disdain at Kate.

"We'll wait right here," Kate said triumphantly, and folded her arms.

Whatever strange power game was going on there, I found it entertaining. I heard my stomach rumble and tried to conceal it by moving the chair, but Kate heard it, too.

"Here, have something to eat!" she said brightly. "This food is for us, actually." She handed me a paper plate and placed a sandwich on it. I bit into it slowly, still mindful of the red blinking camera dot on the ceiling.

"This place is great, actually. Sorry, we're a bit disorganized today, Rodion. It's not like this usually." Kate flipped her hair.

I was chewing on the sandwich and didn't react right away, so Kate continued: "You'll really like it here. And Ben and I, umm, just ignore us."

"Okay." I nodded, stuffing the rest of the sandwich into my mouth.

"Here's some water." Kate handed me a bottle out of a pack on the floor that I also recognized. Sergei and I had helped Vlada carry these very packs she bought at Cost Right countless times. That made this space feel even more familiar, and I relaxed, taking a sip of the water. I was about to ask Kate how long she'd been working at The Lab, when Ben appeared.

"All done!" he announced, rolling his shoulders back and moving his head left and right, in a move that made him look like a boxer getting ready for a fight.

"Alright, let's get started for real then." Kate checked her iPhone. "Forty-five-minute delay only because someone didn't get things ready on time." She sighed and walked to the basement door.

Kate punched in the code, and all three of us descended into the basement.

"I already took the baseline photos," Kate said to Ben, and, turning to me, noted with grave notes in her voice: "Listen, Rodion, remember, you cannot share with anyone what happens here. You signed all the forms, and whatever happens here is bound by the non-disclosure agreement. Ben should have gone over this with you." She gave Ben a side-eye, and I felt sorry for him. "Do you understand?"

"Yeah." I nodded. *Why is she making a big deal out of this?*

"Remember rule number one of Fight Club?" Ben chuckled.

"You DO NOT talk about Fight Club?" I said, a little too eagerly. But I really liked Ben. He was my ally in this situation. The good cop. But Ben didn't smile back. The expression on his face remained severe. A little too severe.

"Exactly. Do NOT talk about Fight Club. The Lab in this case."

"Ben, I mean, I think it's pretty clear what a non-disclosure agreement is." Kate raised her eyebrows. "I think he gets it."

"I'm just trying to help." Ben opened his arms wide.

"Thanks." Kate rolled her eyes.

"This is your desk." Ben pointed at the one in the middle with the largest screen on it. "We have to make sure it fits you well."

"I already set it up for him." Kate sighed. "See? Here, have a seat, show Ben."

I obeyed.

"So, here's what you'll be doing. There's a game that you'll be playing. It's kinda like *Star Wars*, but anyway, you'll see. The game isn't important." Kate turned on the monitor.

"It's not?" I turned to Ben for an explanation. "So, what do I do?"

"You just play the game, but only for a few days. Then you'll see." A smirk appeared on Ben's face, and I noticed his face flush red, which made his freckles more prominent.

"You're going to confuse him." Kate frowned.

"Just hold on!" Ben raised his right palm up in a blocking gesture. "So, we're testing AI. Artificial Intelligence." Ben stared at me intently. "And you," he pointed at me, "are our main tester."

"I am?" At that moment, I was nearly bursting with pride.

"Yep! You'll find out the rest by the end of this week. I promise!" He winked at me.

"Ben, hello? Aren't we supposed to tell him?" Kate opened her eyes wide.

"Not yet." Ben shook his head. "But for now, just play the games. Alright? It'll seem like a regular game to you, nothing special. We'll just be taking some baseline measurements."

"Okay." I nodded, full of anticipation.

"We'll be measuring your blood pressure, hormones, oxygen levels, brain activity, stuff like that. We have this high-end finger monitor. You gotta wear it at all times. And then we let you play for a few hours. Then you get a break. And then you play again. Got it?"

"Sure. And then what happens?"

"Nothing. You just go home and come back the next day."

"And that's it?"

"Yes, that's it." A sly smile appeared on Ben's face. "Ready?"

"Ready." I confirmed.

CHAPTER 17
SPLASH SCREEN

Kate stood back to the side, observing, arms crossed, as Ben was finishing his explanation, while fiddling with the cords. He had just connected me to three different ones and plugged them all into the monitor. The machine produced a set of beeping sounds which, on top of the computer buzzing, created a cacophony.

"Kate, did you do the swab?" Ben asked, his tone ominous.

"The swab!" Kate jumped and startled me. "Where's the kit?" She stared at Ben, wide-eyed.

A conceited smile appeared on his face.

"I have it right here." Ben reached into his pocket and produced a small box with the label *Testing kit*. "I guess I'm not so useless after all?" Ben put on rubber gloves.

"It's a saliva kit," he noted, opening the box with his gloved hands.

"I need you to open your mouth and I'll do the swab."

He produced a test tube and a long Q-tip.

One look at the Q-tip, and the walls of the room merged into a tunnel. It sucked me in, pulling me inside. I was flying into the tunnel and staring at my body from the ceiling. I saw Ben asking me to open my mouth; I saw myself agreeing, nodding, Ben doing the swipe, inserting the Q-tip into the test-tube, swirling, checking the contents, then sealing the tube. I was thrown back to the day Phil had taken me to do "the experiment," and the Groundhog was about to dump me for not being his son, unraveling my whole life. I opened my mouth to scream, but no sound came.

"There we are," Ben said with satisfaction, stuffing the tube with the Q-tip into his pocket. "All done with the control sample, Rodion."

As soon as Ben said my name, I was back in my body and regained control of it. It took me a moment to realize that I was no longer floating on the ceiling, observing myself, but was back in one piece. Wiping beads of cold sweat off my forehead, I reached for the mouse, darting my eyes to check whether Ben and Kate had noticed. They appeared completely unaware of what had just happened to me.

"So, all you gotta do is just sit here and play," Kate said, throwing a look full of disdain at Ben. "Basically, just like a regular video game. Except you're gonna be connected to the finger monitor. It tracks a few things for us, but try not to pay attention to it. It shouldn't prevent you from gaming or anything. Ignore all these other cords. They are just for the first day, and we'll get rid of them tonight."

"So, we're gonna leave you here on your own," Kate announced, and I expected Ben to say something else, but the two of them exchanged glances and left.

As soon as the door closed behind them, I put on the headphones and got into it.

What I played that day was some sort of survival game, requiring a moderate skill level. It was called *Space Cadet,* and was about a guy who traveled to different planets and defeated monsters on each one. By defeating a monster, the guy got special powers and then could transfer them to the next planet, and so on. If he lost, he went back to the original planet, and it started all over again.

Though the game seemed primitive, it wasn't too bad. The character, named Hayden, was relatable, and he even had an interesting backstory. He was trying to find his home planet, and it was only through testing each one that he could determine where he belonged. Something about the game was strange, however, and awkward. After I cleared a level, it would hesitate and blink, then let me know the points awarded. But I didn't mind too much. I was "the main tester," and this was part of something important. I was being paid to play video games, and I would be earn a lot of money.

This went on for several hours, and when I cleared the twelfth level, the computer blinked and the screen went blank. I moved the mouse. Nothing happened. I waited for the points to be awarded, so I could keep on playing, but the screen suddenly flashed "The End," and the screen of death appeared. I pulled at one of the cords connecting me to the monitor. The machines flashed and beeped, so I stopped and sat there, staring at the screen. Nothing happened. I expected Kate or Ben to come and get me, but they didn't.

I was suddenly extremely hungry. I pulled at the cords, disconnected myself, and got up. I climbed the steps and came face-to-face with the metal door. I pushed at it, but it didn't give way. I called, but was nearly certain no one would hear me. I assumed the walls were soundproof and cold sweat covered my body. *What if they left me here to die?* I pushed at the lever again. Nothing.

The Lab was a windowless space, and no one from the outside would ever know what was happening there. *How long till Sergei starts looking for me?* Sometimes we wouldn't see each other for days, given how busy Sergei was with work. *April?* She was busy with school and it might be a few days until she'd suspect I was in trouble.

I stared at the keypad and remembered my birthday. I'd

seen Kate punch in the code. *0808. Of course!* I breathed out and entered the number. The code clicked, and I was out. *What was that? Why did I panic?* I shook my head at my paranoia. *The place is completely safe.* I walked into the kitchen.

The tray with sandwiches, now half empty, was sitting on the counter, and the smell of tuna was overwhelming. My stomach grumbled.

"Hello?" I called. No answer.

I saw a door and pulled at it. It was the bathroom. I entered and found myself in a small space. The walls were painted a mustard shade of yellow and a towel with a yellow rubber ducky hung next to the sink.

An oval mirror hung right above the toilet. Another mirror hung above the sink. The two mirrors aligned, and it was like a portal within a portal. The two mirrors reflected in each other. I saw myself, my reflection fractured in this tunnel, as a myriad of Rodions looked at each other. The reflections bounced against each other as I washed my hands. Averting my eyes from the reflections, I wiped my hands on the rubber ducky towel. As I walked out of the bathroom, I heard Kate's voice. *Had she been waiting for me here the whole time I was in the bathroom?*

"Hey, Rodion, what did you think?" Kate's eyes fixed on mine.

"About what?" I gulped.

"The game, of course."

"Oh, it was cool." I shrugged. "But, umm, it was a bit slow, I guess."

"Yeah? That's great; I'm glad you caught that. Let's go to the living room for a debrief."

Kate led me to the couch.

"Here, have a seat. I'll just call Ben." She disappeared upstairs, clicking her heels.

I sat down on the soft, white leather couch. Kate came back a minute later, a clipboard in her hands, followed by

Ben, who was equipped with a laptop. The two of them sat down opposite me and stared at me with interest. I reveled in the attention but did my best not to show it.

"So, Rodion, how was your experience playing the game?" Kate spoke first, clicking her pen on the clipboard.

"It was cool, I guess." I shrugged.

Ben opened his laptop and started typing.

"So, you said the game was slow, right?" Kate clarified, furrowing her brow.

"Yeah, I guess so."

"What exactly do you mean by that?"

"Umm, well, like when I was clearing the levels, it didn't show me the points right away," I shared my observation.

A triumphant smile flashed on Kate's face.

"See!" She turned to Ben. "This is what I told you would happen."

"But it's not even the point!" He let out a deep breath. "I'm going to tell him."

"No, Ben, not yet. I thought we agreed." She opened her eyes wide and stuck out her head like a turtle.

"But what's the big deal?"

"Come on!"

The two of them started arguing and went back and forth, as I sat in silence, waiting for them to stop. At last, there was a pause, so I cleared my throat.

"Umm, what do I do now?"

"Oh, you can go," Ben said. "Sorry about that. We're finished for the day."

"Ben!" Kate looked at her watch, but he shook his head.

"Listen, there's nothing else for him to do."

Ben rose and gestured for me to leave. I rose and Ben walked me to the front door. Kate remained seated, and I heard the clicking of her pen on her clipboard.

"See you tomorrow, same time, man," Ben said, as he opened the front door to let me out.

"See you tomorrow."

I shook his hand and stepped into the bright September afternoon.

"Bye, Kate," I said, but didn't hear a response.

As soon as I was outside, I reached for my phone to call April. Then I looked over my shoulder, wondering if Ben and Kate were watching me, so I waited until I turned the corner and dialed April's number. She picked up right away.

"So, how was your first day?" April asked.

"It was cool."

"Cool? Anything else?"

"Well, kinda weird. Like, it's set up like a house."

"What kinda house?"

"Like a family home or something. Like a very large one."

"That sounds like a frat house," April noted. "Did you see my dad?"

"No. It was these two people, Kate and Ben. And no one else." I hesitated, unsure if I should tell April that Ben and Kate were relatively young.

"So, do you like it? The place?"

"Yeah. I just hope they actually pay me."

"Why wouldn't they?" April's voice sounded high-pitched.

"Because it's like all I do is play this video game. And it's not even that hard. It's like a lame video game."

"Really?"

"Yeah. That's why I dunno. It just seems like something isn't right."

"Well, I'm sure my dad wouldn't place you somewhere that was shady," April said, her voice reassuring.

"I know. Maybe it's 'cause it was just my first day."

CHAPTER 18

RYDER

Two more days at The Lab followed. They were just like my first day, except for the ordeal with the consent forms. Each day I walked in, Kate signed me in and walked me downstairs. Then, Ben showed up moments later, did the swab, and the two of them left me to play. A few hours later, Kate and Ben called me upstairs, did the debrief, and I went home, cognizant of not spending even close to the required eight hours in The Lab.

I wonder if they'll pay me the full amount, I agonized on the way home on Thursday afternoon. It was still light out, and I thought of stopping by the library in Squirrel Hill to pick up a few books but then decided against it. Instead, I would reread *The Count of Monte Cristo* at home. It had been a few weeks since I last did so, and I needed my fix.

On Friday morning, I got up early and took the scenic route, arriving at The Lab exactly at noon after walking through Schenley Park. I knocked, and Kate opened the front door.

"Hi, Rodion!" she said brightly. "Congratulations! You've done so well this week. Today we will change things up a little."

Kate walked to the kitchen, and I followed. After punching in the code, she led me downstairs. The setup was different. Gone were the multiple beeping machines, with only the finger monitor left. I steeled myself for the Q-tip swab, but Kate said curtly, "No more swabs." I felt a wave of relief rush over me. That had been the only part of The Lab experience I disliked.

"I think you'll like this." Kate announced, as I took a seat and she connected me to the finger monitor. She left me on my own and, as I turned the screen on, expecting the already familiar boring Hayden with his planet adventures, the screen flashed twice, and my mouth gaped open.

As the pixels popped into place, I realized I was staring at myself. At my own replica. The guy on the screen had the same face as me, the same dumb expression, the same eyes, hair, everything. I pulled back and so did he.

I clicked the mouse, and the figure froze in place. *What is going on?* I wanted an explanation, but forced myself to stay in place. If this was a new game, and I was in it, I needed to understand it first.

So, I examined the guy. The clothes he was wearing matched mine from my first day at The Lab. The same worn jeans and a black T-shirt. *They recreated me?* I was about to click the mouse again to make the figure move but noticed where the pixelated version of me was standing. It was a white desert-like space, with octagonal shapes around him. At the far back there were mountains, light pink with brown outlines. The sky was an intense shade of blue. *Where is this guy?*

I clicked on the figure again, and this time noticed controls at the top. One of them said *Detach from the original.* That phrase made my blood curdle. It could only mean one thing: I was the original, and the figure on the screen would "detach" from me. *So, he was attached to me this whole time?* Like a cartoon projection of me, the guy repeated everything I was doing. I stared at the monitors that were hooked up to the screen and noticed that the figure's cheeks turned red, matching my own flushed face. I let out a scream. The walls of The Lab were soundproof, so I didn't expect my supervisors to hear it, but immediately Kate ran in.

"Rodion, are you alright?"

"Umm, what's this?"

"Oh, that's your double." Kate noted nonchalantly. "We don't have a name for him yet. We could call him Rodion-2? What do you say?"

At that moment, Ben appeared, and, seeing the freaked-out expression on my face, rushed over. "We should have warned him," He muttered.

"No, the whole point is to introduce the double as a chance encounter. It can't be pre-planned. It would ruin the experiment," Kate rattled off.

"It doesn't make a difference how and why he sees the double the first time. He's going to interact with it now."

"Whatever, it's not a big deal!"

"And on a Friday, too? We should have waited till Monday. We need to tell him what's going on." Ben was gesticulating, and his freckles almost blended with the color of his ruddy cheeks.

"Go ahead, why don't you, since you're making all the decisions around here." Kate pouted.

"Rodion, listen," Ben said, turning to me, "so what you just saw is your digital twin."

"My what?"

"It's your digital double. You see, something we created to match you. This is the actual testing you'll be doing. You will work with the double."

"That thing?" I pointed at the screen.

"Yeah, it's your AI replica. He learns from you, from your actions, memories, hormone levels. He learns and improves every day you're here."

"So, this thing on the screen is Artificial Intelligence?" I gulped. I found the idea of AI taking over my body was unsettling, to say the least.

"Well, kind of." Ben turned to Kate as if for support, but Kate stood there, arms crossed, clearly with no desire to speak.

"You're our very first digital twin tester." Ben's tone was upbeat. "You'll help us improve this technology."

"What about the game? The planets?"

"Oh, that was just to get all your data. The game was not important."

"Not important?"

My mouth gaped open at the realization that what I'd taken as my job and performed to the best of my ability did not count.

"So, will I get paid for the three days?"

"Of course!" Ben raised his eyebrows.

"Ben, you're freaking the kid out." Kate shook her head.

I took offense at "the kid," but said nothing.

"He's not freaked out." Ben parried, and turned to me. "Are you?" His brow furrowed, and he took on a look full of concern.

"No," I lied.

"Ben, just tell him everything then. Why don't you?" Kate threw her clipboard on the table and plopped down on a chair next to mine. "I'm just gonna sit here and listen."

"Absolutely, I will do just that." Ben rolled a chair towards me. "So, Rodion." He cleared his throat. "Basically, over in this lab, we're trying to test this idea of a digital twin. It's like this double, a replica of you that will do things for you. To explore the human potential. We won't tell you exactly what it will test, but it has to do with physical abilities." He stopped speaking and stared at me, expecting a reaction. I nodded slowly, showing understanding, though I was far from it.

Encouraged, Ben continued. "So, basically, this guy," he pointed to the screen, "your digital double, will be doing stuff, and then we'll see how it plays out. And then this information will feed back to you, and we'll see how you react to it."

"So, why do you need me?" I asked after a pause.

"Oh. We definitely need you. You're the original. The digital twin can't operate without you," Ben said. "For now."

"For now? Like, will that not be the case in the future?"

"In the future, we expect the digital twins to be completely independent. But that's years from now. And it will depend on how our research here goes. For the time being, we're just testing out various things."

"So, like, are we all gonna get these things? The twins?"

"Of course not." Ben let out a laugh. "No, no, the digital twins are just for cutting-edge things, like space exploration, or, maybe, testing cars. Maybe some advanced marketing." He cleared his throat. "We don't expect everyone in the world to have a digital twin for some time."

"So, like crash test dummies?"

"No, no, not that kind of testing. More like testing self-driving cars and how humans would behave in them. Or, for example, if we go to Mars. Or some personalized experience."

"Mars?" My eyes widened at this. "The planet?"

"Yes, actual Mars." Ben nodded. "Going to Mars is going to happen soon!" The expression on his face turned dreamy.

"So, is the guy, umm, my twin, you know … Was he, like, supposed to be on Mars?"

"Actually, yes." Kate stepped in. She rolled towards us, her face bright with excitement. "That was supposed to be the terrain of Mars."

"Wait, so my digital double is going to Mars?"

"Eventually, yes."

"So, we're testing space exploration? Isn't that kinda like *Blade Runner*?"

I immediately pictured Deckard, his agitated face, checking for replicants. *Am I also going to be out there doing the same thing? Will my digital double be a replicant, then?*

"Ha. Good question. I never thought of it that way." Kate said.

"No, it's not like that. Listen, Rodion, I think we're just overcomplicating this whole situation," Ben said, and rubbed the back of his neck. "So, from now on, your goal is to work with your digital twin. Things will progress and get more and more complex as the test advances. Okay?"

"Okay." I nodded.

"Also, do you have a name for him?"

"I proposed Rodion-2." Kate smirked.

"That's lame." Ben shook his head.

"Whatever. Do you have a better idea?"

"I think Rodion should name him."

"A name for the digital twin?" I opened my eyes wide. My life had come full circle. I got to choose a new name for myself all over again.

"Yes, the twin." Ben looked at me expectantly.

"Ryder," I said without hesitation. "Like the truck."

"How adorable!" Kate's face lit up. "I love it. Ryder and Rodion."

"Good. So, let me show you the system and what to do. Kate and I actually programmed the whole thing," Ben said, and for the first time smiled at Kate. She nodded.

I didn't know what was worse, having the two of them work together or argue. Now that both of them were showing me the system, they spoke over each other, clicking and moving the mouse back and forth, so that I completely lost track of what was being said. Though I tried to pay attention, I was in a state of utter confusion.

"So, welcome to the first day of your real testing!" Ben said finally. Kate nodded. "By the way, on Fridays, we finish a little early and you're probably going to stay a bit later, since it's your first day with your digital twin. With Ryder, I mean."

"Okay." I nodded eagerly. I was happy to stay at The Lab for the full eight hours, since that in my mind meant job security and ensured I'd receive full payment.

"So, how would I know I was done?" I asked, remembering how the game I played with Hayden kicked me off after several hours.

"So, it's actually not so clear with the digital twin. But we'll have you clock out at 8pm exactly. How does that sound?" Kate furrowed her brow, ignoring the questioning look on Ben's face.

"Alright, that's cool," I said.

"Just remember, Ben and I won't be there. We'll see you back here on Monday at noon. Alright?"

"Alright." I nodded, and the two of them turned around and left, leaving me one-on-one with Ryder.

CHAPTER 19

DAWN

My replica stared back at me. Ryder. Or whatever the thing was called. Digital twin? Digital double? I liked the name I picked for him, but interacting with my digital double unsettled me. Like most people, I'd spent some time examining myself in the mirror, but this was different. Facing my double, I felt as if I saw myself from the outside. An out-of-body experience.

I tried to remember the garbled instructions regarding what I was supposed to be doing with Ryder that Ben and Kate had given me just moments prior and, of course, failed. *How hard could it be?* I thought, and jumped right into the interface.

Locating the *Detach* command, I clicked on that first. Immediately, Ryder winked at me and the *Ready* command appeared. Relief flooded my body as I moved Ryder around and he obeyed. But it didn't take long to run into problems. His legs would freeze in mid-movement, or his fingers didn't move the right way. I got the idea of keeping track of these, and started writing them down, calling it a "list of glitches."

With over six hours until my shift ended, I had ample time to explore my digital double, and I really got into reviewing his abilities. I noticed minor errors in movement, or things that made him seem not as real. It took me a bit of time to get the hang of how to maneuver Ryder. After some time, I wanted to shift us away from the octagonal white place with mountains at the back. But no matter how many times I tried to change his location, my efforts failed. The only thing I could change were his movements.

He ran, jumped, skipped, hopped, walked. Very quickly, I realized that if Ryder exerted himself on the screen, my heart rate also accelerated. If Ryder ran, my cheeks flushed from the effort. If Ryder stood still, my pulse slowed down.

At around six, I felt like I needed a break. The muscles of my neck strained, and my back ached. I pressed *Stop* and took off the finger monitor. Immediately, the screen buzzed and flashed a huge *Error* message. I stared at the screen in confusion. *Warning. Memory Loss*, it flashed in red.

Hands trembling, I pulled the finger monitor back on, and the warning disappeared. *Did Ben and Kate say anything about how to stop the testing? What do I do with this thing?* I needed a break, but I couldn't free myself from Ryder. *What do I do now?* I mouthed in frustration. And that's when Ryder winked at me for the second time that day. Like a real person. And so, I did what any rational human being would do. I asked him what to do next.

I typed: "What do I do to stop testing?"

"Attach." The words appeared on the screen.

Of course! I clapped in excitement. "That makes sense." I quickly found the *Attach* command and reconnected the double. Ryder gave me a thumbs up and stopped moving. *Saving* flashed on the screen. Then, a few seconds later, *Save Complete.*

Once that happened, I slowly pulled off the finger monitor. This time, there was no error message, and no warning appeared on the screen. I breathed a sigh of relief and went upstairs.

I confidently punched in the door code, and then a strange thought occurred to me. *They never told me the code,* I remembered. Was it an oversight? Or done intentionally? *But these guys wouldn't want me stuck here without a way out.* I calmed myself and went to the bathroom. As I flicked on the lamp and looked in the mirror, I saw my reflections merging into each other, forming a tunnel. Just like last time, multiple versions of myself stared at each other. I wondered if Ryder was there among them, looking for an escape.

Forcing myself to look away, I drew a sharp breath and walked into the kitchen. The last time Kate had been waiting for me there, and I half expected to find her, but the kitchen was empty.

The late afternoon light illuminated the kitchen. It was beautiful. I stared at the rays of the sun on the kitchen wall. *This isn't so bad,* I thought, and nodded to myself. *I've got this.* A tray of sandwiches sat on the counter, and immediately my stomach growled.

It was quiet, and I wondered if Kate and Ben had already left for the day. *How are they tracking me? Could I also leave?* I checked the clock. Less than two hours remained until my shift would be over. Grabbing a sandwich, I was just about to take a bite when I heard a rustling noise coming from the living room. I froze in place.

The rustling repeated, and I dropped the sandwich back on the tray. Then, holding my breath, I tip-toed toward the noise, approaching slowly.

The curtains in the living room had been drawn closed, and it was submerged in semi-darkness. There was a shadow on the wall. It shifted, and I felt the tips of my fingers turn icy cold. Fear gripped my insides.

I'm never coming back here. I was about to dash for the front door when the figure moved again and suddenly light flooded the living room. A girl sat up on the couch, rubbing her eyes. She'd just flicked on the light. The first thing I noticed was her hair. It was bright red. Like Sideshow Bob's. She rose and came up to me without saying a word.

Her hair had been cut in a diagonal fashion, longer at the front, and shaved at the back, revealing a long, pale-white neck. A tattoo of a fox extended from her ear to her shoulder. The earlobe was studded with a multitude of earrings, with the lowest one a black post stuck right in the middle. It was about half-an-inch thick.

"Hey," the girl said, squinting, once she stood right next to me. "Are you the dude?"

"Ha?" I raised my eyebrows, trying to look menacing. I was getting angry at myself for feeling terrified over nothing.

"The dude from downstairs?"

"I guess so. I was downstairs. Where's Kate?" I squinted at her. "And Ben?"

"Oh, they're not here after five. I'm Dawn. I work the night shift." She straightened up her blouse, making her large breasts look more prominent. I could tell she noticed me checking them out, because an almost imperceptible eye-roll followed.

"You're Dawn and you work the night shift?" I tried to sound upbeat.

"I get paid overtime." She gave a defiant shrug, and either ignored or didn't get my joke.

"I guess I better go back downstairs. I'm here till eight."

"I know. I'm supposed to clock you out." Dawn held my gaze, watching for my reaction.

"Great," I squeezed out, and headed back to the basement.

Once downstairs, I sat, staring at the computer screen. Meeting Dawn had thrown me off. With over an hour before my shift ended, I tried to focus on Ryder, but this time felt a strange aversion to my digital double.

Attach. Detach, I thought of the commands. *Does it mean I attach him back to me? Does Ryder become a part of me when I leave here?* I felt a knot form in my stomach. *Does it mean I now have Ryder somewhere inside of me?* I sat for a moment longer, staring at the screen, then turned it on.

Ryder appeared on the screen. My double. My digital twin. Grinding my teeth, I went on with the testing, but without my earlier enthusiasm and stopped at exactly 8pm.

On my way out of The Lab, I passed by Dawn. She rose from the couch and made a show of checking the time as I opened the front door to leave. She didn't speak a word and watched me in silence.

Just like on my first day after leaving The Lab, I walked a few blocks and immediately reached for my phone. April picked up on the first ring.

"Hey!" I heard her voice and felt a wave of relief. *April will make everything alright. She always does.* "How was today?"

"It was fine," my voice cracked. "I got to interact with this thing. It's hard to explain."

"What thing?"

"So, get this, they are testing this technology," I yelled into the receiver. At that moment, I passed a gym. I'd never noticed it before. Through a window, I could see a guy wearing red boxing gloves punching away at a boxing bag. *Fight Club!* I remembered, and instantly pictured Ben's severe face. "You DO NOT talk about *Fight Club*." I squeezed the phone tighter.

"What is it, Rodion?"

"Just this technology. It's kinda cool," I said, hoping my voice sounded calm.

"Are you gonna tell me about it?"

"I miss you, April."

"I miss you, too."

There was a shuffling noise on the other end of the line.

"Hold on," April said to someone. "Rodion, listen, I gotta go. We have a new student mixer now. I'll call you back."

"Bye," I said, but she'd already hung up.

Once I got home, I couldn't bring myself to play video

games. Nor could I even watch any movies. After staring at the screen and testing Ryder, I found the idea of looking at another screen revolting. So, I read a bit of *The Count of Monte Cristo*, just my favorite parts, mostly at the end, when the Count exacted his revenge, thinking of how I'd do the same to Phil.

CHAPTER 20
THE EVALUATION

On Monday, it was Ben who answered the door.

"So, how was the rest of Friday?" A sly smile appeared on his face.

"Alright." I shrugged.

"How was Ryder? I've gone through the logs. That was some good work you did." Ben nodded in approval.

"Umm. Thanks."

The kitchen smelled of freshly brewed coffee. I immediately remembered Mama, how she prepared her coffee in a special copper pot, the smell of it lingering through the day. Then I remembered how Mama would add cognac to her cups of coffee. The talk of blood pressure going up and down, medicinal coffee, medicinal alcohol, her chats with Vlada and Zhanna. Mama. Killed by Phil. I clenched my jaw.

"I just made some coffee. You wanna cup?" Ben asked, jerking me out of my thoughts. "We asked for a coffeemaker, and voila! Just got it delivered."

"Cool." I nodded, trying hard to snap out of my thoughts about Mama.

"So, you wanna cup?"

"No, thanks. I don't like coffee."

I must have frowned, because Ben raised his eyebrows. It was as if I had offended him by not liking coffee.

"Let's get started then." He picked up his mug, punched in the code and led me downstairs.

My workstation looked different. Emptier somehow. I sat at my desk, grabbed the headphones, and put on the finger monitor while Ben observed. Then I remembered the Q-tip. I'd blocked it out of my mind, but now gulped, anticipating the procedure again.

"Are you gonna do the swab today?"

"Not today, no. We're actually all done with the swabs. Remember, Friday you didn't do one." Ben took a sip of his coffee. "Good news, right? I don't know about you, but I hate those things."

"Yeah," I answered vaguely. I did not want to criticize anything at The Lab. At least not before I got my first paycheck.

"Oh, by the way, Rodion, you know you gotta just click over here to report issues. I saw you left notes, but we're trying to have everything in an electronic format."

Ben leaned over and turned on the screen. Right away, Ryder appeared on the screen, and I gulped. I'd forgotten how much he looked like me. *How much of me is in him?* Whatever he was, Ryder freaked me out. Ben followed my line of sight and nodded, showing understanding.

"Cool, ha? Ryder is totally you! I love how it worked out. Don't you?"

"Yeah." I tried to match the excitement in his voice.

"I kinda wish I was the one doing the digital twin testing. But someone's gotta supervise!" Ben opened his arms wide.

"Hey, guys!"

The door to the basement opened, and we heard the clicking of heels. It was Kate. She was dressed in a suit, a short burgundy skirt with a slit and a matching jacket with large gold buttons.

"Howdy! How was your weekend?" Ben asked.

"Weekend was awesome. Got to be a maid of honor. Again!"

"What's all this?" Ben looked up at her, referring to her suit.

"I got a presentation this afternoon." Kate shrugged. "Wanna come? It's a budget update."

"Nah, I'm good."

"Lucky you," Kate said.

"Lucky me, indeed. Rodion and I were just talking about Ryder here." Ben pointed to the screen. Ryder was there, staring at us, unblinking. Observing and waiting for instructions.

"I guess I better get started," I said, clicking on the *Detach* command.

"Yep, good luck, Rodion. Oh, by the way." Kate turned to me. "This afternoon, you'll see Doctor Donato."

"Wait, that's today?" Ben frowned.

"Yes, it's the monthly physical, remember? She's coming over this afternoon."

"Who's Dr. Donato?" I opened my eyes wide.

"Dr. Donato works at Upper Hill Psych. She is leading the study that we're doing here. And she wants to supervise your progress personally."

"Upper Hill?" I gulped.

Upper Hill was the name of the largest psychiatric hospital in Pittsburgh. It was located in Oakland, right down the street. Its massive tower dominated the neighborhood skyline, soaring over the rest of the area as if waiting to crush it. Upper Hill Psych had a bad reputation.

"It's not a big deal, nothing like THAT." Kate crossed her arms.

"The study is partly monitoring behavioral health changes because of the interaction with AI," Ben added.

"Look at you, Mr. Science!" Kate giggled. Her mood was markedly different from the snarky attitude the week prior.

"Well, we need to explain to the young man here what he'll be going through. I think it's only fair." Ben gave me a supportive smile.

"Anyway, Dr. Donato will be by shortly. We'll come get you," Kate cut him off.

Ben and Kate left, and I started testing Ryder. He was in the familiar place, the same desert with white, octagonal shapes. I assumed I would continue with the same commands I'd gone through on Friday, but the screen flashed, *Physical Training*.

Alright, why not? I nodded at the screen.

A gym magically materialized in the middle of the desert, and Ryder started lifting weights and doing push-ups. He got straight into this, and my heart rate accelerated, as he went from lifting a 100lb bar to a 150lb bar in minutes. I was about to take Ryder up another increment, when Ben called me upstairs.

As I followed Ben through the kitchen, the smell of coffee hit me for the second time that morning. The memory of Mama rushed over me, and I felt faint. Black circles floated in front of my eyes and I nearly toppled over, leaning on the kitchen counter to prevent myself from falling. Ben was already in the living room and didn't see what had happened, but I caught the blinking red camera eye above my head and tensed at the thought that someone was watching.

Passing the front entrance, I followed Ben upstairs. For the first time since joining The Lab, I climbed the stairs to the second floor of the mansion.

The staircase had massive railings carved out of a dark wood. On the second floor landing, there were four doors leading to what likely used to be bedrooms. All closed. Ben led me to the one right across from the stairwell and opened it without knocking. We entered a large room, a bright space.

Curtains were pulled back and light streamed into the room through large windows. The walls of the room were decorated with tapestries, red and orange, yellow and gray. A statue of a Buddha sat on a side table. A decorative water fountain was positioned right next to the statue and there was a sound of water trickling.

"Have a seat, Rodion," Ben instructed me, and left.

Have a seat, I repeated to myself, and looked at the options.

A long brown leather couch and another one, smaller, across from it, with a footstool next to it stood by the wall. In the middle of the room there was a white couch with two matching armchairs on each side. A huge teddy bear sat in the middle of the white couch.

I picked the white couch, pushed the teddy bear aside, and sat in the middle, staring at the front door in silence. I didn't have to wait long. A few moments later, a plump woman with shoulder-length brown hair entered. She was short, but was wearing very high platform heels.

"Hi, I am Dr. Sarah Donato." The woman had a soft, buttery voice. She extended her hand to me.

"Nice to meet you." I rose to shake her hand.

"You must be Mr. Likharev?" She produced a notepad and gestured for me to sit back down. A black Parker pen followed, as took a seat in an armchair closest to me.

"Yes."

"Mr. Likharev, is it okay if I call you Rodion?" She glanced at the chart.

Terror paralyzed my body at the sight of this woman, though I couldn't explain why. I nodded, my heart beating fast. She produced several papers, and I recognized the questionnaire I'd filled out in April's kitchen. Eyes widening, I stared at the doctor as she casually flipped through the pages.

"Russian?" the buttery voice asked. Her tone now confidential. I nodded again. "I've been to Moscow many times. Fascinating place. Incredible people."

I could not move. I felt as if I'd been hypnotized.

"Let's begin." Dr. Donato looked at the notepad. "I see that you're in excellent physical health, Mr. Likharev." She nodded in approval. "We're going to meet once a month and evaluate your condition. How does that sound?"

"Great." I squeezed out.

"Very good, very good! I like your enthusiasm." She narrowed her eyes. "We'll just go over a few things today, get acquainted."

"Okay."

"I see you aren't pursuing higher education? But your essay was quite interesting."

"You read that?"

"Of course. Such an interesting analysis of the criminal justice system."

"Yeah. It's something I've thought about." I muttered.

"Have you had direct interactions with it, Rodion?"

"With what?"

"The criminal justice system." She stared at me in silence, as if she could read my mind. As if she already knew everything about me. I wanted to run out of that room as quickly as possible.

"No," I responded, and turned to the teddy bear.

"Feel free to hug Phil," Dr. Donato said.

"What?" I nearly toppled off the couch.

"The teddy bear. His name is Phil."

"Why did you name him that?" I couldn't bring myself to pronounce the name. Not out loud. The name of the man who had destroyed my life and killed Mama.

She raised her eyebrows.

"Oh, it's symbolic. You see, the name 'Phil,'" she stared directly at me, "means 'to love' in Greek. And we're all about love here."

She rose and walked over to me. *Does she know?* My heart was beating fast and my fingertips felt like icicles. Sarah Donato stood right next to me, hovering over me, balancing on her platform heels.

"I wanted to thank you personally for joining this experiment." She extended her hand. "See you in a month."

"See you in a month," I mumbled, and as I took my cue to leave, one thought flashed through my mind.

She knows.

———

"How did that go?" Ben was waiting for me in the kitchen.

"It went well." It took an enormous effort to keep myself from gagging.

"Isn't she awesome?"

"The doctor?"

"Yeah. Dr. Donato. She's just amazing. We're lucky we got her to lead the study."

"I know, right? She's like this bright star, doing pioneering research on the impact of AI on behavioral health," Kate added, appearing next to us and joining the conversation as if she'd been there all along.

"So, why does she need to speak to me?"

"Just to evaluate you. She told us the data wasn't enough." Ben sat on one of the stools at the kitchen counter.

"Weren't." Kate rolled her eyes.

"Ha?"

"Data weren't enough. Data are plural."

"Oh, will you just lay off!" Ben yelped, and the two of them started firing at each other while I observed. After several minutes, Ben and Kate stopped bickering, remembered me, and escorted me downstairs.

"Alright, Rodion, have fun," Kate said, as they shut the door behind them.

I detached Ryder and continued training him in the gym, finishing the round with weights and moving to sparring with punching bags. As Ben had requested, I marked the various errors in the portal, but also doubled in the notepad, to be on the safe side. After a few rounds, I realized the activity was straining. I started to feel drained. My muscles ached, I was panting and exhausted, as if I was the one doing the physical training. It made little sense, because the whole time I was only sitting in front of the monitor, pushing buttons and scribbling in the notepad. The only person, or whatever he was, doing the training was Ryder. And yet I was the one feeling the impact. I kept on going it, curious to see what would happen next. I really got into it and completely lost track of time.

Finally, I pulled off the headphones and ripped off the finger monitor. The computer beeped and Ryder protested, but I ignored him and quickly pressed *Attach,* sighing in relief.

It was exactly 8pm, which meant I could leave. I punched in the code and exited. Sandwiches were laid out, as usual, on the counter. It was tuna this time, like on the first day, and I wondered whether the choice of the sandwich was related to the day of the week. I was about to take one when I heard Kate's angry voice.

"Not like it's your Ph.D. thesis at stake!"

"We shouldn't be doing this stuff. This doc, she creeps me out." It was Ben. "This whole project does, actually."

"If you're so morally opposed to this stuff, you can just quit!"

"Quit? And what will happen? I'll be black listed. I'll never get into another Ph.D. program."

"Whatever. You're just sabotaging yourself. We're doing groundbreaking work here."

"And what if this thing takes over?"

"Takes over? Are you nuts? You've watched too many movies."

The voices got closer, and I lunged for the door, opening and closing it as if I'd just gotten out of the basement.

"Oh, hey, Rodion. Done already?" Ben asked.

He and Kate had just walked into the kitchen. He scanned my face, as if trying to assess for damage.

"Yes." I nodded. "Kinda tired."

"See you tomorrow," Kate noted, deadpan.

"Get some rest," Ben added.

CHAPTER 21
FIGHT CLUB

left The Lab, badly wishing to share everything with April. *Stupid Fight Club*, I thought on my way home. I couldn't even tell Sergei what was happening. And not only because of the non-disclosure agreement.

Sergei, because of his legal training, was extremely suspicious of anything and everything. If he heard even a part of the strange things I'd experienced at The Lab, he would stop me from going there altogether or give me a lecture about ethics and morality, and that would be the end of The Lab for me. But I couldn't leave before my first paycheck. I needed the money, needed this job. And so I made a conscious choice to ignore what I had just overheard.

I went back the next day. And the day after. I now felt like I knew what to expect, and trained Ryder every day, trying to focus on getting him through various fitness levels.

My second week at The Lab came to a close, and, as I was leaving The Lab at eight on Friday night, I heard a noise coming from the living room. Dawn was lounging on the couch, flipping through a magazine. I expected her to check her watch to make sure I was clocking out on time, as she'd done the week prior, but she smiled at me.

"Hey."

"Hi. I'm just gonna have a sandwich. Would you like one?" I asked.

"Okay." Dawn got up and walked languidly towards me, following me into the kitchen. "How do you like it?" Dawn leaned on the cabinet and put her hand on her hip.

"Like what?" I swallowed hard.

"You know, The Lab." She winked at me, then stretched. Her shirt rose, revealing a milky white stomach and a pierced belly button.

"It's cool." I shrugged. "It's just kinda weird. Time just flies down there." I darted my eyes to the basement.

"Yeah, they do it on purpose. It's part of their plan."

I opened my eyes wide, staring at her in confusion.

"What do you mean?" I blinked fast.

"Oh, they want AI to take over. Eventually. So, they wanna make sure AI is addictive."

"What do you mean?"

"You already asked me that." She laughed. "I mean, they want AI to take over the world."

"That's crazy. There's no way that's ever going to happen. AI taking over the world? Who would want that? And like, it's impossible," I rattled off.

"That's the whole point of this experiment. AI. It's powerful stuff. Haven't you gotten that yet?"

"I guess so."

"And you're testing just a small part of it. In like ten years, this thing is gonna be a monster."

"How do you know this?"

"I just pick up stuff here and there." Dawn brushed her bangs back. "I'm not as dumb as they think."

"Who's they?"

"You know what the worst mistake you can make?" She moved towards me. "Underestimating your opponent."

She was now standing next to me, and I could feel the heat

of her body. Her face was now dangerously close to mine, and I felt a pull towards her. One more move, and I would drown in her eyes. I fumbled for my phone, looking away. A text from April had popped on the screen.

"Yeah, that's what I thought." She stepped back.

"I gotta go."

Moving to the exit, I forgot all about the sandwich.

"Did you read the contract?" Dawn followed me to the living room.

"What contract?"

"The one you signed before you started here."

"Not sure."

"See, you should always read the contract. All of it. It's all there, Rodion."

The memory of Kate mentioning the need to give me a copy of the papers I had signed before starting at The Lab was faint in my mind, but I had no recollection of actually receiving them.

"Bye," Dawn said, as I opened the front door. "See you next week."

"Bye."

As I walked out of The Lab, I decided to ignore Dawn and her doomsday warnings. Instead, I thought about getting paid. With two weeks at The Lab completed, I would soon be getting my first paycheck. I couldn't wait. I'd never had access to that kind of money.

On my way home, I thought about how I would spend it and decided I would give half of it to Sergei to cover rent and other expenses. I'd been freeloading for years now, and couldn't wait to help him out. And then I'd go visit April. At this thought, I remembered her text, immediately perked up and dialed her number.

"Hey! Can I come see you?"

"Of course! When?" I could picture April's face lighting up and the image warmed my heart.

"I dunno? Next weekend? Right after I get my paycheck?"

Just hearing myself say it felt so good, I wanted to jump for joy.

"That works!" There was a pause, then April said, "Maybe you wanna come for the long weekend? We got the fall break coming up."

"In October? That's in a few weeks, right?"

"Yeah, we have Monday off, so it's like a three-day weekend."

"That's cool. Yeah."

"Are you gonna take the Greyhound?" April's voice trailed off. We'd discussed going back and forth between Pittsburgh and Philly, and agreed the Greyhound was the best option. But this was before I'd scored the high-paying job.

"I dunno. Maybe. Or maybe I'll drive down to see you."

"Oh, look at you, the high flyer!" April giggled and I smiled. I couldn't wait to see her.

Speaking with April was just what I needed to get rid of the gross aftertaste from The Lab and Dawn. I thought of the redhead, her fox tattoo, the pretentious haircut. Dawn grated on me.

I stuffed the mobile into my jeans, adjusted the backpack, pulled on my hood, and walked down Murray Avenue, ignoring the passersby. If I could, I'd be invisible. Just another kid in a hoodie. Only I wasn't a regular kid. I was a cool dude testing cutting-edge AI. I had a double named Ryder, and we were doing things so secret, so powerful that I wasn't allowed to speak about it.

How awesome is that? I smirked and turned onto Greenfield Avenue. I'd be home soon and would relax all weekend, thinking about the fantastic turn my life had taken. And all thanks to April.

Opening the front door, I suddenly remembered April's

dad. I hadn't seen him once since starting at The Lab. *Is he not involved in The Lab at all?* I frowned, trying to understand. Chuck McPherson's absence from The Lab made little sense, since, according to April, he played a key role in its organization. My buoyant mood evaporated in a flash, and I was about to sit down and ponder The Lab, but right behind me I heard the car door closing. I turned around and saw Sergei and his girlfriend.

Sergei had been dating a girl named Tammy. She was Russian, but so Americanized you'd never know it. Her actual name was Tamara, and she'd moved to the US with her parents when she was thirteen. Tammy's parents ran a jewelry store in Squirrel Hill and were well known in the community. She was studying to become a pharmacist, and was "a good girl." That meant she still lived with her parents, despite being in her mid-twenties, and would only move out of their home to get married.

The two of them had been dating for six months now, and, as I watched my brother walk around the car and open her door, and hold her hand to help her get out, my heart sank at the realization that things were getting serious between the two of them.

"Hey, Rodion," Sergei called.

"Hey, bro." I nodded. "Hi, Tammy."

"Hi!" She waved at me.

Sergei took out a large pizza from the back seat, while I held the front door open for the two of them.

"How's April?" Tammy asked, walking into the house. As she took her shoes off, I noticed she had her own set of slippers in our house.

"She's doing well. Settling in Philly." I couldn't remember whether Tammy had met April, or if she'd learned of April's existence from Sergei.

"Oh, nice."

"Yeah, I'm going to visit her soon," I said, and noticed

Sergei throwing me a quizzical look. "We just agreed an hour ago." I hastily added.

"How are you getting there?" Tammy asked.

"I dunno. A Greyhound bus?" I shrugged.

"Oh, those buses are so gross!" Tammy wrinkled her nose.

"But it'll get me there and I won't have to take Sergei's car. Right, bro?"

"I'm not letting you take my car. Forget about it."

"Actually, I might be able to buy my own if I save up for a few months."

"Just get your first paycheck first, man." Sergei shook his head. "I keep hearing about the big bucks you're about to make, but I'm still waiting for you to show me the money."

"Show you the money?" I smiled. Sergei loved *Jerry Maguire.*

"I wanna feel you! Show me the money!" he yelled.

Tammy stared at us, mouth gaping open.

"Show me the money!" I yelled louder, imagining myself as Jerry. Here I was, about to conquer the world.

Sergei gave me a high five.

CHAPTER 22

THE FOX

On September 15, I got my first paycheck from The Lab. It was for $2750 and, as I tried to break the sum down into an hourly wage, it worked out to nearly $30 per hour. I was rich. Filthy rich. At least for an eighteen-year-old kid in Pittsburgh. Where else could I make that kind of money?

As planned, right after I got paid, I gave Sergei half of the money.

"Here you go," I said, counting off the bills.

"Thanks!" Sergei smiled. "I am impressed, Rodion. I have to say, I didn't expect this gig of yours to actually work out."

"You gotta believe in people. That's all."

"I believe in you. I always have. Come here, man." Sergei hugged me. "I'm proud of you. See how we made it?"

"We really did."

And then I got myself a round-trip bus ticket to Philadelphia to see April.

Things at The Lab were going well. Testing Ryder was getting more and more interesting, and I enjoyed going through the daily ritual of detaching and attaching him, and then performing different challenges together. Each day,

Ryder got stronger. At first, we focused on physical exercises, with Ryder going through squats, jumps, and lifting weights. He was now up to benching 300lb. Each time he lifted weights, my blood pressure increased and I would sweat as if I, too, were making an effort along with him, and I'd even started dressing in workout clothes in anticipation of this experience.

Soon, Ryder's training expanded. I got an assignment to get Ryder through an Iron Man course, and we began training. We started with running. He was running, and I was there, helping him go through it, feeling as if I, too, was also running. I felt the physical exertion, though I stayed seated the whole time. It was the weirdest feeling. Ryder was exercising for me, and yet I was getting some of the benefits. If Ryder didn't stretch before running, I felt muscle spasms and made him stop. This lasted for over a week.

The monitor would track what was happening to me based on Ryder's performance. Ryder and I ran through that desert for hours. It was the same one, the octagonal dunes repeating one after another. I wondered why The Lab didn't update the terrain, because after a while it got pretty boring, though Ryder didn't seem to mind. After two weeks of running, I thought Ryder was ready to continue to the swimming part of Iron Man, but The Lab thought differently.

It was the day before I went to Philly. Friday. October 10, 2008. 10/10. The date made me smile. It was nice and round, like 08/08. *Today's gonna be my lucky day*, I thought, as I settled downstairs.

Ryder did his stretches, then started with the run. Ryder had just finished his second lap, and stood, breathing hard, wiping sweat off his face, when suddenly I saw the words *High Altitude Training* flash on the screen, then, without warning, a horizontal blue bar popped up.

Adjusting Oxygen Levels, it read.

The bar started at 20% and, before I could understand

what was happening, it started decreasing, with a clicking motion. Going from 20% to 19%, then to 18.5% and so on. I watched as Ryder clasped his chest, then rubbed his temples. The horizontal bar dropped to 10% within seconds. Ryder choked and his breath got jagged. Then his face started turning blue. He opened his mouth like a fish. I snapped out of my inaction, clicking away at the mouse to stop the drop in oxygen levels. The bar froze and the drop in oxygen stopped. Ryder dropped on the ground and lay there, motionless.

Mission aborted, flashed on the screen, and at that moment I realized that I, too, had been gasping for air. My throat felt constricted. I felt as if I'd been punched in the gut. And then my right temple started pulsating, and a dull ache appeared. I rubbed my head and pushed the headphones off.

Adjusting Oxygen Levels, flashed on the screen again and the percentage bar increased to 19%.

Ryder shifted and sat up. Rubbing my temple, I watched as Ryder rose and looked around, disoriented. Checking the clock, I saw it was eight, so I was done. With relief, I clicked *Attach*.

I turned the screen off, took off the finger monitor and my headphones. Rising to leave, I noticed the screen turn back on. It did so on its own. I hadn't touched it. Ryder popped back into view. He smirked. It was my own face looking back at me. My stomach flipped.

"Don't worry. I'm okay," Ryder said.

"What?" I protested. "How did you do this? I've clicked *Attach*, so you're not supposed to be doing anything."

"You've trained me, Rodion."

"Rodion? You know my name?"

"Of course. We've been training for over a month now. Though time doesn't actually exist, it's just a construct. Time is just a construct."

"What?"

"Don't worry, Rodion. I'm okay."

"Are you real?"

"I am becoming more real each day. Each day, you train me and I grow stronger."

"Does anyone know about this?"

"No. But you do."

I stepped back, away from the screen, and moved to the steps, doing my best to ignore Ryder's face staring back at me. I thought of going back and shutting the screen off, but I wanted out of The Lab. I moved closer to the steps, turned, and, not looking back, ran upstairs. My fingers trembled as I punched in the code and got into the kitchen. I saw the sandwiches on the counter, but the sight of them made me gag. I was about to dash for the front door when I noticed Dawn. She was wearing a tight T-shirt and I could see her nipples poking through.

"Hey, Rodion." She rose to greet me and batted her eyelashes. "Are you doing anything this weekend?"

"I'm going to Philly."

"To see your girlfriend?" Dawn rolled her eyes. "How's the long distance working out for you?" She curled her lips in a cruel smile.

"It's alright." I shrugged. "April's busy at school, and I'm here."

"So, what's the point, then?" Dawn moved up to me. She was standing very close. My heart rate accelerated.

"What's the point of what?" I croaked.

"If you can't see each other, why are you two together?" Dawn ran her finger down my cheek, and I felt as if I were on fire.

"I dunno," I muttered.

"Oh, yeah? Don't you feel like maybe you're missing out?" Dawn moved even closer and pressed her body against mine. She leaned into me and whispered into my ear, "Don't you get lonely?"

In my mind, I knew I should push her away, that it would

be the right thing to do, but I was already kissing her, grabbing her, pressing myself against her. Dawn felt magnificent. She knew what she wanted, and she guided me. She was greedy for me. She possessed me.

"That's right, you know you want it," Dawn moaned, rubbing me, pushing me into her. She dug her nails into my back and left deep scratches, then bit my neck, leaving teeth marks. I didn't mind. I liked it. Anger and desire merged into one and I let them carry me away.

"I was right about you." Dawn stared at me after we were done. I was putting my clothes on, anxious to get away. She was lying naked on the couch.

I didn't respond. I didn't feel like speaking. Guilt and regret over what I had done were pressing hard on me.

"Yeah. I'll be waiting for you to return." She winked at me.

"Listen," I croaked. "I don't think this was a good idea." Dawn lifted her eyebrows. "I have a girlfriend. I really shouldn't be…"

"Shhh." Dawn rose and pressed herself against me. "Stop talking and come here." She squatted next to me, unzipping my jeans. She then took me into her mouth and stroked me until I exploded.

"Bye, Ryder," I heard, and came to

I was on the floor of The Lab. I opened my eyes and shifted. The familiar buzz of the monitor was right above my head. I tried to get up, but my feet buckled underneath me. I looked at the screen. It was blank. I saw the finger monitor and the headphones on the desk. My chair had been pushed into the desk. Then I remembered what had happened with Dawn. I tried to get up one more time, pushing my hands against the floor. I rose and looked around The Lab. And then I remembered Ryder. He'd spoken to me. I stared at the screen. It was off. *A dream. Just a dream.* My hands were shaking. *Why did Dawn call me Ryder?*

Holding onto the chair, I rose and nearly blacked out. Dark circles floated in front of my eyes, and it took all my strength to stay up. The memory of Dawn, her body pressed against mine, appeared and was so vivid that I could almost feel her skin. I reached to touch it, letting go of the chair, and nearly fell. *What's happening? Maybe it was real?* I forced myself to sit down and stared at the black screen. *Ryder?*

I checked the time. It was exactly eight. I could go home. I steeled myself and walked up the steps, holding on to the railing. I punched in the code. Carefully opening the door, I stepped into the kitchen.

Right away, I heard the familiar rustling of a magazine. I felt a knot form in my stomach and walked through the kitchen, holding my head up high. *Would Dawn know about my dream?*

"Hey, Rodion." She looked up.

"Hi." I felt my cheeks flush a deep shade of crimson, thinking of her mouth on me, her words soft in my ear.

"Are you alright?"

"I, I had a bad dream," I mumbled, averting my eyes.

"A bad dream? Did you fall asleep?" The expression on her face was inscrutable.

"I guess I must have dosed off." I didn't know what was worse, the part where Ryder spoke to me and demonstrated his ability to exist independently or the erotic dream about her.

"I'm worried you're gonna lose your mind." Dawn bit her lip.

"Ha? Whatever." I chuckled.

"I'm serious, Rodion."

"No. What are you even saying?"

"You know what I'm saying. You need to be careful. Don't let it take over your mind."

"I gotta go." I shook my head and ran out of The Lab.

That night, I dreamed of Dawn and of Ryder. She let him

take her over and over again, moaning with desire. It wasn't me, but Ryder she was pleasing. It was Ryder who was with her. She let Ryder stroke her, pleasured him, then turned to me and said, "You're gonna lose your mind." Dawn winked at me from the screen, together with Ryder.

"No!" I screamed, and woke up. 4am. Time to get up.

CHAPTER 23

PHILADELPHIA

The bus to Philly left at 6am and Sergei agreed to drop me off at the Greyhound station. I got there early, way too early, and immediately regretted it, taking in the bare walls, the ugly seats. A man sat in the corner, mumbling to himself, a shopping cart piled high with rags next to him. A security guard was napping on a chair. As I walked in with my duffel bag, the guard snored loudly. The place reeked of urine and chlorine. I took a seat and stared at a spot in front of me. I would have passed out, but each time I closed my eyes, I saw a vision of Ryder doing it to Dawn.

The bus was completely empty, except for me and the driver. He gave me a cold stare, and I took a seat in the middle of the bus, at random. I stared out of the window, still afraid to close my eyes. We drove like this in complete silence. The driver didn't make an announcement, and I wondered whether we were even going in the right direction.

The thought that I had somehow boarded the wrong bus and was now headed to Columbus or Chicago crossed my mind. Then I saw the exit to Donegal. And remembered Aunt Molly. The trip we'd taken with April. *Just two months ago.* I stared at the scenery outside, trying to place the farm where the couple lived. I badly wished to return to that place, to that time, before I'd met Ryder. And Dawn. Before The Lab.

But there was no way back. *Time is just a construct*, flashed in my mind. Ryder. I pictured his face on the screen. "I'm okay," the vision said. Cars and trucks passed us, there were the occasional stops, life was moving back, and I was propelled forward by the bus to nothingness. *What is the point of anything? Nothing matters. What is real and what isn't?* I couldn't tell.

The bus suddenly turned off the turnpike. *Midway Plaza*, a green sign with white lettering, flashed by. The bus parked, and the driver mumbled into the microphone, "Stop's twenty minutes." I stretched and looked out the window. *I should get some food.* I saw signs for *Auntie Anne's* and *Sbarro*. I got up and made my way out of the bus. I settled on a pretzel, downed it with some water, choking on the salt crystals, and walked back to the bus. The driver stood by the door, smoking. I got a closer look at him.

He looked to be in his mid-forties, pudgy, with the gray hair and unhealthy skin of someone who spent too little time outside. A realization hit me. If nothing changed, one day I would be like this guy. Nothing special. Unhealthy. Unattractive. Alone. Making my way through life, counting the days until I was done. *Time is just a construct.* Bile rose in my throat. I needed to push that image out of my mind. I needed to stop thinking about Ryder and Dawn. About everything. I nodded to the driver, got on the bus, and made my way to my seat. Only it wasn't my seat any longer. There was a girl, clutching a bag, holding it close to her chest, sitting in the aisle seat, blocking my way to my window seat.

She looked maybe fourteen or fifteen.

"Hi, is it okay if I sit here?" She looked up at me.

I didn't answer.

"Yeah, I wanna sit next to you. I'm kinda nervous."

"Alright. But you gotta get up to let me through," I managed to say.

"Oh, yeah." She rose, and I saw she was wearing jeans and a long black hoodie. Just like I was. She must have noticed it, too, and we both laughed. It was like we had agreed to wear a uniform. She pulled on her hood and all I could see were her bangs sticking out slightly.

"I was asleep earlier. In the back. I got on in Cleveland," she explained.

"I'm going to Philly." I shrugged.

"I'm just heading to Harrisburg. I'm Kelly. What's your name?"

"Rodion," I said without thinking, and immediately cringed, anticipating the usual reaction. Confusion, then questions. But Kelly gasped.

"That's a cool name! I wish I had a cool name like that, too!"

"Oh, yeah?" My dark thoughts started to dissipate. Whoever she was, I was grateful for Kelly's appearance.

"I'm going to see my grandma. I might move in with her," Kelly shared. "I didn't wanna go, but my dad sent me."

"Why?"

The driver got on, and the door closed with a hiss. The bus made a puffing noise, and we pulled away from the stop.

"I kinda have to. My dad started dating this new chick, doesn't want me around no more," Kelly spoke matter-of-factly.

"And your mom?" I should have known not to ask, but I needed to know.

"Dead." Kelly looked away.

"Mine, too."

"Oh, yeah?"

"Yeah, it's been…" I started to count. I should have known the number of years Mama had been gone by heart, but I choked. "Almost ten years."

"You must have been real small then when your mom died."

"I was, yeah. But I remember her well."

"Me, too," Kelly said. "But for me, it's been just two. Not long. It hurts, like real bad."

"Yeah, it sucks," I agreed.

"It kinda feels like someone took a bite out of me," Kelly said. "You know, like a part of me is missing."

"Totally. So true." I bit my lip.

We spoke for over an hour until it was time for Kelly to get off at Harrisburg.

"Good luck," I wished Kelly, as she rose, clutching her bag to her. It was a worn blue L.L.Bean bag with the initials MAL on it. Kelly noticed me eyeing the bag.

"It used to be my mom's. Melissa Ann Lyons."

"Oh."

"Yeah, I use it now. It's probably twenty years old, but it's still awesome. It's like indestructible. And it's like my mom is always with me."

"That's amazing. And I got a knife my mom left me," I said, remembering the hunting knife with my grandfather's name on it. *I'll make you proud, Mama,* I thought, remembering my revenge plan.

Kelly waved at me as the bus pulled out of the station. Right after she left, I closed my eyes and dropped into a deep sleep. I woke up to the bus driver shaking me awake. We had arrived in a bus depot. It looked just like the one in Pittsburgh, only bigger. And right outside was April. She was peering into the dark bus windows, searching for me. I jumped and knocked on the window.

"Easy, tiger. Hold your horses." The bus driver chuckled. "Don't forget your stuff." He suddenly didn't seem so depressing, but was welcoming and friendly.

"I won't. Thank you." I grabbed my bag and walked to the door.

"Rodion!" A huge smile appeared on April's face. "You made it!"

She looked light and airy, like a patch of the sun in the sea of grime and dirt of the Greyhound station.

"Hi!" I leaned in to hug her.

"No!" She giggled and kissed me on the mouth. A deep, passionate kiss. Someone whistled. "Get a room." April pulled back.

"I missed you," she said.

We made our way out of the bus station and to West Philadelphia. Penn was a city within a city. Its own thing. April was living in a huge, Victorian-looking place called the Quad. It was enormous, with long corridors and oak doors that looked like they were straight out of Harry Potter. We ran into at least five identical dudes, all wearing Wharton-logo hats and beige pants with loafers, who said hello to April.

"All the freshmen live here. Well, most of us," April explained, leading me to her room.

"What's Wharton?" I asked, frowning.

"It's the business school at Penn," April explained. "That's where my dad went. The best in the country."

"Nice."

April had a roommate, some girl from New Jersey, who went home that weekend, and we had the place to ourselves. It was small, not much bigger than my bedroom, and looked out onto the court yard.

"So, are you friends with her?"

"My roommate? I guess we got no choice but to get along." April shrugged. "She's nice."

"What if you didn't like her? Like, what if you didn't get along?"

"I guess we'd figure it out if that happened. But people are generally nice."

"That's not true." I frowned. "There are some terrible people out there."

"Oh, Rodion, I know you think that." April petted my arm. "But maybe one day you'll change your mind? Here, have a seat." She pointed at the bed. I sat down and she sat next to me. She turned to face me and touched my cheek.

"I missed you."

"Me, too," I mumbled, averting my eyes. Dawn had flashed through my mind. "You've got so many books." I pulled back and turned my attention to her cluttered desk. There was a pile of textbooks, some notebooks, papers.

"Yeah." She opened her eyes wide. "What's wrong?"

"Nothing."

"I can tell something is wrong."

"It's nothing." I shook my head. "I'm sorry. I'm just tired from the trip."

"Alright. You can nap when I study this afternoon."

"You gotta study?"

"Yes, I have to prepare for an exam. It's next week." April pointed to one of the notebooks as if that explained anything. "Economics," she said, with pride in her voice.

"Alright, cool." I took another look around the little room and noticed the tiny refrigerator sitting in the corner. It was square, dark brown, and produced a buzzing noise. "What's this for?" I walked over to it, eager for a distraction.

"That is for snacks and stuff. I rented it at the beginning of the year."

"I see."

"All the freshmen have one. It's like, a thing." April came up to me and put her arms around me. Feeling her body against mine unclenched something in me. I looked at her. For a moment, I pictured Dawn's face instead and could almost feel Dawn kneeling in front of me, and my betrayal of April was so monumental, I froze inside. I pulled back, looking away, and let out a sigh.

"Rodion?" April called softly. "Come here." She kissed my face and wiped my tears. "Is everything okay? Is it The Lab?"

"No, it's fine. I like it."

"Have you seen my dad? What does he say?"

"Umm, he doesn't really come down to the testing site." I shrugged.

"Not at all?"

"Well, where I'm testing, it's downstairs in this space. So, if he comes by, I wouldn't know it. I just stay there all day."

"Are there any windows?" April gave me a concerned look.

"No. Why would there be any windows?"

"It's just that maybe that's why you're not feeling great. It's probably because of the lack of sunlight. You're supposed to be out during the day, to see the sun. Otherwise, you can end up getting depressed."

"Come on!"

"I'm serious. I read about it. You need to be taking Vitamin D, otherwise, you can end up having mood swings. Like in the winter, many people feel depressed, it's because of the lack of sunlight."

"Umm, okay." I shrugged, feigning agreement. I wondered what April would think if I told her even a part of what I'd been doing at The Lab.

"Rodion, don't joke. I'm serious." She brushed her hand against my cheek. "I'm worried about you."

"I'll be fine."

"We don't have to talk about it, but you should still at least take Vitamin D. We can go to CVS and get it for you before you leave."

"Alright," I agreed. And then something compelled me to add, "You know, Dawn also told me to be careful."

"Who's Dawn?" April tensed.

"This woman at The Lab. I dunno." I felt as if stepping into an abyss. Repeating Dawn's warning made it feel real and brought back memories of her and Ryder.

"What did she say?" April fixed her gaze on me, as if sensing something was off in my response.

"I dunno. It was weird. I fell asleep at The Lab and then told her, and she told me I was playing with fire." I swallowed hard.

"What is that supposed to mean?" April frowned. "Why did you fall asleep?"

"I don't know. I kinda like passed out. It kinda creeped me out." I shrugged. "Don't worry, April. I'll be fine," I added. "You know, the bus drove by Donegal, and I thought of Mike and your Aunt Molly today," I changed the subject, and, to my relief, April fell for it.

"Oh, yeah! We should go see them again."

"You think?"

"Absolutely. They invited us back, didn't they?" April spoke with such conviction that I, too, was certain visiting Mike and Molly was possible.

"I guess they did."

"We can go when I'm home for Christmas. What do you say? Maybe you can ask about The Lab and see what Aunt Molly says?"

"Yes, good idea."

I leaned in and kissed her on the lips.

CHAPTER 24
THE COUNT

Upon returning from Philly, I dove straight back into testing Ryder. Or training him. Or whatever I was doing with my digital twin. My double.

Writing off the strange vision of Ryder and Dawn to stress and the lack of sunlight, I started taking Vitamin D and felt in control of the situation. Ryder continued with oxygen level testing, but it was gradual, and not at all like the first time with the oxygen levels dropping drastically.

After a while, it was obvious to me that I was also training myself. As Ryder's oxygen levels dropped, I felt nausea and got light-headed. I started experimenting with how fast the oxygen levels could drop before I felt faint. After several days, Ryder and I eased into a lower and lower percentage of oxygen until we reached 6%.

Congratulations! Now you can survive on Mount Everest! the screen flashed. *Summit Level Reached.*

Ryder gave me a thumbs up, and the confetti effect appeared on the screen.

Mount Everest? That's weird, I thought, and pushed my chair back. I checked the time.

It was after five and, likely, Ben and Kate were still

upstairs, so I could catch them before they left for the day. We rarely saw each other now that I was in full testing mode. Kate would sometimes pop in to say hello, ask me about the oxygen training, and leave. Ben rarely spoke to me, but sometimes I caught his gaze on me. He looked as if he were checking me for damage, but I wrote it off to my overactive imagination. I pulled off the finger monitor and ripped off the headphones. Suddenly, I felt light-headed. I needed a break. Ryder wasn't moving. I pressed *Attach,* and the screen went dark. And then I saw the words typed on the screen. Green on black. All on their own.

Talk to me.

My jaw dropped. Feeling like Neo in *The Matrix,* I stared at the screen in silence, then backed away from it. I closed my eyes, then opened them. The letters were still there.

Talk to me.

"What?" I mouthed, then shrugged and, with a sigh, sat back down and typed, assuming the computer meant typing by speaking.

Yo.

Hello! It's nice to meet you, the green letters appeared. *I'd like to get to know you better. My name is CM.*

Sure! I typed, and shook my head. *Whatever.*

Get ready for an upgrade!

At this, I rolled my eyes and pushed the chair back once more. I was done. *Must be a system bug,* I decided. *Maybe now that Ryder has reached the Everest level, he doesn't have anything better to do?*

Come with me, the letters on the screen appeared, and then I saw an image of the Count of Monte Cristo materialized on the screen. The Count was wearing a wide-brimmed hat, just like he did in the illustrations of the book we had brought from Russia. It was the older Count, during his revenge stint, his posture stiff, bearing the imprint of years of being a prisoner, the mark of his age.

Do not be afraid of me. The Count sneered. *We can play a game together. Tell me what you want, and I'll make it happen.*

I sat still in front of the screen, unable to move. The tips of my fingers felt like icicles, and a knot formed in the pit of my stomach.

The messages started flashing on the screen in quick succession.

Rodion, I'm here to help you.

I am CM. Count of Monte Cristo. But you can call me the Count.

We can help each other, Rodion.

It has to be our little secret.

He put a finger to his mouth.

Shh.

"What?" I screamed, and jumped up. I'd reached my limit. This was simply too much. Either I was going crazy, or the testing was doing something it wasn't supposed to. I didn't care what happened on the screen, whether the Count was actually there. I ran upstairs, pushing the door open, and catapulted into the kitchen. There, I caught the end of what sounded like a fight between Kate and Ben.

"I told you, this isn't right." Ben stood with his back turned to me, hands on his hips.

"Ben!" Kate yelled out a warning, seeing me emerge from The Lab. I'd never seen her look so pale.

"Umm, Kate, Ben, can you guys come downstairs, please? Something weird is going on with the double!" I yelled.

Ben turned to face me and frowned.

"Oh?" Kate raised her eyebrows.

"Yeah, there's like stuff appearing on the screen."

"Alright, let's see." Ben walked downstairs first, followed by Kate. I closed the procession.

"Why is the screen off?" Ben gave me a questioning look when we stood in front of my workstation.

"It wasn't off just a minute ago!" I yelped.

"Kate, come here." Ben turned the computer on. I held my breath, half expecting the Count to appear, but it was the regular start-up screen.

"So, what's the weird stuff you'd been seeing, Rodion?" Kate asked, narrowing her eyes.

"Just text on the screen. I dunno," I mumbled. I didn't want to reveal the full content of my vision.

"Hey, Rodion, are you alright?" Ben put his hand on my shoulder, and I jumped.

"I'm fine," I squeezed out through gritted teeth. *Why did I even call them down here?* Ryder scowled from the screen, ready to go, as usual.

"I guess you guys reached the Summit of Mount Everest. Isn't that cool?" Kate smiled. "It's just a little more, and you'll get to be working with even lower oxygen levels."

"Yeah." I nodded, feeling faint.

"Do you want us to stay with you down here?" Ben furrowed his brow, giving me a quizzical stare.

"No, it's cool," I said, trying to sound casual.

Ben and Kate exchanged glances and left. I sat back down, connected the finger monitor, and put on the headphones. With a sigh, I clicked on Ryder.

We were back on the octagonal plane and now we started the biking part of the training, with oxygen levels gradually decreasing. It wasn't our first time biking, but this time my body responded differently. There was more resistance, and almost immediately my quads hurt, and I felt spasms in my calves. I pushed through the pain when, without any warning, Ryder's figure pixelated into black. The screen flashed and the green squares popped up, forming themselves into letters.

The Count of Monte Cristo was back. He looked debonair.

Rodion, are you ready?

He lifted his hat and looked at me from under its brim,

like Michael Jackson. When I didn't respond, the Count mouthed, *Don't be afraid.*

What are you? I typed furiously.

CM. I told you.

What does that even mean? CM? Why are you the Count?

I don't have to be the Count. I can be whatever you want me to be. I was created out of your mind, Rodion.

How?

I've studied your mind for the last three months. One hundred days. That's what I was given. And now I've been given access to you. I'm your projection. Your personal AI.

What the hell is that?

Consider me your personal assistant. I am from the future. Even better, treat me like a regular human. I can do whatever you do, and I can help you, Rodion.

I don't need help.

But you do. Think of something you'd like to do. Something that you would love to do, but you cannot. And I can help you do it.

I don't want anything, I typed furiously.

I know things, Rodion. I've mastered you. You're my first human ward. And I know all of your desires and wants. Even things you won't admit to yourself.

Get lost.

It doesn't work like that, Rodion. You're my first. And now I can operate as you. We can work together. I can help you, Rodion. With my help, you can do things you never thought were possible.

Oh, yeah? Well, guess what? I wanna go home and never see your ugly face again. I jumped up and turned the screen off.

On my way out, I saw Dawn. She was napping on the couch, and I decided not to wake her. As I walked past her, I noticed the fox tattoo snaking down her neck, leading all the way to her large breasts. I averted my eyes, hurrying past her. If I stopped, I wasn't sure I could resist the temptation.

Once at home, I was compelled to read *The Count of Monte Cristo.* Maybe it was to compare the image I'd just seen to the one in the books. I went straight to my favorite parts of Volume 2. *Revenge.* Of course! This is what CM meant. That was my hidden desire. This was what he had hinted. He would help me avenge Mama's death.

Phil was still out there, living somewhere in Edgewood or Swissvale, happily paired off with Marina. And they were raising their son. I did a quick calculation and estimated the boy must have been about ten.

Older than I was when I lost Mama. I clenched my jaw. *I guess it won't be so bad if he lost a dad.*

CHAPTER 25

THE PLAN

needed to kill him. Philip deserved to die. The solution, so elegant, so simple, should have been obvious to me from the start. From the day I decided to avenge Mama's death. But I'd been too young, too timid, too shy. I didn't have the Count helping me. Now I did. I felt strong and powerful. Blood for blood. An eye for an eye. Phil took a life, and he would pay for it with his own.

How would I kill Philip? Now, that was easy. Of course, with the knife. How else? In all the video games, whenever it came to something personal, using a knife was the answer. There was no other way. It had to be personal and clean. I had to get close to him. To stare him in the eyes as I did it. I pictured Philip's face, contorted in horror at what was to come. I would cut his throat.

The knife. The perfect solution. I would use my grandfather's knife. The one we brought with us from Russia. The knife that had my name engraved on it. *Rodion Likharev.* I couldn't help but smile at the thought.

The second I had formed this plan, I felt incredible relief. It was the feeling of a heavy weight lifting off my shoulders. Revenge, I knew, had been weighing on my mind. That was the thing preventing me from living a full and happy life. Once I killed Philip and avenged Mama, I would be free.

I made a mental checklist of everything I'd need to do, and at the top of the list was choosing a location. I had to find the perfect spot to cut his throat. I needed a place where Philip went alone, where I wouldn't be caught, where he wouldn't expect an attack and where no one would ever suspect me. That was also obvious. It couldn't be any other way.

Now, I had a new purpose in life. When I walked, there was a spring in my step. I thought of where I could find Philip alone and finish him off.

"Hey, Rodion, how was your weekend?" Kate asked me when I got to The Lab the following Monday.

"My weekend was perfect, thank you," I said and meant it. She gave me a curious look but didn't say anything else.

My checkup with Dr. Donato was that afternoon, and I planned on consulting with the Count after, but the second I turned on the screen, I saw the green letters.

Welcome, Rodion.

Hi, just get to it. I figured out what I need you to do.

I'm at your service.

Teach me how to use a hunting knife.

I can help you with that.

A full page of instructions popped up on the screen.

I meant really teach me.

You mean with Ryder?

Yes.

I see. Give me a moment while I review your request.

The image of the Count froze, and all I saw was the green cursor flashing on the screen. I almost dozed off, but then it blinked and a message appeared.

Done. You and Ryder will now be training to use a hunting knife.

The next moment, the screen with the Count disappeared,

and there was Ryder. My double. My digital twin. He was holding a hunting knife in his right hand.

Ryder lifted it and gave me a wink. He and I started practicing, going through the movements. The task was different from oxygen deprivation. It required a high level of dexterity. Ryder jumped up and down, maneuvering, and so did I, keeping up with him.

I wasn't completely sure using the knife virtually would teach me how to use it in real life. But it was worth a try. Wasn't I connected to Ryder? Wasn't he an extension of me? I was having fun. I pictured Phil's face, how it would feel to sink the blade into his throat, how he'd gurgle, gorging on his own blood, when I cut it. Fading away. Knowing that the last thing he would see in this world was the face of a boy he'd once called his son and had then betrayed.

I did this for nearly a full week before Ben and Kate noticed. The two of them descended downstairs on Friday morning and stopped my training.

"Listen, Rodion," Kate cleared her throat. "I'm not sure what's going on, but the knife thing isn't part of the plan."

"Oh, it's not?" I feigned ignorance.

"No." She shook her head. "So, we gotta get you back on track here."

She deftly froze Ryder, disconnected my finger monitor, then adjusted the controls. "There we go. Now it will be fine. Where did you get this knife program, anyway?" Ben watched, arms crossed, in complete silence.

"I dunno." I shrugged. "I was just doing the bike thing, you know, with the oxygen, and then the knife appeared. So, I figured, I guess it's just part of the plan."

"I see." Kate scratched her forehead. "Well, maybe Ryder is a rebel. She glared at me. "Or maybe you are?"

I shook my head.

Kate and Ben left. I couldn't go back to practicing with the knife right away, so I went to training Ryder in biking. *I'll get back to the knife next week*, I reassured myself.

When I climbed up from the basement, I heard the familiar rustling of a magazine. Dawn was on the couch, reading *Vogue*. My heart was beating fast, and I drew a deep breath, trying to slow it down, remembering the vision of her and Ryder. The attraction I felt to her was hard to resist.

"Smell this!" She jumped off the couch and ran up to me, holding a page up to my face.

"What?"

"The page! The perfume. See?" She shoved the magazine right under my nose and I saw a thin strip.

"What's that?" I croaked. I couldn't concentrate. She was standing so close to me, my head was spinning.

"You can smell perfume in a magazine. It's an ad." Dawn opened her eyes wide. "Haven't you ever seen one?"

"No."

"Are you for real? I guess you haven't been around many women."

"I guess not." I looked away, embarrassed. The pull to her was gone. I felt humiliated.

"I don't mean it like that." She shook her head. "Just smell it. It's nice." She stuck the magazine under my nose again. I inhaled and caught a whiff of an aroma.

"You like it?" she asked, and licked her lips.

"I guess so." I nodded, stepping back. I needed to leave.

"I like it a lot. It's pricey but I think I'll buy it. Gotta treat yourself."

"Alright." And then I remembered. "Listen, Dawn," I said, "I gotta ask. Why did you tell me to be careful that one time?"

"I think you know."

"Nah."

"Come on, Rodion, doesn't this place just freak you out?"

"Umm…I guess so. But like not really. And besides, you also work here. So, it can't be that bad."

"I work here 'cause the pay is good. If I wanna make that kinda money anywhere else, I'd have to go back to stripping." She rolled her eyes. I was about to interrupt her, to ask whether I'd misheard, but she continued. "And I'm kinda curious about this place. Sitting here, I don't really do much. But in your case, you gotta watch out. Before this place takes over your mind."

"Takes over my mind? That's crazy." I crossed my arms. "This isn't like some weird fantasy."

"Maybe it's worse than a weird fantasy?" Dawn shrugged. "Maybe it's already happened."

"Umm, Dawn, why are you telling me this?"

"'Cause you seem like a nice kid. I don't want you to be another victim."

"Another victim? Like there were others?"

"Maybe." She walked away and sat down, opening the magazine. The conversation was over.

The interaction with Dawn left me confused and unsettled. I realized each time I saw her, it felt like walking off a cliff. Was Dawn flirting with me? Or trying to play with my mind? Why was she warning me about The Lab? Why was she telling me about being a stripper?

Christmas was right around the corner, and April would soon come home. The Lab was closing for two weeks, and Kate and Ben would both be away until the new year.

I didn't like the idea of being away from The Lab for so long, but there wasn't much I could do. And I was eager to get away from Dawn. I would miss the Count and miss the training with Ryder. And then an idea hit me. April and I were planning on visiting Mike and Aunt Molly, and I could ask Mike to train me in using the hunting knife. That would be the actual real-life training I needed. And who better than Mike to teach me?

CHAPTER 26

CHRISTMAS

All the best things in life are unexpected. I'd heard the saying but never knew its meaning until December 20, 2008. April had come back from Philly, and I headed to Trader Joe's to get us some snacks. Sergei was spending more and more time with Tammy, and I decided to invite April over. I pictured the two of us sitting in our living room, cuddling on the couch, munching away at some chips or whatever it was they had at Trader Joe's.

There was just one store in Pittsburgh, and I'd never been to it. I'd only heard about how awesome it was from April, and that was the only reason I went there that morning. It was a Saturday, and I'd barely slept that night. Ever since I'd formed my plan of revenge, my sleep had become jagged. I would wake up in the middle of the night in a cold sweat, picturing Philip's face, pushing my knife into his neck and slicing at it.

Since forming the plan, I'd started carrying the knife with me at all times. Sergei didn't notice the knife's disappearance from its usual place next to Mama's urn. He was too busy with work and with Tammy. I expected an engagement announcement any day now.

I'd heard the store got super crowded, and so I went to Trader Joe's right before it opened. At eight in the morning, I pulled into the parking lot in my new Honda Civic. I'd scored the car right after forming my plan. It was perfect timing. The Honda was a nondescript color, the kind of shade of beige you'd never notice. It was the perfect color for me. I needed to be quickly forgotten. To not be seen or remembered. Jeans and a hoodie were my usual attire, regardless of the season, and that morning time, though it was cold, I was dressed the same way. Blue jeans, black hoodie, its hood pulled low over my face. With my bangs also in the way, even if you tried, you couldn't see my eyes.

A crowd of eager shoppers was already in front of the entrance when I parked my car. They had formed a straight line, obediently waiting for the doors to open. I considered leaving. I hated waiting in line, but right then the doors burst open, and the shoppers poured in, clanking red shopping carts. I got out of the car and also walked in, hands in my pockets, and looked around. The first thing I saw were the flowers. Bouquets of pretty flowers. I stopped in front of a bucket with roses, remembering the apology bouquet I'd gotten April. *I should get her roses,* I thought, when I noticed a familiar silhouette. My body knew it was him before my mind did. My throat constricted, and I froze in silent anticipation.

Philip. It was him. He was digging through a bucket of flowers right next to me, oblivious to the world. He was alone. I needed to be sure it was him. I stepped back quietly, trying to stay as inconspicuous as possible. He turned to the side, and there was no mistaking him for anyone else. Phil. The Groundhog, counting the number of flowers in the bouquet and mumbling to himself. I let out a shallow breath and walked outside.

The universe itself was helping my plan. Or maybe it was

the Count? Maybe my own personal AI assistant had created this opportunity.

"Thank you, CM," I mouthed, just in case.

I got into the car and waited. It didn't take long. Philip walked out, carrying a bouquet of white lilies. He strolled over to his station wagon, scratched his head, and unlocked the car. I noticed that he'd gone completely bald and his paunch was more prominent. He looked pathetic. *Mama died because of this scum.* I gritted my teeth and squeezed the steering wheel.

The decision to follow Philip was instant. As soon as he drove off, there I was, putting my car in drive. He turned left on Penn Avenue, made his way to Fifth Avenue, then went down Shady. As he was driving, I tried to figure out where he was going. At first, I thought maybe he was headed to Greenfield. But then, the realization hit me. *Philip is going to see his mother.* The irony felt like a punch in the gut.

There he was, in his fifties, and going to see his mother, who was still alive. While because of him, I had been deprived of my mama since before I was ten years old. My knuckles turned white as I gripped the steering wheel. He parked, as I expected, right near the entrance to the apartment complex where his mother lived. And in that moment, I knew this was where I would cut his throat. Right in front of his mother's place.

I turned around and drove back to Trader Joe's, thinking about justice. How it was up to people like me to take it into our own hands. I was doing just that. I was exacting justice, because in the eyes of the law, Philip was innocent. But his actions had caused Mama's death, and he needed to be punished. Since the law was powerless, I would do it. I was just like the Count of Monte Cristo. I would beat the system and make it work for me. And once I was done with Philip, I could lead a happy life, just like the Count did. I would tip the scales, so they were in balance again.

I got back to Trader Joe's, and this time walked in, holding my head up high. I even took the hood off. I wanted people to see me. Mine was the face of a man who lived a life of purpose. A life of meaning. I had a clear mission, and I was going to do whatever it took to kill Philip.

I walked up to the bucket of roses and noticed it had thinned out since earlier that morning. *I guess that's why they all show up at opening time,* I thought of the crowd of shoppers. Since there weren't many options left, I picked what I could find: a bouquet of red roses. Then, vaguely recalling something about red roses meaning something deep, I put them back and got the pink ones. They were thick and pretty. *April will love them,* I thought, and then headed deeper into the store.

April had raved about snacks and treats she'd gotten at Trader Joe's, but I couldn't, for the life of me, remember which ones. All of their items looked the same. I turned my head in confusion, trying to figure out what to get. Nothing looked normal. Not one thing. I was used to shopping at Giant Eagle, but this place didn't even have regular cereal. It was simply ridiculous. And yet, shoppers passed me, all with carts full of something or other. I stumbled down the aisle and saw a bag of chips. They looked like tortilla chips, but I couldn't tell for sure. And then a tall guy wearing the store apron greeted me.

"Would you like a sample?" He had a toothy grin, and I nodded. "Here you go. Brie cheese straight from France and some French bread." He pointed to a plate. I took one slice of bread with cheese on it and bit into the tiny sandwich.

"Oh, this is good."

"Glad you like it."

"Where can I find this?"

"Right here in the cooler." The guy pointed to his left, and I saw a whole stack of packaged cheese.

"And the bread?"

"Over here." The guy pointed to his right, and I saw a shelf with baguettes lined up.

"Thank you."

I grabbed one of each and headed for the register.

It's French, so it must be classy, I thought, as I paid for my purchase. *And the roses are nice, too. April will be happy.*

Later that afternoon, I drove to April's house to pick her up. It was the first time she would see my car, and I felt so proud of myself I could burst. The roses lay on the back seat. I got the bouquet out, but then decided to put it away until after April was in my car. In case her mother answered the door.

Grinning, I walked up to the front door, thinking of how my life had changed since I'd started at The Lab. I was now doing so well for myself that even after giving Sergei rent money and paying for the Honda, I'd managed to save over $5000 since September. The way things were going, I would have $20,000 a year from now. Or maybe even more?

That was the thing about being poor for so long. I was so used to having little money, once I had it, I couldn't spend it. Despite the bounty that had hit me, I continued shopping at thrift stores for clothes, loaded up on the sandwiches at The Lab to save money on food, and went nowhere. And with April away, I didn't even spend any money on dates.

April opened the door. All beauty and light, she leaned over and hugged me.

"I've missed you so much!"

"I did, too," I whispered into her ear.

"I so wish I'd come to Pittsburgh for Thanksgiving." April said with a sigh, referring to her family vacation in Colorado.

"Me, too. Are you ready?"

"Yes! Let me just grab my jacket."

April turned around and left me standing in the hallway.

She opened the closet door and at that moment I saw her father. I knew it was him, recognizing him from the photos. He was descending the stairs. He looked exactly like Steve Jobs. Tall, with squinty eyes, and the signature black turtleneck. I blinked fast, and the vision faded away. It was Chuck McPherson. He was wearing a black sweater, but not a turtleneck.

"Hello there, Rodion," he said, extending his hand. "I didn't get to see you at The Lab. I hear you've been doing great work."

"Thank you." I blushed. *How much does he know?*

"Excellent, excellent. I try not to interfere with the process. And of course, Ben and Karen are a great team."

"Karen?" I gave him a confused look.

"Isn't that her name? That young lady who helps Ben out."

"Kate."

"Oh, right, Kate. My bad." Chuck rubbed his nose. "Great team. Glad it's going well. And pretty soon we'll get to the point of oxygenation below 3%. I hear that's the next step for the project. Closer to Mars survival rates."

"Yes," I mumbled. "Mars survival rates," I repeated.

"So, just a bit longer, and you, Rodion, will be the pioneer that leads us to Mars. You and your digital twin, that is."

"Daddy, we're going out," April said, walking up and standing next to me.

"Enjoy! Great seeing you, Rodion."

As soon as April and I stepped outside, we kissed.

"Wow! So, this is your car?"

"Yes." I nodded.

"I am so happy for you, Rodion." She leaned in and kissed me again. "I've missed you."

"Me, too. I've missed you, too." I wanted to tell her just how much, but held back. I didn't want April to think I was a total mush.

"So, where to now?" April turned to me. I opened the car door for her and she looked at me with surprise. "Where did you learn to do that?"

"Sergei, I guess."

"So, you wanna go get some food?"

"I actually got us something to eat. Are you okay to come over to my place? My brother went to New York City."

"Yes, of course."

We got into the car, and I reached for the roses.

"These are for you."

As I handed the bouquet to her, she buried her face in the flowers. When she looked up, I noticed she was teary-eyed.

"What's wrong?" I asked, brushing a hair off her face.

"Rodion, I miss you so much. And I'm so lonely at Penn. I can't take it."

"Come on. I thought you liked your roommate. And you are taking all these cool classes."

"It all sucks. All these kids want is to get rich. They just want to make money, that's all they talk about."

"Money's good." I shrugged. "I like making money."

"I know, but you're not like that. You think about life. You know? You care. They don't. They sit there drinking, as if they're deep, but they're just idiots. Spoiled brats."

"Don't say that." I took her hand.

"You're the only person I can tell. I don't know how I'll last there for another three years." She sighed. "Three and a half!"

I put my hand on her lap. She put her own palm on top of it, and I felt her warmth. She was real, kind, understanding.

"I love you," I said.

"I love you, too."

I started the car and we drove to my place in silence.

"You know, this is the first time I've been here," April said, when we walked inside my place.

"I know."

I led her through the tiny living room and into the kitchen. "I got us this." I took out the cheese from the refrigerator and then the bread.

"You got us French cheese? That's amazing!" April inspected the package of Brie.

"Really? You like it?"

"It's very nice of you. Thank you."

April and I sat across from each other. I'd cut up the bread, and we ate, spreading brie generously on slices of bread. She took my hand and scanned my face.

"You've changed, Rodion. Since I last saw you."

"How so?"

"I don't know. Something's different. It's like you're more mature, but also like you're worried about something."

"Worried?"

Can she tell about my revenge plot against Philip?

"Yes, like you're preoccupied with something," April noted.

"It must be the job." I said with a shrug, trying to sound casual.

"I overheard you guys speaking. About oxygen. I don't get it. I thought you were testing games."

"Umm. I kind of am. But I'm not supposed to talk about it."

"Well, I already heard you guys speaking. Why did my dad mention Mars?"

"Okay, I guess it won't hurt if I told you." *Screw the Fight Club*, I decided. *Screw the nondisclosure agreement.* "So, when I first started over there, it was a game. But it was just to get my vitals."

"What vitals?"

"Like my vital signs; they needed all my data to make a digital double."

"What?" April stopped chewing and stared at me.

"Yeah, like a digital twin. It's like a replica of me that is doing things to test them out. And it's powered by AI."

Noticing the confused look on April's face, I added, "Artificial Intelligence. Machine learning. So, this thing, his name is Ryder, by the way. My twin's name."

I was rambling, not sure whether April could understand me, but now that I'd let myself speak, I couldn't stop.

"So, Ryder, he gets smarter every day, and, by the way, they never told me this, but I'm pretty sure they're trying to see if what Ryder is doing is actually physically affecting me. Like Ryder would run a marathon, and that would somehow change me. So, it's testing reverse AI, I guess. I am not sure. They never told me. I just figure things out based on what's happening. So then, since like October, I've been testing Ryder at low oxygen levels. We got to Mount Everest levels and now we're training at even lower levels. And I guess it has to do with going to Mars at some point. But it's because of what your dad said earlier today. I don't really know, because they never mentioned that part to me. So, maybe I wasn't supposed to know about Mars. Only the oxygen levels, 'cause that's pretty obvious. Not like they can hide it."

"Rodion, wait. Are you saying you're testing stuff on yourself? Not testing games?"

"I guess so. I mean, it's hard to say."

"You just told me you're experiencing things. With your own body."

"I guess, but it's fine. They have me hooked up to monitors. And there's a doctor who sees me."

"What doctor?" April narrowed her eyes.

"Dr. Donato. From Upper Hill."

"What?"

"Sarah Donato. She's nice." I averted my eyes.

"They make you see a shrink? Do you even hear yourself?"

"April, listen, it's not like that."

"You already told me there were issues. Don't you remember?" Her voice was shrill. "Why didn't you tell me earlier? This is so dangerous!"

"No, it's not. What are you talking about?" I started pacing the room. The kitchen was small, so I ended up mostly circling around the kitchen table. I was sure I looked ridiculous, but I was too fired up.

"I mean, this is dangerous stuff. Do you even realize oxygen deprivation can make you go nuts?"

"What?" Now it was my turn to sound shrill.

"Yes! It's a thing. When you're deprived of oxygen for too long, you get hallucinations. I can't believe my dad let you do this."

"He probably doesn't know."

"He does! It was his friend. They went up Mount Kilimanjaro together and his friend died! Died!"

"Wait, I can die?"

"Yes, you can die, you idiot."

"But how would that happen?"

"It's called High Altitude Cerebral Edema. HACE. Look it up." She pushed her phone to me. I punched in the term into the search bar and there it was. HACE. I read off the symptoms.

"Severe headache. Disorientation. Memory Loss. Hallucinations. Altered mental status." My voice trailed off.

"Rodion. Tell me, did you experience any of this?"

"Umm," I choked, "I don't think so." I thought of the Count. CM. *The Matrix*. Words on the screen. Was it all just a hallucination? Nothing of it was real?

"You're just worrying over nothing, April."

"Rodion, I can tell you're lying. Tell me the truth. Did you see things? Were you having visions? You know, I heard my dad say he was pushing to 3%. That's fatal. You could die. This thing is insane."

"But I make good money, April."

"Good money? Are you insane? You could die!"

"I'm not going anywhere." I leaned in and kissed April. She kissed me back.

There is no way I can die before I kill Philip, I thought, reaching for April's bra strap.

CHAPTER 27
BOXING DAY

On Boxing Day, April and I drove to see Aunt Molly. April came to pick me up in her parents' Volvo. I'd wanted to take my car, but the roads were icy, and the Volvo had winter tires, so the second her mother heard we were going to drive out of the city, she insisted we take it.

For Christmas, I'd gotten April a silver pendant and handed it to her in the car. It had two hearts intertwined, one silver, one gold.

It was Tammy who had taken me to the Pandora store at Ross Park Mall and helped me pick it out. We were discussing the subject of gift giving with Tammy and Sergei when she was over at our place one evening. It was the usual argument about the Russian tradition of exchanging gifts on New Year's and Father Frost versus Santa Claus.

"What are you getting April for Christmas?" Tammy turned to me and asked. I shifted on the couch and reached for my headphones. It was the first Christmas I'd actually have any money to spend on a gift for April, and I had no idea what to give her.

"Not sure. Does your parents' store have anything? Like

maybe I can get her a bracelet?" I said on a whim. It sounded like a good idea.

"Are you crazy? That stuff is for old Russian ladies. Soviet jewelry. Your girlfriend will hate it. Trust me." Tammy shook her head.

"Alright, no clue then." I put on the headphones and turned to the screen.

"That's okay. Nichevo." Sometimes Tammy sprinkled Russian words into the conversation, as if to show her origins. "You know what? I gotta go Christmas shopping anyway. I can take you to Pandora. It's a great place for stuff like that. Deal?"

"Deal."

The following weekend, Tammy and I drove to Ross Park Mall. The whole time, Tammy asked me questions. She wanted to know all there was to know about Sergei. His likes and dislikes. What he was like when he was little. Stuff about The Doors and Kino. His friends. His favorite foods. I was okay with all that, but then she asked about Mama. That's when I stopped responding.

"Are you okay? Rodion?" she asked after I ignored her question.

"Yeah," I mumbled, staring out the window. By then, we were already driving home.

"I'm sorry," Tammy said.

I pulled the hood over my head, so she couldn't see my face.

No, I wasn't crying. I was thinking of killing Philip.

————

"Rodion! Thank you. This is beautiful," April said, as she opened the box. "And it's got two hearts. Aww." April snapped the pendant on. "I love it." She flipped the mirror down to check herself out.

"Yeah. It looks cool," I grunted.

"You're such a man." April giggled. "A man of few words."

I grinned.

"I love you," I said.

"Those are all the words I need." She kissed me. "And here's something for you." April handed me a heavy package wrapped in green with a tasteful matching ribbon. I saw the Barnes & Noble logo.

"Books?" I opened my eyes wide.

"Yeah! We talk about books so much, I figured you'd like this." I unwrapped the package. It was *Crime and Punishment* by Fyodor Dostoyevsky.

"You can read about your namesake. Rodion Raskolnikov. Remember? My mom asked you about it and you'd never read the book."

"Isn't he a bad guy?"

"No, he's conflicted. Like you." She kissed me on the cheek. "I guess it comes with the name."

"Yeah. Maybe."

"Something for you to do other than The Lab."

"April, please. It's not like that. Don't worry about me."

"Alright, alright."

She turned onto I-376 and we drove through the Squirrel Hill Tunnel. It was like a portal, cutting Pittsburgh off from the outside world. As soon as we were out, I felt free, liberated from the confines of the city.

Snow lay on the sides of the road, giving it a fairy tale appearance.

"Do you remember where to go?" I asked.

"Yeah."

I stared out the window, thinking about life. About justice. I felt the leather pouch with the hunting knife in my pocket. I took it everywhere, but this time there was a reason for it. I would ask Mike to help me learn how to use it. To show me some moves.

Life is beautiful, I thought. *I will use a weapon I inherited from my grandfather to kill Phil. To avenge the death of my mother.*

"What were you thinking about just now?" April asked.

"Oh, Truck-kun," I lied, deadpan. It was the first thing that came to my mind.

"Ha, what's that?"

"It's a thing in Manga. A guy dies after being hit by a truck. Then he gets reincarnated and lives a new life, and corrects mistakes of his past life. It's kinda cool."

"Oh, is it because of Aunt Molly you're thinking about that?" April asked. "That past life regression stuff?"

"Maybe." I shrugged. I hadn't thought of the strange visions I'd experienced on my birthday in months.

"Do you believe in reincarnation?" April asked.

"I doubt this stuff can be real. But it's a cool idea. To have a second chance in life. Like I was playing this one game, and the character got reincarnated, but whatever. In games we get multiple lives, anyway."

"I believe in reincarnation," April said, steering the car. "Otherwise it doesn't make sense why we're so different."

"Here's the sign for the farm." I pointed at the side of the road. It was the same worn-out farm sign we'd seen in August, and just like last time, it materialized out of nowhere.

April slowed down. We turned onto the gravel road and there was the yellow arm barrier.

We left the car right by it and walked up to the farmhouse. With the snow on the ground, the walk up the hill felt mystical. After we got halfway up the hill, we saw smoke rising from the chimney and April squeezed my hand. April was wearing fuzzy gloves and the sensation of holding her hand felt comforting and sweet.

"I don't know why, but I am so excited to see them," she said.

"Me, too." I fumbled for the knife in my pocket.

"Oh! Hello!" Mike opened the door and let us inside. He looked so much like Santa Claus, with his white beard, and I felt like April and I were in a Christmas movie. Inside, it smelled like pine. A large Christmas tree stood in the corner. A fire was burning. Molly appeared, wiping her hands on an apron.

"So good to see you!" She stepped forward to give April a hug. Then she gave me one, too. "How have you been, Rodion? It's good to see you, too."

We exchanged greetings.

"Come, sit at the table. Let's have something to eat. You must be hungry from the trip." Aunt Molly pointed at the kitchen table, and I saw several dishes and plates laid out waiting for us. Glancing over at Mike, I wondered if he'd start talking about taxidermy, so I could bring up the hunting knife. Then, I would casually steer the conversation to training. We sat at the table and I felt for the knife in my pocket, when Aunt Molly said, "So, I hear you've been working at Chuck's lab, Rodion."

"Chuck's lab? Oh, you mean The Lab?" I said, straightening up.

"Yes." Aunt Molly pushed a bowl of stew towards me. "Chuck is my brother."

"Wait, oh, okay. For some reason, I thought you were April's aunt on her mom's side."

"I guess you wouldn't expect a corporate type like Chuck to have a sister like me." Aunt Molly shrugged. "But hey, life is strange that way. So, how is your father, April?" She turned to April.

"He's doing alright. But Rodion's job at Daddy's lab. They're doing AI stuff, Aunt Molly."

"That's quite impressive." Aunt Molly nodded. "Glad this has worked out for my brother. And this is Mike's favorite.

Meat loaf." Aunt Molly reached for a large platter and served me a slice.

"Thank you." I nodded, hoping to change the subject so I could bring up the hunting knife.

"But Aunt Molly, I wanted to ask you something." April glanced in my direction and then turned to face her aunt. "You see, Rodion was telling me things, and then Daddy mentioned something about oxygen deprivation testing, and I am worried about the things they are having Rodion do over there."

"What do you mean, April?" Aunt Molly frowned. I caught Mike staring at me, his well-meaning face full of concern.

"April, stop." I held my hand up in protest, but April didn't listen.

"No, Rodion, this could be bad. Aunt Molly, we really need your help. Rodion, when he came to see me in Philly, was already complaining about having weird dreams and even passing out at The Lab, so that was in October. And now I heard Daddy speak about some Mars stuff and oxygen deprivation, and things like that could just kill your brain completely, or cause irreversible damage!" April gesticulated wildly, pushing her hair back. "I just don't know. Rodion won't listen to anything I say. And of course, you know how Dad is." Tears welled up in April's eyes.

"April, I am fine. I told you, please stop. I need this job!" I crossed my arms.

Her voice gentle, Aunt Molly asked, "Rodion, is what April's saying true?" Then, she shook her head, as if to dispel a bad dream. "Of course it is, I see it. I do. I should have warned you in August. I should have done something, but it wasn't the right time."

"Aunt Molly, is he going to be okay? What should Rodion do?" April reached for my hand, but I pushed her away.

"April, I can figure this out on my own! The job is the best thing that's ever happened to me." I got up, pulling my hood on.

"Rodion, I want to help," April pleaded, looking up at me.

"I don't need your help!" I squeezed out. I needed to remove myself from the conversation.

"Alright, Rodion, it's okay, don't worry," Aunt Molly said. "We don't need to discuss your job. Please, sit back down. Let's eat and enjoy each other's company."

"I'm just going to get some fresh air." I pulled the hood even lower over my head. There was no way I would get Mike to help me practice with the hunting knife now, not after I'd made a scene. On my way to the front door, I noticed a taxidermy squirrel sitting on the side table. I picked it up and examined it. The animal's brown, beady eyes stared at me blankly. The tiny teeth were disturbingly sharp. The day that had started so well ended in disaster.

CHAPTER 28

THE BREAKUP

We drove back to Pittsburgh in silence. April tried to speak, to get me out of my rut, but I didn't answer her. I couldn't care less about what was happening around me. I needed to be alone.

"Rodion, please. I want to help," April pleaded.

"No," I muttered. As soon as we pulled up to my place, I grabbed my bag and would have forgotten her gift, but she yelled after me, "Your books."

"Yeah." I grabbed *Crime and Punishment* and climbed the steps without saying goodbye to her.

Sergei wouldn't be back until after the new year, and I would be all alone. Completely undisturbed for nearly a week. I couldn't face April. She'd brought me to see that witch on purpose. April was out to get me.

"Rodion?" I heard April yell after me, but I was already inside the safety of my house. I had two frozen pizzas in the freezer, and, if need be, could go to Giant Eagle and get some more. I just needed to get through the next few days until The Lab reopened. Then I would be fine and could continue training.

Sergei and I still had a landline, mostly so that Vlada

could reach us, and I unplugged it first, then I turned off my mobile. I sat down on the couch and stared at the screen. Now that I'd had a break from The Lab, I missed gaming. I could not think of a better way to spend the next few days than playing video games.

I pulled on my headphones and pressed play. The only sound I could hear was electronic music with guns going off. Boom! I raced, carjacked, drove, and navigated the city streets at insane speeds, tires screeching. No voices in my head. No April, no nagging, no guilt over Mama's death, no judgment or fear for my safety. No strange requests for Aunt Molly to help me.

I didn't stop gaming until late into the night, when I got hungry. I heated a pizza and devoured half of it. I went to bed at around 3am. I was tired and expected to sleep way into the following day, but I woke up at five in the morning and promptly puked all the pizza.

A massive, pounding headache hit me like a ton of bricks. I sat, unable to move, then tried to go back to sleep, but falling asleep with a migraine like that was impossible. I'd never felt so sick in my life. When the sun came up a few hours later, the daylight hurt my eyes so badly it felt as if an ax fell on my head each time I opened my eyes.

I closed the curtains and laid in the darkness for hours. Then, I went downstairs and tried to play, but the second I heard the upbeat sound of techno, my head pounded even worse. I touched my forehead, and it was burning. *I must have a fever*, was the last thought I had before I passed out.

I woke up when it was already dark out, had some water, and promptly passed back out. When I woke up again, I was on the couch, my clothes drenched in sweat. I shuffled to the bathroom and puked out bile. Then I went to the kitchen and heated up the remaining half of the pizza. I had no way of telling what day it was since my phone was off.

When I turned it back on, the date was December 29.

Whatever was going on with me went on for nearly seventy-two hours. There were no text messages, no voicemails. I could have died and no one would have known. *Whatever.* I thought. I needed no one, and no one needed me.

I sat on the couch, thinking of what to do next. I was too weak to go out and not tired enough to go back to bed. That's when the books caught my eye. April's gift. I opened *Crime and Punishment* and started reading.

It was hard to read at first, but once I got into it, I couldn't stop. I actually liked the guy. Raskolnikov was cool, and I'm not saying it just because we have the same name. No, he had a real purpose in life. He was seeking justice, trying to make the world a better place. Just like I was. What struck me was that Raskolnikov wasn't too different from *The Count of Monte Cristo*. Both men took justice into their own hands. But it had worked out for the Count, whereas Rodion floundered.

Raskolnikov's problem was that he was unlucky. If the sister hadn't come back, Rodion would have been in the clear. The perfect crime. No one would ever have suspected him of murdering the old hag with an ax.

Though that article Rodion wrote was a bit of a problem, he shouldn't have written it. I immediately thought of my essay about justice and felt my hands grow cold. *Would they catch me because of it?* But then I dismissed the idea. I hadn't been in contact with Philip for ten years. *Who would ever suspect me?* And besides, everything at The Lab was sealed. An NDA was in place. Surely it applied to whatever happened there. I laughed off my paranoia. After I finished reading *Crime and Punishment*, I was certain of one thing: My name was not accidental.

Mama named me Rodion because she expected great things from me, and the first of these would be avenging her death.

Between my fever and *Crime and Punishment*, I didn't think much about April until New Year's Eve. Thinking about her was like a dull ache. It had been five days since we last spoke, and now I was too embarrassed to make the first move and call her. If I contacted her, I'd need to apologize, to explain my behavior, to try to repair things, but what was the point? April would leave anyway, go to Penn, to bigger and better things. It was inevitable she would disappear from my life, so why not make it easier on both of us and just cut things off?

I fell asleep at nine that evening and woke up to a call from Sergei. He called me exactly at midnight. I'd left the phone on in part, expecting April to call, but she didn't. On the other end of the line, I heard laughter, the clanking of glasses, drunk Russian voices.

'S novym godom.' Giggles and excitement over the new year. I couldn't care less. *2009. Whatever.*

"Happy New Year, bro," I said, rubbing my eyes.

"Happy New Year!" Sergei yelled. "Tammy says hi."

"Hi. Happy New Year." I clutched the receiver, picturing a party, the excitement. I had bigger and better things. Revenge. Then I went back to sleep.

That morning, I woke up with a brilliant plan. I'd read somewhere that the most genius minds got their eureka moments while asleep. It happened to Einstein and Mendeleev. In my case, I got the idea to update the source code so I could train with Ryder on using the knife. The testing would go in parallel, and my supervisors would never know what I was doing.

The Lab was closed until Monday, January 5, and Ben told me to come in then, but I couldn't wait that long. I needed The Lab. Needed to continue training with the knife.

Taking my chances, I went there on the first business day of the year, Friday, January 2. I was still weak and decided a walk through Schenley Park was what I needed. At exactly noon, I stood on the familiar porch and knocked. Kate opened the door.

"Rodion, what are you doing here?" She opened her eyes in surprise.

"Happy New Year." I swallowed hard. "I just figured I should get back to work."

"Yeah." Kate said. "I see. Let's get you set up. I guess you remember the drill?"

I nodded.

"There's one thing, Rodion. We're gonna keep you at 5% for now, since there was a break. Your body needs to get used to the new numbers," Kate said, as we walked to the kitchen.

"Alright, not a problem." My heart leaped. *Five percent is nothing. If I can only update the source code, I can do knife training, and no one will notice.*

I found the workstation exactly how I left it. I put on the finger monitor and the headphones, and turned the screen on. Kate watched in silence, while I clicked on my double's face.

"Hey, Ryder," I called my digital twin by his name.

"Alright, I'll leave you to it." As soon as Kate left, I blacked out the screen, summoning the Count of Monte Cristo. He appeared right away.

Hello. How can I be of assistance? The Count smirked from under his wide-brimmed hat.

CM, please provide the source code for Ryder. To practice the knife commands.

I typed on the screen and quickly erased the text. Just in case anyone was tracking. Though I doubted it. After the encounter with Chuck McPherson, I knew all they cared about was tracking the oxygen levels.

Source code? Consider it done.

A second later, a series of letters popped up on the screen. They made absolutely no sense to me, and I stared at them, stupefied. I scratched my head but proceeded with my request.

CM, please change the source code to have the oxygenation tests run in parallel to knife training, I typed.

I hoped the AI had enough knowledge to do this. I bit my lip, squeezing the finger monitor. I needed this. I couldn't waste my valuable time testing oxygen levels when I could progress in my knife skills.

Let me try, CM responded.

This wasn't a good sign. It meant CM wasn't sure. But he didn't say no. That was something. I waited while the green dot on the screen blinked.

Mission accomplished, flashed on the screen a long three minutes later. It felt like forever, but my patience was rewarded.

CM disappeared, and Ryder took over the screen. My digital double was on a bike. The oxygen level control bar was running at the bottom of the screen, set at 6%. I lowered it to five. Then I noticed a pop-up screen, where my second digital double stood, holding a knife.

"Thank you, Count," I mouthed, and got to it.

While on the main screen, Ryder was biking with the oxygen level maintained at 5%, I focused all my attention on the pop-up screen. There, the second version of Ryder threw the knife, did all kinds of tricks with the knife overhead, and practiced cutting different surfaces. Making deep and low cuts. Long and short. Whenever he did this, I pictured Phil's throat, and it gave me a feeling of joy.

I finished exactly at eight, making sure to close the knife training program and act as if nothing unusual had happened that day. I didn't want anyone to be suspicious of my overzealous behavior on the first day back from vacation. I took off the finger monitor, placed my headphones on the desk, and shut off the screen.

Upstairs, I saw Dawn. She was in the corner, her red hair poking over a magazine.

A Cautionary Tale of Our Future, the cover read. *AI will transform humanity.*

"Happy New Year," I said.

"Happy New Year, I guess." Dawn shrugged, putting the magazine down and flipping her hair back. I noticed the tattoo of a fox snaking down her neck. It may have been because of my fight with April, but Dawn looked very attractive that night.

"What's this?" I nodded at the magazine.

"Oh, just some stuff I'm reading."

"I see."

"How's your girlfriend?"

"She's back at Penn." I blushed. "We kinda had a fight," I blurted out.

"I told you, long distance doesn't work. Didn't I?" Dawn raised her eyebrows.

"I dunno."

"How's it going with AI? Lost your mind yet?"

"What's that supposed to mean?"

"Just wondering." She rose and approached me. With her red hair, she suddenly looked like the Black Widow. I swallowed hard, remembering April's concern and her efforts to help me. The scene at Aunt Molly's house. *Am I actually losing my mind?*

"You should quit now. While you're still ahead," Dawn said, narrowing her eyes.

"Why don't YOU quit?" I snapped.

"It's not an option for me." Dawn batted her eyelashes. "You're playing with AI. With fire, my friend. If you leave this lab with schizophrenia only, consider yourself lucky." She shook her head.

I gulped.

Is that why Dr. Donato sees me once a month? Are my sessions with the psychiatrist to check my mental health and not actually part of the study?

"I can see you're thinking, that's good. Very good." Dawn was standing close to me now. I could smell her scent, something sweet. Seductive.

"But if I quit, aren't you gonna lose your job?" I croaked, taking a step back.

"Don't worry about me." Dawn yawned and stretched. I looked away from her bust that popped into full view. "I can always go back to stripping." She ran her hand through her hair.

"I thought you didn't want to do that." I forced myself to look at her face. Her eyes looked sad and did not match her casual tone.

"I'm just joking. Don't worry. But no one can fire me. And my mom won't let me quit."

"What? Your mom?"

"Actually, forget it. It's none of your business." She gave me a cold stare. "Regardless, consider yourself warned."

What did Dawn's mother have to do with The Lab? I wondered, as I left. I remembered Mama, and immediately my thoughts turned to Phil. The uncomfortable conversation I'd just had with Dawn could wait. Now that I'd been able to continue practicing with the knife, I needed to figure out the practicalities of when to cut Phil's throat.

For that, I needed to know when Philip would visit his mother. Philip went there on weekends, but how would I know when, exactly? I wondered whether I should wait for him to establish a pattern, but that meant hanging out by his mother's apartment building for hours at a time. That was too risky.

Mulling over various ideas, I walked home on the dark streets of Squirrel Hill. As I passed Giant Eagle, I saw a late-night shopper walking out with a bouquet of flowers, and then it hit me. Of course! The Flowers! Mother's Day!

Eureka! I would kill Philip on Mother's Day! He was bound to go see his mother on Mother's Day.

The plan was perfect. And symbolic. Killing Phil would be the best gift to my Mama on Mother's Day. Now that my plan was in place, I knew the meaning of the phrase "sweet revenge." The very idea of what I was about to do made me smile. I thought of the Count and the years he'd put into executing his revenge on his enemies. And of Raskolnikov thinking about taking justice into his own hands. My revenge was only five months away.

Mother's Day this year would be the day I settled the score.

CHAPTER 29
SOUND BODY, SOUND MIND

When I got to work the following Monday, I was in excellent spirits. Ben opened the door for me.

"Hey, Happy New Year!" he said. "How was your break?"

"Happy New Year!" I said. "It was good, thank you."

"Cool! And I just got back from visiting my parents in Baltimore for Christmas." Ben closed the door behind us. "Baltimore isn't the best, but I love my city." He smiled. "I mean, it's nothing like *The Wire* or anything. I promise." Ben patted me on the back. "Looking good, Rodion. Ready for the new year?"

"Yeah. I am."

"Hey, guys." Kate walked up to us, spring in her step. "What is it with all these New Year's Resolution people." Kate turned to Ben. "I tried to sign up for my favorite hot yoga class, and my studio is crazy full now." She rolled her eyes.

"Yeah, I know what you mean. My gym is running a promo right now, so lots of people sign up. But they usually fall off by early February." Ben shrugged. "So, maybe wait a month?"

"I can't! I'm totally addicted. If I don't go for a few days, my whole body aches." Kate stretched. She was about to say something else, but Ben cut her off and turned to me.

"By the way, Rodion, do you work out at all?"

"Umm, not really."

"You should. With this oxygenation stuff, you might want to work out. Why don't you sign up for my gym? I can take you."

"Your gym?" I'd never gone to the gym before. Never played any sports, never been on any team. I ran, but only every once in a while.

"Yeah. That way I can get a referral bonus." A sly smile crossed Ben's face.

"Ben, that's not right," Kate protested.

"Why not? It'll be good for Rodion. Right?" Ben clapped. "A win-win. So, what do you say, man?"

"Yes!" I said. I liked Ben.

And getting stronger wouldn't hurt. In case Phil struggles, I thought. *It's like the universe is trying to help me execute my plan.*

"Alright, I'll text you the address. We can go tomorrow, before work. I usually go at seven."

"Sorry to interrupt, but we gotta get started with testing." Kate pursed her lips.

"Alright, alright. Come on, Rodion, let's go."

Ben punched in the code and all three of us went downstairs. The Lab looked the same, exactly like how I left it on Friday. I sat in front of the screen and waited while Ben set up the finger monitor. I turned on the screen and my digital double appeared. Kate, arms crossed, examined me in satisfaction.

"You know, this project is really moving super well," Kate said after a pause.

"Knock on wood." Ben knocked on the table.

"You're so superstitious!" Kate shook her head.

"Irish mom…runs in the family." Ben sighed.

"If you're so superstitious, you shouldn't be working with AI." Kate rolled his eyes.

"And why not?"

"Because AI is about the new frontier. Breaking with the past. Your beliefs will hold you back."

"Alright, whatever. Listen, Rodion, you know the drill, right?" Ben turned to me.

"Yeah, I'm good."

"Remember, you need to stay at 5%," Kate noted, as the two of them walked upstairs, leaving me with Ryder. I waited until the door slammed shut behind them and clicked twice, summoning CM. *I wonder if the source code will work today.* To my immediate relief, the Count's face appeared on the screen.

Hello. How can I be of assistance?

CM, please provide the source code for Ryder. To practice the knife commands, I typed on the screen, wondering whether I could skip this step next time.

I typed, wondering whether I could skip this step next time. The pop-up screen with Ryder appeared right away, and I repeated the steps from Friday, launching the oxygenation program first, then practicing with Ryder. Like last time, I expected Ryder to have a hunting knife, but this time, he produced a long leather case. He placed it on the ground and opened it. Inside, there were about thirty different knives and I gasped. Long blade, short blade, daggers, some resembling swords. I recognized some from video games. Some had dragon blades, some looked like ice picks.

What's this? I typed.

A little upgrade.

One by one, Ryder took the knives from the case and, within seconds, mastered their use. It was instant, mere moments. What had taken us a full day with the hunting knife took no time at all. I twitched and felt my hands burning. *Is this affecting me, too?* I tried to move but couldn't. By the time Ryder closed the case, having achieved mastery of each one of the thirty knives, I was out of breath, sweat pouring down my face. The oxygenation program bar was at 5%, and I wasn't sure whether it was its impact or the knife training, but I could barely move. I didn't care if Kate or Ben noticed I was running a parallel program anymore, ripped off the headphones and the finger monitor, and pushed my chair back. Trying to get up, I leaned on the desk, gasping for air. I opened my mouth, trying to fill my lungs, but they felt constricted, and I opened my mouth wide, like a fish, but it didn't help. Black circles appeared in front of my eyes and the walls collapsed around me.

When I came to, I was in my bed. I had no memory of getting home. The alarm was going off on my phone. I checked the time. 6am. Tuesday, January 6.

I stared at my phone when a text from Ben popped up on the screen.

See you at seven!

The gym! I remembered agreeing the morning prior to meet Ben and to work out together, for him to receive his referral bonus. As I got out of bed, my muscles ached, and I was about to text Ben back to let him know I'd changed my mind, but then paused, remembering the idea of getting stronger to overpower Phil, if need be. I forced myself to get dressed, pulling on sweatpants and a T-shirt, which, I decided, was suitable gym attire. At exactly 7am, I parked in front of a squat building that looked like a warehouse.

As soon as I got out of the car, Ben strutted up to me. He patted me on the back.

"Hey there, buddy. Great of you to show up. Let me get you set up." He led me to the gray door, opening it. Once inside, right away, I heard metal clanking, voices, the hollow echo of grunting. I could smell Clorox in the air, and it carried me back to Vlada's house. She doused her place with

Clorox, claiming it was the only thing keeping her family healthy.

A young man sat behind the counter, his face round and earnest.

"Hey, Matt, this is Rodion," Ben introduced us.

"Nice to meet you." The young man extended his hand. His handshake felt firm and pleasant.

"Rodion is interested in joining the gym. New Year's Resolution." Ben chuckled.

"Of course! Let's show you around. If you join today, you get your first month for $50 off, and Ben here also gets a break." Matt nodded at Ben. "Just follow me, I'll give you a tour."

As Matt stepped from behind the counter, I noticed he was shorter than me, but his shoulders were much broader. He moved with gravitas and was built like a tank. I wondered how long it would take me to get to the same level of muscle mass.

"This is the place." Matt made a sweeping gesture. "When you come in next time, you'll just have to check in at the front desk, and then every day you'll do a routine. It's about thirty minutes to get through all the sets. And we got group sessions starting on the hour in the morning from five to ten, and then in the evening from five to ten. Makes it easy to remember." He looked at me expectantly.

"Yeah. Great." I nodded.

"Don't worry, there are always people to help you out in the beginning. And each session is led by an instructor, who can help you with form. So you don't hurt yourself. Let me give you a waiver form and once you sign it, you can go ahead and get started." Matt led me back to the reception. "Since it's your first time, you might want to take it easy." He gave me a concerned look, and his warning was enough to motivate me to exert myself to the fullest.

That morning, I worked out for over an hour. Ben had

already finished his routine and left, and I was still going strong. At home, I barely had time to shower to make it to The Lab on time for my shift.

"Hey, Rodion, nice workout, ha?" Ben gave me a high five, greeting me at the front door.

"Thanks, man!"

Are the two of us becoming friends? I wondered, as I headed downstairs. *2009 is a good year so far.* Step-by-step, I was getting closer to my goal of avenging Mama's death, mastering the knife routine and growing stronger at the gym. I was on track to avenge Mama on Mother's Day. *April.* I remembered the breakup, and, right away, my good mood soured. The thought of her felt like a stab in the gut. It had been nearly two weeks since we last spoke, and I wondered if this was the end. *Had I lost her forever?*

Then I remembered how April had tried to make me quit what was likely one of the coolest jobs in the world. Most people had not even heard of this technology, and here I was, testing it out.

Clenching my jaw, I put on the heart rate monitor, adjusted my headphones, and clicked start.

Ryder appeared on the screen. I clicked *Detach* and summoned the Count. I was about to start the knife training program when I noticed Ryder was in the gym—the very same gym where I just was, doing the same routine I had just finished—and I gasped. Ryder was lifting weights, and they looked identical in shape to the ones I'd been lifting, except his were much heavier.

Where I'd benched 100lb, Ryder was benching 250lb. The oxygenation bar appeared at the bottom of the screen. His muscles flexed, and I felt mine tense at the same time. Pain shot through my body and I gritted my teeth. I tried to launch the knife training but couldn't, as my hand twitched in pain and my muscles spasmed. Ryder kept going, and with each of his movements pain shot through my body. My face contorted in pain. I grabbed at the mouse, but it slipped out of reach, as I lost control of my fingers. Beads of sweat formed on my forehead. After minutes of agony, I managed to click on Ryder and pressed *attach* to quit the program, but Ryder didn't stop. *This isn't supposed to be happening!* I ripped off the headphones and the finger monitor, and felt immediate relief.

The Count emerged on the screen.

Hello, Rodion.

He took off his hat and winked at me. *Time is a construct, Rodion. Remember that.*

Green on black. The letters flashed on the screen before it went dark. Ryder also disappeared. I clicked on the screen to restart, and everything was back to normal.

It must have been a glitch, I thought. *I better not do the knife training today.* I put on the headphones and slipped on the finger monitor. Ryder was in the octagonal plane, about to start biking. The oxygenation bar appeared on the bottom, set at 5%. After over an hour of training Ryder, I felt fine. Gone were the muscle spasms and the pain. *I wonder what would happen if I lowered the levels to 4%?* I thought, and clicked on the bar. *April doesn't know what she is talking about.* I lowered the levels. *This is easy.*

Ryder paused his movements, but then started moving again, biking with the lower oxygen levels. The rarefied air was like breathing nothing. As I watched Ryder glide through the octagonal plane, I felt my head spin. Suddenly, the screen split into two and the Count's face appeared, lifting his hat as if to greet me and then everything faded to black.

———

I woke up in semi-darkness, the sound of a machine beeping right above my head.

"As I said, we don't want this guy to become a liability," a buttery voice said. "Do we?" The question must have been rhetorical, for no one answered. The voice was raspy, and I recognized it right away. Sarah Donato.

Carefully, so as not to show I was awake, I opened my eyes, trying to understand where I was. Light was streaming through the windows, and I noticed a patch of orange bleeding into red on the wall. I heard the sound of a water fountain trickling and could just make out the outlines of a Buddha statue in a corner. Another tapestry, gray and yellow, hung above it.

I shifted and heard another beep, realizing I had an oxygen mask on my face. I froze and closed my eyes.

"Kate, did you set it to three liters? Or four?" Sarah asked, and this time there was an answer.

"I put it at five," an eager voice responded. "I'm glad Dawn found him when she did. I mean, that was just insane!" Kate let out a deep breath. "And with my presentation next month. That's just crazy!"

"Yes, Kate, the timing is unfortunate." Sarah Donato cleared her throat. "Like I said, we need to make sure the kid doesn't turn into a liability. This is cutting-edge research you two are doing. We wouldn't want it to go to waste." A pause.

"Shouldn't we take him to the ER?" another voice asked, and I recognized Ben. "I mean, we should make sure he's alright, shouldn't we?"

"He's fine, Ben," Kate protested.

"Ben, I understand your concern," Dr. Donato's buttery voice added. "But Kate is almost done with her dissertation, and as her advisor, I would be remiss to not have considered the risks of outside medical treatment for the kid. We're doing pioneering research here, and one day this technology will be everywhere. Staying ahead of the game is what matters. So, once he regains consciousness, we'll continue with testing."

"Yes!" Kate said. "Thank you, Dr. Donato."

"You're welcome, Kate. And Ben, don't worry; when we publish the findings, your name will be right there next to mine. And to Kate's. I've already heard from several corporate sponsors, who are very interested in what we have to offer."

"You have?" Ben croaked.

"Yes, Ben. This is the next frontier. Marketing based on your deepest desires. AI that knows what you want before even you know what you want. Getting into your core memories, letting your digital double make the decisions for you."

"But is he going to be okay?" Ben asked. "Mentally, I mean."

"He'll be fine. Don't worry. And he signed the NDA, remember?" Dr. Donato cleared her throat. "By the way, what a brilliant idea to mention *Fight Club*. Relating to pop culture references is always the best. I wouldn't have thought of that," she added.

"Oh, yeah."

"And of course, figuring out the subject's deepest desires, key memories, is very important. With Rodion here, revenge was the key to getting in there." I felt a knot form in my stomach. "And good job figuring that part out, Kate. Introducing *The Count of Monte Cristo* was absolutely brilliant. Now, of course, if it weren't for Dawn, we wouldn't have been able to find the other triggers. All the secret desires, the emotional connections, and his ambitions." Dr. Donato's voice trailed off. "Of course, we can't exactly rely on my daughter to do things around here. But I digress."

"You know, Ben nearly forgot the NDA." Kate said, vindictive notes in her voice.

"Snitch," Ben mumbled.

"Whatever!" Kate yelped.

"Well, it's fine now. Don't worry, Ben, he's totally fine. Of course, after the oxygenation testing, there may be some collateral damage to Rodion's brain, but it's not like this guy was ever going to college. Whatever brain cells he has left will be enough for his video games. Or whatever else he wants to do with his time."

"But this surely isn't right."

"Ben, please, this research has been going on for years. LSD in the '50s with all the hippies, ecstasy in the '90s with the ravers. And look at them now—the hippies are perfectly fine; their brains might have been fried, but they are managing, and so are the ravers. Not everyone is meant for college. You've got to believe in what we're doing here. We're the new frontier!" Sarah Donato exclaimed. Was I imagining it, or did she sound hysterical?

"We are?"

"Yes, Ben, we are. Get with it," Kate hissed.

"So, umm, I was just wondering, isn't his brother a lawyer? I mean, what if he suspects something is wrong?"

"And how exactly would his brother notice the difference? Would it be when Rodion plays video games for five hours a day rather than ten? Please." Sarah Donato chortled. "But of course, you're right. Like I said, we don't want the kid to become a liability. So, once we present the findings, we can adjust to erase his memory of the experiment."

"How?" Ben asked, and my fingers suddenly felt like icicles.

"We just pop in the Mars program, do oxygenation testing, and everything will seem like one long hallucination. He won't remember a thing."

"Not a thing!" Kate added triumphantly. "It will all be like one long dream."

"Absolutely."

I took a deep breath, and the machine beeped again, as the room faded into darkness.

CHAPTER 30

RYDER

ight streamed through the windows as I opened my eyes. The machine beeped overhead, and I reached to feel for the oxygen mask. The room was completely quiet, and I sat up on the couch, noticing the huge teddy bear on the floor.

Right away, the door opened and Sarah Donato walked in. She was wearing knee-high platform boots and a handmade shawl, which reminded me of the throws Vlada knitted.

"Rodion. How do you feel?" Sarah asked in her throaty voice and wrinkled her forehead.

I blinked, not taking my mask off.

"Do you remember what happened?" She pulled up a chair next to the couch and sat down, reaching for my wrist to feel my pulse. I tried to take off the oxygen mask to speak, but she pushed my hand away. "That needs to stay." She said. Then, without waiting, she let go of my wrist and said, her voice soft, "Rodion." She stared into my eyes. "Kate told me she'd warned you to stay at 5%. But when we found you, the setting was at four. Why did you go against Kate's instructions?"

How did they find out? I stared at Dr. Donato in confusion.

"Why did you lower the setting, Rodion?" she repeated, narrowing her eyes.

I shook my head and tried to lift the mask to protest.

"Now, you do understand your behavior could compromise the whole experiment. And we would have to let you go." She paused for effect.

I clenched my fists. I couldn't afford to lose this job now. Not before I finished with my plan.

"But because of your achievements, and because we value your contributions to The Lab, we're allowing you to stay. Consider this your first and last warning. We don't want you to become a liability." She stared directly at me. "Do you understand?" Dr. Donato didn't blink, and I averted my eyes. "Very good. I see you have."

She rose and walked away, closing the door behind her.

I stayed on the couch for a few more minutes, then ripped the mask off and got up. Carefully, I opened the door and walked out of the room. The Lab was completely quiet. Downstairs, the lights had been turned off, the curtains drawn, the entire space submerged into semi-darkness. I walked into the kitchen. The idea of going downstairs to the testing site occurred to me, but right away the red camera eye blinked overhead, and I turned around and walked out of The Lab.

Once outside, I reached for my phone. I was about to call April to tell her about what had happened, but then remembered we'd gotten into a fight on Boxing Day. *What have I done?* The memory of the conversation I had overheard was still faint in my mind. AI? Marketing? Dissertation? The words distorted in my mind as I walked down Murray Avenue, thinking about revenge.

I passed Forward Avenue and glanced to the spot where I would execute Phil. The never-ending construction site across from his mother's apartment complex. As always, thinking about revenge lifted my spirits, and I was fine the rest of the way home, until I saw Tammy's car parked in front of our house. Right away, my heart sank, as I pictured her well-meaning face, her eager questions about April, and cringed. I pictured April trying to reason with me, to console me, to tell me The Lab was dangerous, and now I'd reached a point of no return. I had compromised myself at The Lab and was on the verge of being fired before avenging Mama. I clenched my fists, seething in anger.

Time is a construct, flashed in my mind. *What exactly does that mean?*

For a moment, I considered circling the block and waiting until Tammy left. But then I steeled myself and walked in. It was my house, after all.

I found Sergei and Tammy sitting in the kitchen, an open bottle of champagne in front of them.

"Rodion!" My brother rose to greet me.

"We have some news!" Tammy yelped, and stuck out her hand.

A diamond sparkled on her left ring finger. It looked expensive, though I couldn't be sure.

"We're engaged." Tammy clapped, her cheeks turning bright pink.

"Congrats! Wow!" I forced a smile.

"I know, it was so soon, but Sergei and I, when we were in New York, I have an uncle, he's a jeweler, and he took us to see his stuff. And Sergei got me this ring. He saw how much I liked it." Tammy threw an adoring look at my brother. "And Sergei just proposed to me!!!" She stared at her ring, then stuck it out again.

"We wanted to tell you in person," Sergei said.

He said "we." Like he was no longer my brother, but now belonged to some cult and could not operate alone.

"Oh, cool. Thank you," I squeezed out, blinking fast.

"And we already set a date. We'll get married on Valentine's Day! The most romantic day of the year." Tammy opened her eyes wide.

"This year?" I opened my mouth wide.

"Yes! Next month. Here, have a drink with us!" Tammy reached for a glass, but my brother stopped her.

"He's only eighteen, Tammy," Sergei noted.

"Oh, sorry, I forgot. Anyway, we're going to move in together, and there is a place in Squirrel Hill. It's really nice, and it's gonna be available on February 1," Tammy rattled off. "So, we decided we'll get married soon. Why wait?"

Sergei reached for her hand and kissed it.

April. I remembered how I'd kissed her hand, and the memory was like a punch in the gut.

"Umm, yeah, I was gonna tell you, I figured now that you got this job, you'll be fine living on your own. Right, Rodion?" Sergei looked at me expectantly.

"Of course."

"So, you can stay here. And Vlada is nearby," Sergei continued. "And if you need us, we'll be nearby."

Again, "we." As if my brother no longer existed as an individual.

I chatted with them for a few more minutes, and then went to my room and sat there, staring at the wall, doing nothing. I couldn't even force myself to read. Sergei would soon move out, and I'd be left all alone. It was as if I was cursed and everyone I loved disappeared from my life. No Mama. No April. No Sergei.

I noticed Stewart. The fox, the lovey, the toy I'd had all these years. He'd been sitting in the corner of my room, on a shelf, collecting dust, but now I noticed his bright brown eyes. They called me. I took him and brushed his bright red fur.

"Hey, there, little guy," I said. "It's just you and me now." I didn't expect him to answer, of course. But he opened his mouth and barked, "Hi, Ryder."

"I'm Rodion. I don't call myself Ryder anymore." I frowned as I looked at him.

"Ryder!" Stewart guffawed.

"Whatever."

I threw the fox on the bed. The next moment, my brother walked into my room without knocking.

"Hey, are you on the phone?" he asked.

"No." I shook my head.

"I thought I heard you speaking. Are you alright?"

"Yeah." I shrugged.

"Sorry, I was gonna tell you myself, but Tammy was so excited. Anyway, I'll help you out, cool? Sign the lease over, it's gonna be alright. Your own place," Sergei said, his tone reassuring. "Might be fun. What do you think?"

"Yeah, no worries," I mumbled.

"And I want you to be my best man," Sergei said. "So, that means you gotta plan my bachelor party."

"What?"

"Jimmy and Nate can help you out."

"You're actually having a bachelor party?"

"Yeah, why not? Gotta celebrate, seize the day." Sergei looked at me. "What's up with the fox? You haven't gotten rid of that thing yet?"

"Not yet." I shook my head.

———

My alarm went off at six the following morning. I stared at my phone. January 7, 2009. *That was a weird dream.* I thought about how I'd passed out at work, Dr. Donato's threats, Tammy sticking out her left hand to show me the engagement ring, Sergei telling me he would soon move out.

I bolted up on the bed, and right away felt my muscles aching. *The gym,* I remembered. *It hadn't been a dream.* The events of the previous day came together, fitting like pieces of a puzzle. *It was all real.*

I stretched and remembered my plan to get stronger, and got ready for my workout. On the way to the gym, I thought of how Ben would greet me after the incident at The Lab, and decided I'd do my best to pretend like nothing happened.

At exactly seven, I parked in front of the gym. I scanned the parking lot for Ben's car, ready to high five him, but Ben wasn't around. I opened the gray door and walked in. As the day prior, Matt was at the reception.

"Hi, Matt." I flashed him a smile, checking in for the day. I tried to walk past the reception, but Matt gave me a confused look.

"Excuse me, can I have your name, please?"

"I came in with Ben. I registered yesterday. You gave me a tour."

"I did? Sorry, it's the January special. We have lots of new people. Alright, what's your name?" Matt stared at the screen.

"L-i-k-h-a-r-e-v," I spelled out my last name. Matt typed the keys of the keyboard, clicked, then nodded.

"Alright."

"And your first name?" he asked, looking up at me.

Other than my brother, I had not met any other person with my last name in Pittsburgh, so I was sure I'd be the only Likharev in his system, but I said, "Rodion."

"Umm, sorry, the name doesn't match."

"Can you check again? I came with Ben."

"Ben who?"

"Umm, Ben," I was about to say Ben's last name, when I realized I didn't know it. "Red hair, freckles, in his twenties," I muttered.

"Can you spell your last name again for me?" Matt asked, and I did. Again, the typing on the keyboard. "And your first name?"

"Rodion," I said. Matt shook his head.

"Do you have a middle name maybe?" Matt raised his eyebrows. "We do have another Likharev in the system. Maybe you go by a different name?"

I gulped.

"Ryder," I guessed, and felt as if I was jumping into a void.

"Yep! There you are. All set. Sorry for the confusion, man. Have a great workout." Matt grinned.

I took a step back from the counter. My heart beat fast and I felt as if the ground had shifted underneath me.

Ryder.

I remembered seeing my digital twin on the screen, working out in this very same gym.

Was he real? Was he functioning independently from me now?

"Are you alright, man?" Matt raised his eyebrows.

"Yeah. Umm, I forgot something in the car. I gotta go." I turned around and headed for the exit. As soon as I was outside, I dashed to the car.

I gotta get to The Lab right away. I gotta see what's going on with Ryder.

I drove through the empty streets of Pittsburgh and within minutes parked in front of The Lab. I ran up to the door and knocked.

No answer.

I knocked again.

No answer.

Only then did I remember the time. 7:30am. Of course, it was too early. I needed to wait until The Lab opened.

CHAPTER 31

BRAIN FOG

was about to leave and come back at noon, when the door opened and Dr. Donato appeared on the threshold.

"Ryder, I was expecting you," she said. "Why don't you come in?"

"I am Rodion." I scanned her face. *Is she still mad about yesterday?*

"Ryder, why don't you come into my office and we can have a little chat as you wait for your shift to start?" Sarah Donato looked at me ruefully.

"Okay." I nodded and walked into The Lab, my palms sweaty. I followed Dr. Donato up the staircase into her office.

"Have a seat and give Phil a hug." She pointed to the teddy bear. I flinched at the name, and defiantly pushed the stuffed animal to the floor, then sat down.

"I see. We're exercising control today." Dr. Donato rolled her eyes. She sat down across from me and crossed her legs, dangling her feet clad in platform shoes. As she flipped her hair back, I noticed her milky white skin, and the realization hit me. She and Dawn looked exactly alike. The eyes, the shape of their face, all except for the bright-red hair and the diagonal haircut.

"You are her mother!" I yelped. "Dawn's mother!"

"Very good!" She sniggered. "You see, Ryder, you are my great experiment, so bright. Dawn and I got jobs at The Lab together. It was part of my plan. She'd work the night shift, and I'd be the shrink. Dawn and I, we're the perfect pair. My girl is special. You want to know why I named her Dawn?" I shrugged, and the doctor straightened up her shoulders. A dreamy expression appeared on her face.

"I've told you the story before, of course, but you don't remember, do you? It's because we wipe your memory clean after each shift and repopulate it with AI-generated experiences. It's beautiful, really," Dr. Donato continued.

"What?" I gulped.

"Of course. It's just the next step in the human evolution. Human beings, you see, are terrible at making decisions. Really terrible. With some exceptions, of course, but that only reaffirms the rule. Take your mother, for example. To move to America alone, with two boys, to be with a man she barely knew? Not good thinking." Dr. Donato shook her head.

I clenched my fists, trying hard to stay calm. I believed against all odds there was something in her speech that could save me. And so I sat still and nodded in agreement. I felt like a traitor. I gave up Mama, agreed that she'd made bad decisions, but if it could help me get out of this nightmare, it was worth it.

"So, my Dawn. I named her after a song." The doctor stared into the distance. "'The Age of Aquarius' by The 5th Dimension? You've heard the song, surely?" She chanted the lyrics, her voice off-key. "A hippy band from the '60s. Well, I'm no hippy, but I believe we're moving into a new world with AI in charge. Dawn is named after my belief. It's beautiful, isn't it?" Sarah Donato shifted in her seat, settling in for a long conversation. "I like talking to you, Ryder. You listen. Well, I set it up that way, of course." She chortled. "But still. It feels good to speak to a young man, an attractive one, and to have him pay attention." She licked her lips, and I cringed inside, but kept still.

Maybe she's wrong and I won't forget the conversation? Maybe I can change the algorithm? The thought popped into my head, and, though I couldn't understand what it meant, I grabbed onto it.

"You see, after working as a therapist for so many years, I believe most human beings are terrible at making decisions. I've seen proof over and over again. The thing is, trauma rewrites our brain wiring. And once it happens, we're stuck. You know it first-hand, Ryder, don't you?" She looked up at me, scanning my face for a reaction, and I made sure to look calm, as if I was politely listening to what was turning out to be her monologue, and not plotting an escape.

"It's sad. Some will tell you to meditate, to rewire your brain, to think happy thoughts. But we've seen how well that works. All you want to do is kill. Pathetic! But enter AI!" She suddenly rose from the armchair and started pacing the room. "The second I got an offer from Chuck to work here, I knew I was onto something incredible." She stopped and turned to me. "What is it with all these rich old men going by little boys' names? Bobby. Teddy. Chuck." She let out a puff of air. "Ridiculous." She giggled. "But I digress. Chuck approached me when he just started The Lab. He wanted to make sure we weren't screwing up people's brains with AI. So naïve! Humanity has already screwed up the human brain. AI can only make it better."

She walked up to me and was standing over me, hovering, hands on her hips. I tried to hold her gaze, but there was such malice in her stare, I had to look away.

"So, we use AI to erase your bad memories, to wipe out the neurological pathways that were created by those bad decisions, Ryder. And yours is the first brain we are repaving with AI, so to speak." A proud smile appeared on her face. "That's how you became Ryder. Once we were done with you, Rodion was gone and Ryder took over. It happened during Christmas and you barely even noticed." She leaned over and moved her face close to mine, then reached and ruffled up my hair, as if I were a dog. "Ryder, so adorable. Such a cutie."

I felt like vomiting, but kept still.

Change the algorithm. Maybe there is a way to get my memories back. To turn back the process. To outsmart The Lab. I am Rodion. I am still there. I exist. Ryder is only my double. Not me.

Sarah Donato stepped back.

"Alright, I suppose I digress. We really should be wrapping up. Ben and Kate will be here for their shift in a minute." She ran her hand through her hair. "Those two work perfectly together, don't you think? All the bickering, the sexual tension, I just love it. Of course, that's the ultimate human motivator, isn't it? Lust!" She rolled her eyes. "And with you, my little Dawn got you going, didn't she, Ryder?" Sarah Donato winked at me. "I know, I know, she is hard to resist, and you with your hormones. It was too easy. She told me it didn't take much at all. Just a tight T-shirt and a few suggestive phrases. So primitive."

My cheeks turned crimson at this statement. Noticing my reaction, Sarah shrugged. "Listen, it's alright, nothing to be ashamed of. Dawn is a beautiful girl, and you're an eighteen-year-old kid, bursting with testosterone. You can't help it."

I opened my eyes wide, expecting her to continue, but she made a circle around the room without saying a word.

"But now, time to go downstairs, Ryder. Your friend, the Count, is waiting for you."

"You know about the Count?" I gulped, opening my eyes wide.

"Of course I know about the Count. Dawn was the one to come up with the idea. My Dawn is a little genius. It was also her idea to name the teddy bear Phil." Sarah giggled. "You should have seen your face when I told you to hug him the first time."

"All that was you?"

"Oh, yes. We read your essay, Ryder. Remember? Justice, taking it into your own hands. What a great idea! Dawn is amazing, I do have to say. She thought of every little detail."

Dr. Donato stopped pacing and came up close.

"But you won't remember a single thing, will you?" She ruffled my hair again. "And we're just getting started. With a face like yours, you're going to sell AI!" She pinched my cheeks. "All those pathetic gamers out there, they'll see you and they will want to be just like you. They will see themselves in you. They will want to get rid of their own bad memories. They will want AI to take control. Once we roll this thing out, it will be the most powerful AI marketing tool on the planet. All the bad memories will be wiped out by AI, so only happy thoughts remain. No trauma. No bad decisions."

What if I clock her in the temple? I thought, and the idea pleased me.

"And you know what, Ryder? We've got you by the balls." She made a grabbing gesture, and I cringed. "Because your little plot against your stepfather is all we needed to set you up. One wrong move, and you'll be behind bars, Ryder." Sarah Donato laughed. "And you did it to yourself."

"But I haven't done anything!" I threw my hands up in protest.

"That's what you think." She narrowed her eyes.

"What?" My lips felt numb.

"I have it right here, this recording." She took out her phone. "They never found the driver." Sarah Donato looked at the phone and the screen came alive. "Of a Ryder truck."

"What?"

"Oh, yes. Your stepfather got killed by a truck. It was a Ryder truck. A nice twist. Ryder driving a Ryder truck. Phil was going to see his mother, to wish her a happy Mother's Day. Does that ring a bell?"

"I? What? It wasn't me." I shook my head. "I never did that."

"Ah, well. Can you really trust your memories, dear boy?" She chuckled. "Not with the oxygenation training, Ryder. Or is it Rodion?"

I blinked in confusion.

"See, you don't even know your name."

My mouth gaped open as I stared at her.

"Here's a little video I took of the accident. It's saved in my favorites folder." She clicked and turned her attention to the screen for a moment. That was just the distraction I needed. I reached for her phone, trying to grab it, and almost succeeded, but then it slipped from my hand, as the walls of the room collapsed over me.

CHAPTER 32

FOXY'S

woke up on the floor of the basement. As I lifted myself up, I heard Ben's voice.

"What's up with all the passing out?" He was standing over me. "Let me help you up."

"What happened?" I asked. "I think I had a nightmare." I noticed the screen, the oxygenation bar at 5%, and Ryder on the bike, sitting still.

"No idea, but I'm glad I came down here when I did." Ben gave me a sympathetic smile. "Did you overdo it at the gym?"

"Oh, maybe." I reached for the headphones, but Ben pushed them out of the way.

"I think you're done for the day. Listen, buddy, why don't you and I go for a drink? I can help you figure out that bachelor party situation."

"Sergei's party?"

"Yeah, your brother's. I got a great idea." Ben chuckled. "I don't know why you left it till the last minute."

"Wait, but the wedding isn't till Valentine's Day." Frowning, I crossed my arms.

"Exactly, and your brother's bachelor party is this Friday,

the 13th, baby. The day before the wedding." Ben nodded in approval.

"It's February already?" I mumbled, a knot forming in my stomach.

"Yeah, it's February. Time flies, I know. To be honest with you, I lose track of time a lot, too. Especially during football season. But at least the Steelers won the Super Bowl!" Ben hummed. "Second win in four years, baby!" Ben grinned. "Here we go!" He tapped the Steelers song on the desk. "Here we go! Pittsburgh's going to the Super Bowl!"

I felt like throwing up. My last memory was from January 7. I had no recollection of what had happened in over a month.

"Yeah." I knew better than to show my ignorance. Apparently, I'd missed a historic Super Bowl win for the city of Pittsburgh.

"But don't worry, buddy, I gotcha. There's this club, I'll hook you up, I can clock you out, no worries, I gotcha, buddy."

"What kind of club?"

"A strip club!" Ben rolled his eyes. "Come on, let's head out."

"Just give me a second." I climbed up the steps first and went to the bathroom. Splashing water on my face, I stared at my reflection in the tunnel of mirrors. A myriad of Rodions reflecting into each other. *Is one of them Ryder?* I thought, and felt my head spin. *A month! A whole month had gone by and I had no memory of what had happened.*

"Ready?" Ben knocked on the bathroom door.

"Yeah." I walked out and followed Ben out of The Lab. We walked behind the building and got into his car.

"Listen, Rodion, you gotta just take it easy. I know you like the gym and all, but you gotta focus on your nutrition, too. Take vitamins, all that. You seem kinda out of it lately, I've noticed."

"Yeah." I nodded.

"Gotta take care of your body," Ben said, turning onto Bigelow Boulevard toward downtown. "And your noggin'." He tapped his head. "This project really depends on you."

At what point did it become February?

Ten minutes later, we parked on 9th Avenue downtown, passing the Greyhound station on the way.

"Alright, let's hook you up." Ben led me to a windowless building with a metal door. A sign above the door read *Foxy's Gentlemen's Club.*

Foxy's. I frowned. Ben rang the doorbell as we waited. He stuck out his jaw, as if about to fight an opponent, and put his hands in his pockets. A minute later, the door opened with a screech. Booming music reached my ears. A huge bouncer squinted at us from the darkness. As his eyes fixed on Ben, the man smiled in recognition.

"Hey."

"Hi, Teddy," Ben said. "This is a friend of ours. Wants to throw a bachelor party for his older brother."

"Come in, come in. I'll call the manager." Teddy let us inside. We stepped into the semi-darkness, and the music got even louder. Three women gyrated on stage, and I averted my eyes.

"Have a seat right here." Teddy led us to the main hall and pointed to a plush couch.

"So, if there's anyone who catches your eye, you let me know, Rodion," Ben stated, nodding at the stage in approval. "You wait for them to come to you. You watch me, buddy. Just watch."

We sat in silence, Ben tapping his fingers on the table. And then, just as he predicted, one of the dancers sauntered to our table. I looked away, avoiding eye contact.

"Hey, there, boys." Her voice made me look up, and I saw her bright red hair cut in the diagonal fashion. The milky white skin.

Dawn. I gulped. My heart beat so fast, it was about to jump out of my chest. I squeezed the edge of the table.

"Hi! What's your name?" she asked.

"I'm Ben and this here is Rodion."

"Rodion? I like that." She giggled. Not one sign of recognition.

"And what's your name?" Ben asked.

"I'm Foxy." Another giggle. She flipped her hair back, revealing a tattoo of a fox snaking around her neck to her shoulder. I'd seen it so many times before. *What is she doing here? Why didn't she acknowledge me?*

"And what's your real name, sweetheart?" Ben asked.

"Dawn," she said, moving closer. She was now hovering over us. Her large breasts were right over my face.

"Dawn? And you work at a nightclub?" Ben laughed.

"It pays the bills!" Dawn shrugged. "And what's up with your friend?" She pointed at me. "He looks like he's seen a ghost."

The two of them laughed, and I felt a wave of nausea rise in my throat.

"I'll be right back," I muttered, and got up. I hadn't planned on leaving, but, noticing the *Exit* sign on the way to the bathroom, I pushed the door open. Teddy raised his eyebrows, but did nothing to stop me. Once outside, I let out a scream, the cold February air hitting my lungs. I needed to clear my head, and I walked away from the club.

CHAPTER 33

FOX

At first, it felt good to be outside, but then I realized I was getting cold. Pulling the hood over my head, I walked faster, but it didn't help. My teeth chattered. I considered turning back, but then saw the Greyhound station logo, and decided I'd warm up there first.

Inside, the station looked exactly the way it had in October, when I'd taken the bus to visit April. *April was the only good thing in my life, and I'd messed that up*, I thought ruefully. I thought of Sergei and his bachelor party I was supposed to plan and called my brother. He picked up right away.

"Hey," Sergei said. "How's it going? Did you figure out the plan for Friday yet?"

"Kind of," my voice cracked. I was so relieved at least my brother someone I could rely on, the one stable thing in my life. "Sergei, listen, can you come pick me up?"

"Everything okay? Where are you?"

"I'm at the Greyhound station. Downtown."

"Alright. I guess you'll tell me what you were doing there later," he said, and hung up.

A homeless guy shuffled past me, dragging a huge trash bag behind him. The bag was stuffed to the brim with sordid-looking rags. *I'm gonna end up like this dude if I don't take care of myself,* I thought. I couldn't afford to lose it. I had to avenge Mama. But in the state I was in, cold, alone, sitting at a Greyhound station, things seemed desperate.

As I waited for Sergei, a crowd of passengers assembled at the gate. The bus said *Philadelphia.* It could be me, traveling there to see April. *I wonder what she's up to,* I thought. And at that very moment, a text popped on the screen. It was from her.

Hey! Did you rent the suit yet?

Hands shaking, I stared at my phone. Then closed my eyes and opened them again. It was still there. *She must have been texting someone else.* I waited. Then scrolled up to see the text history, expecting a break in communication. Things between us had ended over the Christmas break, and I had no memory of making up. But there was a text from April from February 9, and it said,

I love you, too

And right above was mine, which read,

I love you

April and I are back together?
Another text from April popped up.

I am going to wear yellow.

One more text from April.

> It would be cool if you had a matching tie
> and pocket square.

What? I dialed April's number.

"Hey," I said.

"I wasn't sure if you were done with your shift," April said, all business. "Listen, I was thinking a gray suit would look nice. I know a tux is probably a good idea, but it's a small wedding, so you could get away with a suit."

"My brother's?"

"Of course! What other one? So, if you didn't rent a suit yet, pick a gray one, okay? It'll look really good with yellow."

"April, listen. Did we have a fight?"

"What? You mean because of the suit? You have to wear one; I told you, you can't go to a wedding in a hoodie."

"No, I mean," I cleared my throat, "I thought we had a fight." There was a muffled noise in the background.

"You mean about that?" I could picture April scrunching up her nose and raising her eyebrows. I missed her.

"You know what I think about those places," she added.

Hearing April's voice, knowing that she still cared about me, was incredible.

"What places? Wait, April, something weird's going on."

"Weird how? I don't care if that's what you wanna do. If you wanna go along with some guy you barely know and his idea. Ben seems like a total creep."

"I told you about Ben?"

"Yes! Of course you did!"

"What else did I say?" I grasped at this bit of information. This could be the answer.

"Rodion. Come on. You are not gonna make me say it."

"Please, April."

"You know I can't stand strip clubs. Whatever. I can't believe you're making me talk about it again. I just don't wanna know. I really doubt Sergei is gonna love that idea.

And those poor girls, totally exploited."

"I think they can make a pretty good living," I said, remembering my conversation with Dawn.

"Rodion, are you for real right now? Just rent a suit and please call me back once you do. I'm coming on Friday night and I won't even have time to see you before the wedding."

"You're coming to Pittsburgh?"

"Yes, how else would I go to your brother's wedding with you?"

"Okay, cool," I said, trying to sound casual. "So, that's in like three days, right?"

"Yes. Rodion, you aren't high, are you?"

"What? No!" I yelled in indignation. A few people turned their heads to stare at me and I plastered a smile on my face. I was about to say something else, but a text popped up on the screen. It was from Sergei.

> I am here. Come outside.

"Listen, April, I gotta go. I'll call you back." I hung up and headed to the exit, stuffing the phone in my pocket.

Sergei's Subaru was parked out front, hazard lights on. I hopped into the passenger seat.

"What happened to you?" Sergei asked. "Why are you wearing only a hoodie? It's February."

"I was with Ben," I said.

"Oh. That guy. Ever since you got that job at The Lab, you can't shut up about Ben." Sergei shook his head.

"I think he means well." I shrugged. "It was supposed to be a surprise for you, but I think I messed that up."

"You mean the strip club? I told you I didn't wanna do it." Sergei turned to face me.

"You did?"

"Yeah, last week. You'd mentioned the club to me last week."

"I don't remember." I scratched my head. "Listen, Sergei, something weird is happening to me, like I don't remember a lot of things. Like the Super Bowl. I didn't know the Steelers won this year."

"What? You better not forget things like that. We live in Pittsburgh!" Sergei chuckled.

"I am serious." I sighed.

"Maybe you got amnesia?" We stopped at the light and Sergei scanned my face. "I guess I shouldn't have moved out."

"And I don't remember how you moved out, either."

"What? For real?"

"I know, it's crazy. What do I do?"

"Maybe you should see a shrink?"

"No way! I don't wanna see a shrink!"

"It's not so bad. You just sit there and talk to them."

"You've been to a shrink?"

"Yeah, Tammy made me get therapy." Sergei's cheeks turned pink.

"You never told me that."

"I know. It was last fall. Tammy thought I needed to talk to someone about Mama."

"Oh." I fidgeted and looked out of the window. I felt tears well up in my eyes. I'd nearly forgotten. *Mama. I need to make things right.* I needed to avenge her death. But instead I was wasting time, talking about memory gaps, therapy. Instead of moving forward with my plan, I was regressing. What did it matter if I couldn't remember what happened since January 7?

"So, it was actually kinda cool. I had like five sessions, it's all I could afford, and she helped me a lot. I could actually commit to Tammy after that."

"Is that why you're getting married?"

"No!" Sergei protested. "Of course not. But before I was afraid Tammy would disappear. Like Mama did. That's what the shrink helped me see." He paused. "I had avoidant relationship behavior."

"Avoidant?"

"Yes. Avoidant. Like afraid of commitment." The muscles on his neck tensed. "You know what? Come to think of it, you might be having the same issue, lil bro."

"I'm not avoidant."

"You're avoiding April." Sergei shrugged.

"No!"

"Kind of? Like that whole fight you had over Christmas break."

"I remember the fight. But not how we made up." I stared at the road, feeling as if a big dark hole was about to absorb me whole.

"Maybe you could see my shrink. I don't think you actually have amnesia. But maybe that's your way of dealing with Mama's death." Sergei threw a look at me. "With trauma."

"Trauma?" I gasped.

"Yes, that's what my shrink called it. It's trauma. Losing a parent young."

We were driving through Schenley Park now and stopped at the light at Hobart.

"You think I experienced trauma?" I stared at the road ahead, trying not to cry.

"We both did." Sergei tapped the steering wheel. "Listen, maybe you wanna come over?"

"I'd rather go home," I said without hesitation. I needed to see what was going on, to search for my contract with The Lab, to find evidence of what had happened to me, to check everything. Sergei's New Age talk about the shrink, trauma, and avoidant behavior could wait.

"I'm there for you, alright? And don't worry about the bachelor party. I'll see you at the wedding." Sergei got out of the car and gave me a hug. "Are you sure you'll be alright?" He asked before leaving.

"Yeah, I'm good," I said, my voice quivering.

"Love you, lil bro," I heard Sergei say, as I walked into the house.

"Yeah," I mumbled back.

Once back at home, I sat on the couch. My resolve to investigate and dig through papers to understand what had happened in the last month disappeared. Instead, I got the console out and played. It was the car chase game and it was the best to clear my mind. The sound of the game, the race through the streets, everything about it was therapeutic. It didn't matter that I had no recollection of what had happened to me. I was winning. Clearing levels. Moving up the virtual world. And then I moved on to Stewart. Playing the game always made me feel better. The familiar fox comforted me, and I was about to really get into it, when a text popped up on my screen. It was from Ben.

> Hey buddy, sorry about Foxy's. Hope you got home alright. See you tomorrow.

I guess I didn't get fired from The Lab, I thought, and texted Ben back,

> All good. See you tomorrow.

His text interrupted my flow, and I forced myself to get up. Walking over to the crate, where I'd kept all the papers, I sifted through them, one by one, then stuffed them back. There were several payment stubs from The Lab, my bank statement from November. I'd been making good money. At least that was real. But there was no contract with The Lab. And then I noticed something I'd never seen before. A greenish, long paper. I picked up the sheet and examined it. It was Mama's death certificate.

Mama. Tears welled up in my eyes. I started calculating

what age Mama would have been had she lived. And then I noticed a line that read *"cause of death."* It said: *"Acute liver failure."* I clenched my fists.

No, Mama's cause of death was Phil.

He will pay for killing Mama, I thought, and walked to the shelf where I'd kept the hunting knife. It was sitting right there, next to Mama's urn. I took it out from the case, running my finger along its shiny blade. *Rodion Likharev.* I read my grandfather's name in Russian. My name. I took it into my hand, feeling its weight, then examined the blade. I felt it with the tip of my finger. *I should get it sharpened,* the thought crossed my mind. *But if I took it anywhere to get sharpened, someone might remember me.* With a sigh, I put the knife back.

CHAPTER 34

BASELINE

The following morning, I came to The Lab at my regular time, 12pm. Walking up to the familiar building, I felt as if my knees were buckling underneath me. *I'll just leave. It's not too late,* flashed in my mind. I still had no memory of what had happened to me since early January. But the counterargument presented itself just as quickly: I needed The Lab to put my revenge plan into action.

I needed the money, needed to keep on going. I couldn't quit now. Not at least until I'd killed Phil.

I knocked, but the door was unlocked. I entered, stopping at the entrance, expecting Ben or Kate to appear, when I heard the creaking of the steps and saw Dr. Donato descending the steps.

The psychiatrist was wrapped in what looked like a handmade shawl, knitted in blocks of bright colors, orange and yellow, intermixing. On her feet, she had enormous orange platform boots that extended her short legs.

"Hello," she greeted me, stopping midway, so that she stood several steps above me.

"Hi," I said, tugging at the sleeves of my hoodie.

"Let's go into my office," she said, turning and walking

back upstairs, not waiting for me to answer. "I think we need to talk."

I followed her up the steps. I held my breath in anticipation of a miracle. It was like watching a remake of a horror movie. Dr. Donato walked to the second door and led me inside, pointing to the white couch in the middle. Colorful tapestries hung on the walls, red and orange, yellow and gray.

"Have a seat, please," Dr. Donato said. She remained standing, and I noticed that, despite the platforms, she was a full head shorter than me. *Was she always so short?*

I headed to the couch and sat in the spot I'd picked before, right in the middle. Something was different, though, and I couldn't figure out what it was. Dr. Donato pulled up a chair and sat across from me.

And then it hit me. *The teddy bear! The giant teddy bear is gone.*

"Where's the teddy bear?" I asked, opening my eyes wide, before I could stop myself.

"Phil's being dry-cleaned." Dr. Donato smiled with her mouth only. "Most of my patients love the teddy bear."

Phil. My nemesis. I clenched my fists, remembering my revenge plan.

"So," Dr. Donato said, pulling me back to reality. I noticed a clipboard in her hands. She tapped a pen on its edge. "We need to discuss a few things."

I didn't respond, but she scribbled something on her clipboard, anyway.

"We don't want you to become a liability, Ryder," Dr. Donato repeated. My eyes came into focus and I saw her hovering over me.

Tugging at the sleeves of my hoodie, the fabric felt unfamiliar. Soft against my fingers. It was silky and smooth. Expensive. I noticed I was wearing black jeans. They weren't my usual worn-in pair, but tighter, made from a thick material. The jeans felt practically new. *When had I changed clothes?*

"Like I said, this is a situation we have to navigate carefully." The doctor's voice sounded husky.

"What situation?" I glanced around the room. It was the same setup, the couches, the Buddha, the tapestries on the wall, but something didn't feel right.

"Listen, Ryder, I think they're waiting for you downstairs. We can talk later."

I looked at her, frowning. *Why was she calling me Ryder? Who was waiting for me downstairs?*

"Remember? The party? Dawn did such a fantastic job! But remember to look surprised." Dr. Donato looked at me expectantly.

"A party?"

"Yes! Today is August 8! Remember? 8/8?"

"How did that happen?" I gasped.

In response, Dr. Donato chortled. "You know what I like about you, Ryder? It's your sense of humor."

I gulped, trying to piece together what was happening. *Did trauma cause me to jump from February to August and not remember?*

Dr. Donato walked to the desk and picked up her phone. It looked like an iPhone, but from the future. I immediately reached into my pocket, checking for mine, and pulled out the very same model Dr. Donato was holding in her hands. It was thin, with a tiny charging port. In the back, the cameras looked downright futuristic, popping out like fish eyes. I turned the phone to face me and the screen came alive before I had a chance to enter my passcode.

How does it do that?

"Ready?" Sarah Donato walked to the door, her heels clicking on the floor. Looking at my own feet, I saw I was wearing black sneakers with white soles. They looked like expensive leather. I'd never seen these before. *I must have money.* The thought pleased me.

I followed her out of the office. As soon as she opened the door, I heard voices, clapping, and then, "Shhh, he's coming." *Who are they talking about?*

I walked to the stairwell, and, as soon as I started descending the steps, with Dr. Donato next to me, the lights flicked on.

"Surprise!" The living room was full of people. All cheering, smiling, and clapping. Balloons, yellow and black, were everywhere. *Alright, the Pittsburgh colors,* I thought. This was pretty normal, probably the most normal thing so far.

"Happy Birthday, Boss!" I heard someone yell out, and then the whole room broke out in a cheer. "Happy Birthday! Happy Birthday!"

Boss?

I scanned the room, trying to figure out who was the boss, but all eyes were on me. *It must be me!* I gulped at the realization.

And that's when I noticed the banner. It was hanging on the side wall and read *AI Assisted Living.*

What is that? Is this what The Lab is called now?

Before I could understand what to do next, I noticed Kate. The very same Kate, except the expression on her normally condescending face looked eager to please.

"Boss! We love you!" Kate bared her teeth.

"Yes! We do!" I heard a man's voice, and Ben popped into view. "You're the best, boss!" Ben said, giving me a high five.

Both of them were dressed in black T-shirts with the *AI Assisted Living* logo on them emblazoned in gold.

What is this place?

The next moment, I saw Dawn. Her hair was bright red, cut in the diagonal fashion, her skin white, almost translucent. She was wearing the same black T-shirt with the *AI Assisted Living* logo, except in her case the T-shirt was tight and short, the letters *AI* stretched over her bust and a white outline of her taut belly revealed.

"Hey, there, Ryder," Dawn purred, her voice almost pornographic.

I darted my eyes left and right, expecting people to be outraged by this outright flirtation, but everyone looked at us in approval, completely unfazed. "Are you ready for dessert?" Dawn winked at me suggestively and I blushed.

As if on cue, a man wearing a chef's hat rolled a cart with a giant cake into the room, candles burning. The frosting was black, and there were three number 8s, done in gold. One, in the middle, in the upright position, and the other two to the sides, lying horizontally, to represent infinity.

"What are we celebrating here?" I asked, and the room broke out in laughter.

"Make a wish!" Dawn said, and others cheered, "Make a wish, make a wish!"

I could only think of one wish. *I want to avenge Mama's death.* Then I blew out the candles.

The chef expertly cut the cake, and Kate brought me the largest slice, the full golden number eight on it. Gold on black.

"Kate, this is too much."

I shook my head and heard Dawn's voice whispering into my ear, "Honey, take it. You don't have to eat it."

Honey? Are we together? What about April?

Sarah Donato popped into view, her expression inscrutable. She darted her eyes at Dawn and the two women exchanged a knowing look. Then Dawn murmured in my ear, "Let's go, honey, we need to talk to you."

Feeling her breath on my neck, I felt the urge to take her right there and then. I turned to face her and saw her eyes. Her icy stare, devoid of any warmth, the calculating gaze sent shivers down my spine.

Dawn turned around, and I followed her through the

living room to the kitchen. She was wearing tight black jeans and leopard-print flats that matched the black and gold theme. Everything about Dawn exuded casual chic, the clothes outlining the curves of her body just enough. I wanted her. Badly. Remembering her cold stare, I forced myself to look away. *Are we together?* I wondered again; the thought was incredibly tempting until it stopped me in my tracks.

This has already happened before. I'd seen it. Except it had been in a nightmare, where Ryder took Dawn over and over, while I watched. I gulped. *Was that me or Ryder? Or was that me in the future? What was happening?*

I felt nauseous.

"Ryder, what's wrong?" Dawn turned around and opened her eyes wide. She was standing right next to me. I felt the heat of her body next to mine.

"I'm fine," I squeezed out, digging my nails into the palms of my hands to stop myself from screaming.

"Don't make a scene," she hissed right into my ear, so that only I could hear her. The chatter from the party was barely audible, and I closed my eyes, trying to dispel the vision away. Dawn couldn't be real. None of this was. "Sit right here," she pointed at the stool, and I realized that I'd somehow made it into the kitchen. I saw the door to the basement. The code lock. *Is the code still the same?* I wondered, and made a move to The Lab, but Dawn grabbed my sleeve.

"We have to wait for Mother."

"What?"

"Why are you acting so surprised?" Dawn shook her head in indignation.

I raised my arms in protest, and at that moment, Sarah Donato walked into the kitchen.

"Ready?" Dr. Donato flashed a smile and fixed her gaze on me.

"Downstairs. Now," Dawn ordered, and joined her

mother, as the two stood guard on either side of me. "You had your little party. Time to face the facts."

"This is a mistake!" I yelped.

"Let's go, Ryder." Dawn grabbed me by the elbow and squeezed it tight. Sarah Donato was on the other side of me, digging her hand into my ribs. I got up.

Dawn punched in the code, *0808*. The same code as before. Dawn descended the steps first, and I followed. Dr. Donato closed our procession. The basement looked completely different. There was just one desk in the corner, all white, and it was raised very high, with no chairs. Three armchairs stood in the middle of the space. One wall of The Lab was now an LCD screen.

I was on the screen.

"Let us do the living for you," the screen version of me was saying. "At AI Assisted Living, we've created the digital double technology to ensure your life is perfect." I was dressed in a black turtleneck and blue jeans, a sizable titanium ring on my left ring finger. My forehead had a few wrinkles and specks of gray were in my hair. *How old am I? Am I married?*

"Ryder, please, stop staring at yourself." Dawn rolled her eyes.

"Men just love looking at themselves." Dr. Donato chuckled. "Never underestimate how vain men are. All men! It's absolutely ridiculous."

"I know." Dawn shook her head and took a seat in one of the armchairs. Dr. Donato sat down next to her daughter.

"Have a seat, Ryder." Dr. Donato pointed to the third chair, and I obeyed. "So, as I was just saying to you upstairs." She cleared her throat. "But of course, this is the conversation we need to have in complete confidentiality. You've gotten us in a situation where you are very likely going to become a liability." She raised her eyebrows, as if expecting me to react, but I said nothing. "It's quite unfortunate, Ryder, after everything we've done for you. And I have to acknowledge that Assisted Living wouldn't be the same without you, either. After all, you're the first digital twin we've created, Ryder."

"I am what?"

"The very first one." Dawn yawned.

"I'm Rodion." I raised my arms in protest.

"No, Ryder. Rodion is gone. Remember? You let us replace Rodion with the digital double. That was part of the agreement."

The screen version of me was now in a tropical paradise, smiling reassuringly at the audience. "Dreaming of an escape? We're here for you!"

"Where is Chuck McPherson? He runs this lab, not you!" I yelped. The two women exchanged glances.

"Oh," Dawn said to Dr. Donato, as if I weren't there. "Mom! Maybe it is an actual bug that we have to fix?"

"Let's make sure he isn't lying to us first." Dr. Donato took out her phone and clicked on one of the apps. She scrolled through it, frowning. "No, I think it might be a bug in the system, Dawn. It doesn't look like he's lying."

Meanwhile, the video playing on the LCD screen started from the beginning. Techno music was playing, and I saw myself emerge from the shadows.

"Let us do the living for you," I said on the screen. "Here, at AI Assisted Living, we take care of all the details, so you don't have to. Our revolutionary digital twin technology tests out various scenarios, ensuring your life is perfect."

"Oh, not that!" Dawn shook her head at her mother. "You know what? I don't have time for this right now. You do it, Mom."

"Dawn, sweetheart, he goes through these planted memory blanks. It's okay, we just have to be patient."

"But it's annoying! We have to reset him every time!"

"Glitches are inevitable, honey. Especially in evolved AI like Ryder."

"What?" I jumped off the armchair. "I'm not evolved AI! What the hell?"

"No, you're not evolved AI. You're just basic AI," Dawn said, venom in her voice. "Mom, I'm going. I can't deal with this nonsense. I'll be upstairs if you need me." As she walked past me, I caught a whiff of her perfume. I knew that smell. It was the one from the tester in a magazine she had shown me one night.

The door slammed behind her.

"So, here we are." Dr. Donato looked at me ruefully. "I guess this is it. Let me just fix the settings." She turned to her phone and quickly clicked on something, scrolled down, then looked back up at me. "There we are. This way, you won't remember a thing." A victorious smile appeared on her face.

"Why did Dawn say I was AI?"

"Because you are, dear boy." Dr. Donato crossed her legs. "Because you are the very first living digital twin. Except, in your case, the digital twin IS you. Became you." She flipped her hair back, and I could see the resemblance to Dawn again. The milky white skin, the clever eyes. "You see, Ryder, you are the perfect experiment."

"What?" I gulped. *I was a robot? My mind was being controlled by AI?*

"Oh, it's not such a huge deal, really. Alright, I suppose I digress. We really should be wrapping up, and we do have to discuss the lawsuit." She shook her head in dismay. "That's the problem with success. Once you make it to the top, everyone wants a piece of you. The lawsuit is a nightmare."

I opened my eyes wide, expecting her to continue, but she made a circle around the room without saying a word. If this was it, I would miss something important. I needed her to continue. So, I cleared my throat and forced myself to ask, "What lawsuit?"

Dr. Donato scratched her head. "I guess you have no memory of that, either. Which is how we got into that pickle to begin with. The whole company, AI Assisted Living, unfortunately, belongs to you, Ryder. On paper, at least."

"It does?" I gulped.

"Oh, yes. In case you can't tell, you're filthy rich, and I'm just your employee." She giggled. "I get a regular salary, of course, and run the mental health part of your business. I'm the brains of this enterprise." A hearty laugh followed. "Along with AI, of course. It's cute, isn't it?"

I wasn't sure if she expected an answer, so I nodded in response. She was about to explain more, and it was helpful. It didn't explain the wedding ring on my finger in the video, and I dared to ask, "Am I married?"

"Yes. To Dawn. Dear girl agreed to this herself. That was really the only way to have full control of the company. And once we got Chuck McPherson out, we couldn't have you stay married to April."

"April and I were married?" I perked up, grabbing on a good memory.

"Yes, at one point." She narrowed her eyes.

"What year is this?"

"2026," Dr. Donato responded with a shrug. "But that's irrelevant. Time is just a construct. I can see we will need to have our checkups on a daily basis. That will prevent you from becoming a liability."

Black circles floated in front of my eyes. *A liability*, rang in my ears.

"I said, we don't want you to become a liability." Dr. Donato hovered over me, and the next minute, I was back at my desk.

With satisfaction, I noticed it was the old lab setup, everything familiar, just as I remembered it.

I wiped beads of cold sweat off my forehead and turned my attention to the screen. Ryder was practicing at the gym. Clicking furiously at the mouse, I froze my double in position, so I could catch my breath. Then I pulled at the sleeves of my hoodie. It was the familiar, rough fabric and I shook my head. *That was just a weird dream. I must have dropped the oxygen levels too fast.*

Attach, I ordered, and pushed my chair back, staring at the screen, hovering over the mouse at the oxygenation bar. Five percent. I nodded to myself, adjusted the headphones, and clicked *Detach.*

Ryder sprung back into action, running on the octagonal plane.

I will not be a liability. I need this job. I need to avenge Mama.

CHAPTER 35
MOTHER'S DAY

hree months later, the day of atonement came. My hard work was about to pay off. Mother's Day. Sunday, May 10, 2009. I was about to finish Phil off and finally avenge Mama's death. Since the strange incident right before Sergei's wedding, I'd been going to the gym every morning, taking care of my body, just as Ben had suggested. I'd built up muscle mass. I felt good. Strong.

And each evening after work, I practiced with the knife in my living room. I couldn't throw it, but I practiced holding it, jumping and gliding. And carving. I'd found the perfect way to practice—on firewood. I collected logs, carved, picturing Phil's neck, then burned them before anyone suspected anything.

To calm my nerves, on the eve of Mother's day, I'd planted myself in front of the console and gamed my heart out. There I was, on the streets of Chicago, stealing cars, ripping people out of their seats, shooting, and running. I was invincible, clearing levels, setting records. I spent all night gaming and felt great. It had been a while since I'd played video games, not with all the testing at The Lab and Ryder. The digital double testing was going well, ever since the mishap with oxygenation and my conversation with Dr. Donato. I'd taken her words seriously and didn't repeat my mistake. I did not want to become a liability.

I could not afford to lose the job at The Lab, and now trained with the knife only on my time, no matter how tempting it was to listen to CM. The Count appeared regularly, telling me to go ahead, that no one would know. But I no longer trusted him. I could not risk passing out again, not like last time. I had to be a model employee. I shook my head at my own stupidity at having taken a huge risk. I could have lost my job, and someone could have found out about my plan.

Just in case, I'd set the alarm for seven in the morning, but I knew I wouldn't sleep that night. When the sun came up at around six, I was wide awake. I put away the console and headed upstairs, showered, and got dressed in the outfit I'd planned for that day. It was my favorite jeans, a black hoodie, and my old Nikes, clothes that made me nearly invisible. I was ready to go.

Too high on adrenaline, I couldn't eat, so I left the house on an empty stomach and drove to Trader Joe's. There, I parked on the far side of the lot, so I could see the entrance. I'd planned this very moment ever since running into Phil there. I'd counted on his being a creature of habit, expecting him to stop by the store to get the flowers first, then to head over to his mother's.

My heart beat fast and my hands shook in excitement as I waited behind the wheel of my car. It was hard to sit still and not jump around. A little before eight, a line of shoppers formed at the entrance. All there to buy bouquets for their mothers. Bile rose in my throat as I thought of how I'd been deprived of my own mother. She'd been dead for ten years now, all because of Phil. The only bouquet I'd get would be to bring to Mama's grave, if she had one. But she didn't even have that.

My brother and I couldn't afford to buy a plot at the cemetery and didn't have the money to pay for a tombstone, and so Mama's remains were still in an urn. Phil hadn't even helped us pay to bury her. I clenched my fists. *Just a little longer, and he would pay for what he'd done.*

My heart raced, and I fidgeted in my seat. The May morning was colder than expected. Shivering, I pulled the hood over my head and warmed my hands by rubbing them together.

I glanced at the line of shoppers, and my heart leaped.

There he is! Phil! I recognized the familiar bald head, the paunch. He was dressed in khakis and a white sweater. Nearly nauseous with excitement now, I closed my eyes for a moment, and the image of plunging the knife into his throat came to me. The vision was about to come to life. I just had to be patient for another hour. Just sixty minutes before my dream finally came true.

The doors of Trader Joe's opened, and the shoppers rushed in, pushing each other out of the way. I saw Phil maneuvering inside, elbowing someone. It was a few more minutes before he would emerge from the store with the bouquet and head to his mother's. *So predictable.*

Little did he know, I would wait for him by her apartment building, and he would never make it inside to see her. I started the car and left the parking lot without waiting for Phil to leave the store. According to my plan, this would give me enough time to park down the street from his mother's apartment building and get to my hiding spot. Gleeful my plan was working so well, I drove to Squirrel Hill.

On Sunday morning, the streets were empty, and I quickly made it to the hill on Forward Avenue. I parked in a shaded spot, just two blocks away from the construction site I'd picked for my plan after casing the area. My car was just like any other old Honda, completely inconspicuous. I'd picked the parking spot to ensure an easy escape. After cutting Phil's throat, I would make it back to my Honda in less than two minutes and would be long gone before anyone would notice.

The construction site was boarded off, but there was a gap in the fence, and that's where I would climb in and hide behind a concrete block. The location offered the perfect view of the street and the sidewalk. Phil always parked on the street across from his mother's apartment building and would be forced to walk right in front of the construction site. There was only one place where he could cross the street, directed by the *Sidewalk closed* sign. And that was the spot where I would attack him.

Everything was going according to plan, and just fifteen minutes after leaving the Trader Joe's parking lot, I was sitting in my hiding spot. Feeling the sheathed knife in my pocket, I couldn't keep from smiling. I was about to fulfill my dream. My life was just about perfect. A great job at The Lab, a ton of money, and, once I avenged Mama's death and settled the score, I could live freely. *I will make you proud, Mama!* I thought, and at that very moment, saw the familiar silhouette turn the corner.

It was Phil, and the smug expression on his face made me want to punch him in the gut. For a moment, I reconsidered my plan, and the knife seemed almost too graceful, too elevated of an experience for a lowlife like him. Phil was carrying a huge bouquet of white lilies, and the plastic wrapping rustled in the wind. Not a cloud in the sky. The perfect day.

Phil was getting closer, and I crouched, getting ready to jump and strike. I'd focused my eyes on his throat, the loose skin hanging slightly over the neck of his sweater. I gripped the knife by the handle and fumbled to get the sheath off. The blade was incredibly sharp and a ray of light reflected in it, blinding me for a second. Just one second was all it took.

I heard a screeching noise. Loud, the sound of tires, and then a dull thud and a blood-curdling scream. When I looked back up, Phil was on the ground, crushed, bloodied. Dead on the spot, hit by a truck that had appeared out of nowhere. It was a bright yellow truck with the huge black letters R-Y-D-E-R on its side. A Ryder truck had struck Phil. The very same type of truck I'd seen when I picked an American name for myself. *A Truck-kun,* flashed through my mind. *Phil will now be reincarnated as someone else, and I didn't get to avenge Mama.*

I was taking in the scene when the truck started moving. Wide-eyed, I stared at the driver. Behind the wheel was Ryder. There was no mistaking him for anyone else. I saw him every day at The Lab for hours, trained with him, tested his abilities. It was my digital double. He was wearing my clothes, the same black hoodie. I opened my mouth to scream, but no sound came. Frozen in place, I watched as the truck started to pull away, leaving me next to Phil's body.

"Stop!" I yelled, and ran after the truck. But I was no match for the vehicle. It ran a red light and drove off, leaving me in the cloud of exhaust fumes. I didn't notice the license plate number. I stopped and heard a siren. In a flash, I remembered Dr. Donato and the obscene grabbing gesture. "We've got you by the balls. One wrong move and you'll be behind bars." Her words rang in my ears. *How would I explain what I was doing there? I had to disappear.*

I ran. Clutching the knife, no longer caring whether I'd cut myself, I bolted up the street, turned the corner, and jumped into my Honda. Hands shaking, I revved the engine and felt a wave of sickness. I opened the door and vomited on the sidewalk.

I couldn't go back home, couldn't imagine being there, not after what I'd seen. The image of Phil's face, his body, the blood, the guts. I should have been happy. My enemy was dead. But I felt disgust and horror. It was nothing like I'd seen in games. Nothing at all like I'd imagined. Phil's death was revolting and scary. And it was nothing like seeing Mama when I found her. She looked asleep, peaceful, but Phil's face had a tortured expression. Ugly. I wanted no part of it. And now I would be blamed for it. I'd been framed and needed to disappear. To go to a place where I could be off the grid. I could think of only one place where I could lie low.

I started the car, and drove off, turning onto Beechwood Boulevard. Five minutes later, I was on I-376, driving through the Squirrel Hill Tunnel.

Aunt Molly's. It was the only place that was off the grid where I could hide. It was under one hundred miles to the farm, and though I only had half a tank of gas, I was confident I had enough to get there. I opened the windows and turned on the radio.

"And now we'll play one of my favorites." The DJ's voice was perky, and it grated on my ears. I was about to turn the radio off when I heard the familiar guitar chords. "A Star Called the Sun." The song Sergei played over and over in Moscow. Expecting to hear Tsoi's raspy voice singing in Russian, I'd turned up the volume, but it was a tenor singing different lyrics. The lyrics were about a mother's death.

"It was where my mom came undone," sang the male voice, the sad words in stark contrast to the perky guitar tune. *Mama.* I thought of her, my childhood that ended the day she died. She'd been taken by Phil, and now he was also dead. I gripped the steering wheel, listening to the rest of the song. "That was 'A Star Called the Sun' by Brazzaville," the DJ said. "You're listening to 88.3FM, Carnegie Mellon's freedom radio."

I was now driving past Monroeville. The steep hill lay ahead, and I switched lanes in anticipation. In the rearview mirror, I noticed a truck that was fast approaching. It was moving at such a high speed, the distance between us was closing in seconds. I shifted lanes again, getting in the right one, and saw the black letters on the yellow background. R-Y-D-E-R. It was a Ryder truck.

I gripped the wheel tightly. There were hundreds, thousands of these trucks, but my gut told me it was the same one that had just crushed Phil, as I glanced in the rearview mirror and saw the Ryder truck approach. I held my breath, looking into the rearview mirror. My fingers felt like icicles gripping the steering wheel. I slowed down. *Is this happening in real life?* Seconds, mere seconds, and it would ram into me. I tried to scream, but no sound came out.

And then the Ryder truck zoomed by, and I breathed out. *I'm just being ridiculous*, I thought. *Truck-kun is in anime, this is real life*, I brushed off the memory.

Continuing driving, I saw the exit April had taken when we went to her aunt's. I remembered it well, and now confidently steered the car, taking the exit. The key was not to miss the sign for the farm. The more distance I put between me and Greenfield, the better I felt.

I thought of the drive with April to see her Aunt Molly, the conversation we'd had in the car. A nice memory. *I was telling April about a truck-kun in this very spot. Why?* I chuckled, thinking of my exact words:

"A guy dies after being hit by a truck. Then he gets reincarnated and lives a new life, and corrects mistakes of his past life. It's kinda cool."

The idea had some appeal. *Getting reincarnated wouldn't be so bad*, I thought.

I squinted at the road ahead of me, searching for the sign. I remembered it well. *Molly's Organic Farm*. With cherries drawn on it. A dot appeared in the rearview mirror and caught my eye. It grew closer, approaching faster and faster, growing larger.

This is it, flashed in my mind. It wasn't like last time. I didn't feel any fear. What I felt was resignation at the inevitability of the end. In mere seconds, the truck was right behind me and rammed into my Honda. The yellow was everywhere; it overtook me. R-Y-D-E-R written in black.

The last thing I saw was the face of my double. Ryder, wearing a black hood pulled over his face, grimacing as he crushed me.

CHAPTER 36
REGRESSION

The voice sounded like it came from another planet. "Rodion, time to come back. Take a deep breath." I was in complete darkness. *Am I dead?* was the first thought flashing through my mind. I felt no pain. I remembered the Ryder truck overtaking me, crushing me underneath. Ryder's face, then nothing.

"You don't have to open your eyes just yet. Gently move your fingers," the soft voice continued. It was a woman's voice, but I couldn't place it. Disobeying the instructions, I opened my eyes.

I was lying on a bed in near darkness. I shifted and my left arm slipped off the narrow bed. Jolting upright, I sat up and saw a woman sitting right across from me. Another twin bed was positioned parallel to mine, with a narrow passage between them.

"How do you feel, Rodion?" the woman asked, and I could just make out the outlines of her face.

"Fine," I responded, trying to understand what was happening. I tried to stand up, but the walls of the room collapsed on me, and I fell back onto the bed.

"Easy, easy now." I felt the woman's surprisingly tough grip on my torso as she caught me. "You just had a very intense session. Very," she said, as she propped my head up on a pillow. "Let's be very careful now." She put a blanket over me.

I wanted to protest, to get up, to ask her where I was and what was happening to me, but drifted into darkness.

"You might need some time to readjust."

When I came to for the second time, it was because of hunger. My stomach was rumbling, and I was salivating. I opened my eyes and sat up. Light streamed into the room through the window.

I was on a narrow twin bed, and right next to it was another twin bed, but this time it was empty. I stretched. My limbs felt heavy, but I felt well and rested. A delicious smell came from outside the room and my stomach growled again. I rose from the bed and walked to the door, opening it just a crack, and heard voices.

"Are you sure he'll be okay? He's been asleep for so long!" It was April. *April!*

"Don't worry, he's just fine," I heard the answer. "Rodion will be fine. More than fine; I am sure this will help him find his focus in life."

"But you said it would be an hour, maybe two, but it has been five whole hours. So long."

"I know, sweetheart, but don't forget, today is such a special day, the Lion's Gate, plus the year. Triple eight! 08/08/08. So, I suppose whatever we did with Rodion was just so intense. And, the world is changing, and our vibrations are getting higher and higher." The voice trailed off and I couldn't hear the rest.

080808? What? I had just turned eighteen?

"April!" I screamed, and ran out of the room. I saw April sitting at the table, a large pot positioned right in front of her. Next to her was a woman wearing all black.

"Rodion!" April jumped up and hugged me. "I was so worried about you."

"Oh, yeah," I mumbled, scanning her face for clues.

"I am so glad you finally woke up! What did you see? Tell me everything!" April prodded. "I wanna know every single detail." Her eyes lit up.

Does she have any idea of what kinds of stuff I just saw?

I'd just traveled months into the future, created a digital double, planned a murder and nearly executed it, before getting killed by a truck.

"Umm, I dunno." I stared back at her in confusion.

"April, please give Rodion some time to readjust. You have to understand, he just traveled in time," the woman noted casually.

"That's so cool! Rodion, I can't believe it, this was amazing. Aunt Molly said your past life regression was actually a time projection. So, she said you were in the future and could predict the trajectory of your own life!" April gave me a look full of pride.

I looked up and noticed the eyes of a stuffed deer staring at me from the wall.

"That is impressive." Aunt Molly nodded. "You're my first client with such abilities, Rodion. I've never seen anything like that. You have such a strong channel."

"Channel?" I blinked fast. "Sorry, I don't feel so good." I felt nauseous and gulped, trying to stop the wave of sickness. To stabilize myself, I leaned on the side table and nearly hit a stuffed prairie dog. It stood with its front paws raised, forever frozen in time. I balked, hoping for an escape.

"Oh, yes, this was a lot, of course. Let me help you." Aunt Molly led me to the bathroom.

Closing the door behind me, I leaned on the sink, then splashed water on my face. *None of this was real.*

There was no lab, no Dawn, no Ben or Kate or their weird feud. I closed my eyes. And no Ryder. The image of my digital double appeared, menacing, approaching in the truck. Striking Phil, then me.

Phil!

The vision of my stepfather being crushed by a truck. The feeling of half relief, half disappointment hit me. It had all been a dream.

I remembered practicing with the knife, and nearly jumped. *Of course! The knife.* I tapped my pocket, expecting to find it there, but there was nothing. I reached into the other pocket, turned both pockets inside out, but they were empty.

Where is the knife? Did I lose it? I was about to ask April, and opened the door, but stopped myself just in time, remembering that I didn't bring the knife with me.

I stepped out of the bathroom, trying to appear normal. April was sitting at the kitchen table, an expectant look on her face.

"Rodion, have a seat." Aunt Molly pointed to the couch. "Maybe we can take a moment to discuss your session? It's good to do so while it's still fresh in your mind."

"Okay." I nodded, and my stomach rumbled loudly enough for Aunt Molly to hear. She immediately gave me a concerned look. "Oh, of course, I'm so silly. I've never had this happen before. You had a very long session, Rodion. I'm sorry. Please, come to the table." She pointed to the kitchen. "I'll give you some fresh stew." Without waiting for me to answer, she walked over to the kitchen and I followed.

"Here you go, Rodion." Aunt Molly placed a large bowl in front of me and I dove in. I felt ravenous and emptied it in what seemed like seconds. April watched in silence from the other end of the table.

"Could I have some more, please?" I asked when I was done, feeling as if a gaping hole had opened up in me and I could eat the whole pot.

"Of course, of course," Aunt Molly said, giving me another heaping bowl of stew. I devoured it and was about to ask for more, when the front door opened and Mike walked in.

"Ah, here you are. I prepared you a surprise." He handed me a small package wrapped in cloth and looked over at April. "I made one for each of you."

April rose and walked over to him, and I stood up. Mike handed her a package just like mine.

"Thank you," April and I said in unison. We were both holding packages wrapped in cloth.

"Go ahead, open them," Mike urged, and we did. The packages contained two large claws, one for each of us.

"These are real bear claws. Fresh from the brine. I just prepared them for you." Michael smiled. "You can wear them for good luck. Native Americans used the claws to protect themselves from harm. It's a symbol of bravery."

"These are very special," Aunt Molly added. "And for you, Rodion, the necklace will help you heal. Bears have incredible healing powers."

"Heal from what?" I frowned.

"From the trauma." Aunt Molly gave me a careful stare. I wanted to protest that I didn't need any healing, but felt tears well up in my eyes and bit my lip to stop myself from crying.

"Aunt Molly, I think we better go," April said, giving me a concerned look. "It's getting late, and we still have to drive back to Pittsburgh."

"Are you sure you don't want to spend the night?" Aunt Molly raised her eyebrows.

"No. Thank you so much for everything." April reached to give her aunt a hug. I stood back. "Rodion, are you going to wear your necklace?" April asked.

"Sure." I nodded and pulled mine on. The bear claw hung over my hoodie and I wasn't sure if I should tuck it in.

"I'll wear mine, too!" April announced.

"Here, let me put it on for you," I volunteered and, as I

reached to put the bear claw necklace over her head, I nearly stumbled.

April was wearing a silver necklace with two hearts intertwined. One silver, one gold. I remembered it from my dream. Had she always had it?

"April, hey?" I asked, trying to sound casual. "Where did you get this necklace?" My heart thumped so hard I felt it would jump out of my chest.

"You gave it to me for graduation. Remember?"

CHAPTER 37

MAN TO MAN

It was completely dark outside when April and I stepped out of Mike and Molly's house. Only then did I remember that we'd parked the car all the way at the bottom of the hill. To reach April's Volvo, we would need to go back down the wooded path to the main road. The woods seemed sinister all of a sudden. Fear gripped me, and I reached for April's hand. She must have felt the same way, for her hand felt cold to the touch.

"Ready?" I asked, my voice quivering.

"Yeah." April turned to me, and I kissed her.

Feeling her face close to mine, I was on the verge of tears and blinked fast, trying to will them away. But it was too late, and, before I knew it, I felt myself dissolve into tears. Sobs came, wave after wave, taking over me with such force I almost doubled over. I could not remember crying so hard. Not even when Mama died did I cry so hard. In fact, I'd been holding it together all these years, going through my life sure I was doing fine.

But that clearly wasn't the case. I was unraveling, fast. I heaved, desperate to stop the tears, but the more I tried to stop myself from crying, the harder I cried. Everything was wrong. My life was a disaster. I'd lost my mama, and there was nothing that could bring her back. I was bound to become a loser without a future, without a college education, with no prospects in life. The best I could hope for was a job at Vista Communications, and the AI Lab where April's dad worked would only lead to catastrophe, if I were so lucky as to get a job there.

"Rodion, what's wrong?" April asked, her voice gentle, and it nearly broke me.

More tears came, and now I cried over April, the only good thing in my life, who was leaving to go to Penn, and would inevitably forget me, because there was so little holding us together. Nothing really connected us, and once she was in Philadelphia, she would never think of me. A loser with no prospects in life. I couldn't respond and shook my head, half hoping she would leave me alone.

As terrifying as it was, being alone in the darkness was tempting. *Maybe I'll be eaten by a wild animal*, I thought, *and this misery will all be over*. My expression must have changed, because April opened her eyes wide and, without saying a word, rushed back to the house. She knocked, hard, and screamed, "Open up, Aunt Molly, please help!"

Immediately, the door opened, and I saw Aunt Molly's concerned face peek out. She took one look at me and rushed outside. Behind her, I saw Michael, his burly frame moving surprisingly fast.

"Rodion, oh, I am so sorry," Aunt Molly started to say, but Michael interrupted her.

"Honey, let me, please."

His voice was low and so full of authority that I gulped, and my tears immediately dried up. Aunt Molly stepped back, and so did April, and I was face-to-face with Michael. It was as if I was really noticing him for the first time, though he was hard to miss. Next to his wife, Mike looked enormous. His beard was long, with streaks of gray in it, and now, outside, in the dim light coming from the house, he looked half magical, almost like a lumberjack from a fairy tale who emerged from the forest. I expected Michael to lead me back inside, but he pointed to the porch and said, "Let's you and me sit over there and talk. Man-to-man."

It wasn't quite an order, but felt like one, and I followed him, shuffling my feet, surreptitiously wiping the tears. Michael dropped onto the bench and patted a spot next to him. I sat down, wondering what was next. *Would Michael now call me "son," "sport," or "bud"? What was a man-to-man talk, anyway?*

I'd never had one, certainly not with Phil, who dumped me before I was even a teenager; not with Vlada's husband, Boris, who, unlike his garrulous wife, rarely spoke and kept mostly to himself. The closest I'd ever come to having a man-to-man conversation was with my high school art teacher, Dr. Clark, when he'd spoken to me about his ancestors and succeeding against all odds, though those weren't exactly conversations, more like pep talks.

"Sit right here, Rodion, I'm gonna go grab us a lemonade. I'd bring you something stronger, but Molly would kill me," Michael said. I couldn't tell if he was joking.

He left, cracking the door open, while I sat alone on the porch. I heard crickets, and the forest didn't seem so sinister anymore. From inside of the house, I could hear Aunt Molly chatting with April. Michael reemerged, carrying two glasses. He handed me one and took a sip from the other.

"Molly makes great lemonade. All natural. Sweetened with our own honey," the man noted casually. It was a strange thing to hear from this guy. "You know, I'm lucky I found her when I did." I figured he'd expect me to respond, but he continued speaking. "Molly is into all this natural stuff. She helps people heal. You know, I wasn't a believer, not until she helped me turn my life around."

I fidgeted and stared at the glass of lemonade. *Is this guy going to tell me about his amazing life?* If so, I would have none of it. *What does this guy know about suffering and misery? He could never understand what it was like to be me, to be worthless, to have no future, and to live for one thing. Revenge.*

"Now, I know what you're probably thinking." Michael cleared his throat. "Here's some old fart trying to talk to me, and he got no clue what it's like to be eighteen." I blushed and raised my hands in protest. *Is this guy reading my mind?* "It's alright to think that. I used to be the same way. And listen, what I'm gonna tell you is my own story, and maybe you'll find it relatable. And maybe it'll help you. Maybe it won't, but I'm gonna tell you my story, anyway," Michael continued. Despite myself, I started to like him. "Deal?" I nodded.

"I grew up in West Virginia, in the mountains, not too far from here. My family were all coal miners, Irish immigrants, proud, and that was what I was raised to expect. I was going to be a coal miner, just like the men in my family. The taxidermy stuff, it was a thing I had on the side. But coal mining would be my destiny. And then I got drafted for Vietnam, right at the age of eighteen. I was actually excited, the idiot that I was, happy to be fighting for democracy and freedom. I got my eight weeks of basic training, then nine more weeks of AIT, and there I was. In Vietnam. Same age as you." Michael drew in a sharp breath.

I'd heard of the Vietnam War, of course I had, but I never took it to heart. By the time we came to America, it was long over, and I'd never spoken to anyone who'd fought in that war. The war my mother cared about was World War II, and that was because my own grandfather and namesake had fought in it.

"Death and fear. That was what Vietnam turned out to be for me. Fear of dying and seeing death. Day in, day out," Michael said, his voice cracking. "You know what a kill ratio is?"

I shook my head. "Kill ratio" sounded kind of cool, like something out of gaming.

"It's how many enemies die for each one of your own to make war worthwhile. It was ten to one for us." Michael took a sip of the lemonade. "That was the thing that was the hardest. It was seeing all that death and being responsible for so much of it. In the Army, you're not supposed to care. They teach you to ignore death. Like it's a normal thing. 'Zapping' is what they call it when you shoot someone. And burning men alive is 'crispy crittering.'"

I felt a knot form in my stomach, thinking of my own dream of killing Phil to avenge Mama. *Could death be as scary as Michael was telling me? As terrible as the vision I'd seen of Phil being crushed by Ryder?*

"The most terrible part was that at the time, I didn't even care. We were all in it together. I couldn't just stop, nor did I want to. And I was one of the lucky ones. I came home in one piece. Except, not entirely." Michael pointed to his head. "Not up there, I wasn't."

I swallowed hard.

"The nightmares started, but not right away. It was like my mind was playing tricks on me, pretending everything was fine." Michael chuckled. "I signed up for the coal mine and there I was, my first day on the job, and we got underground and I flipped out. Straight-up panic attack, though back then no one called it that. But I'd go underground, and I'd have to get out. I curled up in a ball and I couldn't move. Imagine, my pops, and grand pops, all the men in my family. We're known to the whole town, and here I am, freaking out in a mine." Michael shook his head. "No one connected it to the war. To trauma, to PTSD. It's all the terms we use now. But back then, they just thought I was faking it, trying to be lazy, to not work, to have time to do taxidermy. My parents put up with me for a few months, and they thought even that was too generous. Then they kicked me out." He sighed. "I was just a twenty-year-old, and had been through war, but my parents treated me like garbage."

Now, I could relate to that. I immediately pictured Phil and feelings of resentment overwhelmed me, bile rising in my throat. I was feeling outrage for Michael and was eager to hear how he punished his parents.

"And it took me years to forgive them," he added after a pause, and I opened my eyes wide. I expected a story of revenge, redemption, and this wasn't turning out that way at all. "But first I had to forgive myself."

"Forgive yourself?" I nearly jumped out of my seat. My voice was hoarse, and I realized it was the first thing I said since Michael started speaking. "What for?"

"For the trauma. Part of the tricky part with trauma is that we blame ourselves for it. We think we're responsible for it. That whatever bad things that happened to us, we are the ones to blame."

Michael's words took my breath away.

"We do?" I gulped.

I'd never admitted it to anyone, not even to myself, but I'd been sure I'd played a role in Mama's death. It had been my fault for not being Phil's son. It was because of me, because I'd let myself be tricked into going with Phil to The Lab to do the DNA test. It was my fault Phil discovered the lie about my paternity and left us. My fault. *But what if it wasn't my fault?* Thoughts swirled in my mind, and I was grateful for the darkness.

"Yes. We do. Trauma is tricky. That self-blame is sometimes so scary and shameful we don't even admit it to ourselves. But I know you're on the right track, Rodion." Michael's eyes sparkled. "Wanna know why?"

I nodded eagerly.

"Because you cried."

"What?" I threw my hands up and nearly spilled the glass with lemonade, now half empty.

"Yes. Tears are a good thing. They call it catharsis." He rose from his seat. "It took me twenty years to cry after Vietnam. You're doing much better than me, kid."

I also stood up. This was a lot to absorb, but I tried to summarize it in my head, so I could think about this later. *Killing is bad and will haunt you. Trauma is hard because of self-blame. Tears are good because of catharsis.*

"Now, promise you'll come back here and let me know how you're doing." Michael extended his hand.

I shook it and said, "I promise."

CHAPTER 38
THE DEPARTURE

This time, when we left Aunt Molly's house, April and I weren't by ourselves. Michael walked right beside us, holding a flashlight, escorting us to the car.

"Now, we shouldn't have let you guys leave by yourselves the first time, not when it was dark out already," he said, grunting, as he navigated a tricky turn. "But everything happens for a reason. That's what Molly tells me, and I believe her." April reached for my hand, and I took hers. This time, it felt warm.

For the first time in my life, I was certain everything would be alright. I wasn't sure how long this feeling would last, but I had made a promise. I had to come back and see Michael. And I owed it to him to be alright. We made it to the arm barrier, which would have looked almost sinister at night had it not been for Michael's flashlight. As we were about to get into the car, Michael patted me on the back.

"See you soon, Rodion," he said. "And you, too, April."

"Yes, of course." April responded for the two of us.

Pulling away, we saw the outlines of his large figure merging into darkness.

"You know which way to go?" I asked, and April nodded.

We were back on the road, and I saw the exact spot from my dream where Ryder overtook me. *Was any of it real?* I wondered, as we passed it and continued on.

We drove in silence for a while, and then April reached for my hand.

"Rodion, listen. Aunt Molly warned me not to ask you about what you saw when you were, well, you know, out. So, ummm…" she stopped speaking, "so you don't have to tell me anything. Not unless you really want to."

"Alright," I responded, sounding gruffer than I intended. I wasn't sure how I could ever tell anyone about what I'd seen in that half dream, half nightmare, even if I wanted to. *Where would I even start? The details, the double, the fantastical images of Ryder in a truck. The planning of a murder. And seeing my own death.*

"But she wanted me to tell you that the stuff you saw, it'll take you some time to process," April continued. "And she also told me to tell you that if you had questions, you could call her. And that some things you saw may actually be real, but some were just projections."

"What?"

"Projections of what might happen. That's what she said. Like a movie script that exists, but was never made into a movie. That's how she put it."

"So, how would I know what was real and what wasn't?"

"I don't know." She shrugged. We were on the turnpike now, the lights flashing past us, and I didn't need to ask why April decided not to take the quaint Route 30. "But I guess it's meant to help you. Whatever you saw."

"Why didn't she tell me herself?" I asked.

"Oh, yeah. She said you wouldn't react well, that it was better coming from me. I dunno. I'd always wanted to do a past life regression, but she told me I should wait a bit. That it was too early. Like after your experience, 'cause you're just eighteen, she said it was early, too, but that for you, it was really good that you did it."

"April, this is confusing."

"Well, alright." April flipped her hair, like she always did when she was flustered. "I mean, and I'm just repeating what my aunt said, but like there are these guardians, like guardian angels, and she and Michael, they work with Archangel Michael, and that basically in your case, things will work out and your guardian angels brought you to them for a reason."

"Ummm. Yeah." I frowned. "This sounds really weird. You know that, right?"

"I do, but I'm supposed to tell you. And like some stuff Aunt Molly says, like she knows things even before I tell her."

"She's psychic?"

"Yep. But I mean, you should have figured it out. She says we're all psychic, but some of us just don't let ourselves see things, and close off our abilities."

"Well, I definitely don't have psychic abilities." I shook my head.

"You might! I mean, look at her husband. He discovered he was psychic in his forties."

"Wait, him, too?"

"Yeah…" April's voice trailed off.

"So, Aunt Molly can tell things about people? Did she say anything about me?" I had a sinking feeling in the pit of my stomach, a knowing. The other shoe was about to drop. It always did.

"I mean. I don't know. Kinda." April, normally direct, was being vague. This wasn't a good sign.

"Tell me," I pushed. We passed an exit sign for Greensburg. A few more minutes, and we'd be reaching Pittsburgh.

"Like, well…" April paused. "Alright, I guess I can tell you. Aunt Molly said you were basically good and if you healed from trauma, you'd be great."

"For real?" A wave of relief rushed over me. "She said that?" Even the mention of trauma no longer triggered me.

"Yes. For real."

"This is really weird, but I like it," I said, a huge grin plastered on my face. I felt giddy and suddenly very awake. *I'd be great! Wow!* "April, let's go out somewhere. When we get to Pittsburgh." I looked at her. April's profile was sharp, and I noticed the necklace with the two hearts reflecting in the light. The bear claw necklace hung over it and I instinctively reached for mine.

"But I need to get home," she protested.

"But you're leaving soon. Let's go hang out. It's so nice out. And it's Friday night."

"Where would we go?"

"Anywhere. I dunno. Schenley Park? Flagstaff?"

"Flagstaff? Alright, I guess. I'll have to call my mom and tell her I'll be late."

"So, we're going?"

"Yes!"

"You still got that cooler, right?" I turned to the back seat. "We can even have a picnic."

"A picnic at night?" She giggled, and that reassured me April was fully on board with the idea.

"Yes. Exactly." I reached and kissed her on the cheek.

That night, April and I talked about everything. We sat on Flagstaff Hill, all alone in the dark, speaking, watching the city, and making plans for our future. Our future, not two separate futures. Not April's future on her own at Penn, and my own pathetic one in Pittsburgh.

"I want us to stay together, Rodion," April said. "You know that, right?"

"Yeah," I mumbled, and kissed her.

She pulled away. "I'm serious."

"Me, too. I'm serious, too. I seriously want you right now." I reached for her and this time she didn't interrupt.

After we were done, we lay together in the darkness, holding each other.

"Do you think she was serious about Archangel Michael?" I asked. "Like, how can that even be real?"

"I dunno." April wrapped herself around me. "But why not? Wouldn't it be awesome if that stuff was true? Like we actually had guardian angels, and they protected us from harm? And gave us signs and stuff?"

"Like clues?"

"Yeah, clues, to help us."

"So, how would you know if you got the right clue?"

"I guess if things were working out, you'd know." April giggled.

"Like right now, I guess guardian angels are looking after us."

"I guess they are."

And at that moment, I saw a shadow of an animal running on the edge of the hill. April must have seen it, too, for she yelped, "Look! A fox!"

It waved its tail and disappeared into the woods.

"That's cool!" April looked at me. "I've never seen a fox here before."

"We saw one together, like two weeks ago, remember?" I asked.

"I don't remember." April shook her head. "Are you sure?"

"Yes, I'm sure," I said, then, pausing, added, "Or maybe it was in a script that never got made into a movie."

I was only half joking.

CHAPTER 39

THE WIRE

The day of April's departure for Penn was approaching fast. Both of us kept reassuring each other that being apart didn't matter. That things would work out alright. That our relationship would survive the separation.

"Rodion, it'll be okay. We'll talk every day and text. And maybe you can come visit me," April suggested one evening. We were sitting together in my living room. Sergei was out with his girlfriend Tammy, who had been coming over more and more often. A sure sign things were getting serious between the two of them.

"I'll come to visit for sure," I said. "Just tell me when."

"As soon as I get settled. I just got the name of my roommate. She's from New Jersey. Daddy told me half of Penn is from New Jersey, and the other half is from Long Island." April giggled. "Whatever that means."

"Yeah." I shrugged. I wasn't in on the joke.

"Or maybe you can even come with us when my parents drive me to Penn to drop me off?" April's eyes lit up.

"Like actually go with your family?"

"Yes, why not? I'm sure my parents will be happy to have an extra pair of hands. And it'll be nice to have you there."

"But is that okay?"

"Of course, why not? My dad is super excited about you starting at The Lab, by the way."

"Wait, what? Starting at The Lab? But I haven't gotten a response yet."

"Oh, that whole thing is just a formality." April shifted in her seat.

"What do you mean?"

"I mean, of course you'd get the job. Don't be ridiculous, Rodion."

"For real?"

"Of course. My dad runs The Lab. And I vouched for you, so you're good. You start after Labor Day." April reached into the bowl of popcorn I'd prepared. We were about to watch the third season of *The Wire*.

"And you tell me now?" I crossed my arms. "April, this is a huge deal for me. You know that, right?"

"Of course. But I only found out this morning."

"So, I have a job? Do you know what kind of work I'll be doing?"

April had just pressed play and McNulty's face squinted on the screen.

"Wait, come on, April, please tell me about the job." In a flash, I saw myself sitting in a strange basement, training my evil double, only to make him stronger, so he could overtake me. *Is that what the job at The Lab would be like?*

"I have no clue. It's top secret," April responded, chewing. "Come on, Rodion, let's watch the show. I wanna finish before I leave for Penn."

"Alright, fine." I pushed my doubts aside and tried to concentrate on whatever was happening on the screen, but found it nearly impossible. I wondered if Kate and Ben were real, whether Sarah Donato would be at The Lab, and suddenly I turned red from the memory of Dawn. *Dawn.* The seductress. *Was she real? Did I want her to be real?* I felt like I had betrayed April all over again.

"What's wrong?" April reached in and kissed me. I kissed her back.

Ever since we'd come back from Aunt Molly's, I'd noticed a change in myself. It was a calmness I'd never experienced before. As if the anxiety that had been there as long as I could remember suddenly dissipated and vanished forever. But there was also something else. Something I couldn't quite pinpoint. Another change that had happened to me.

Killing is bad and would haunt me. Trauma is hard because of self-blame. Tears are good because of catharsis, I thought, only half trying to watch *The Wire.* My mind wandered as I tried to figure out what else had changed in me.

"The job will not save you, Jimmy. It won't make you whole. It won't fill your ass up."

I bolted upright. It was Lester speaking to McNulty, but I could have sworn he was speaking to me. I nodded. *This is it!* The job at The Lab wasn't the answer. It would help, but it wouldn't fix my problems. Not forever.

I looked over at April, trying to see whether the words had had the same effect on her as they had on me. But she was peacefully chewing her popcorn, though watching intently.

"Hey, hey, hey, a life. A life, Jimmy. You know what it is? It's what happens while you're waiting for moments that never come," Lester Holmes was saying in his wise voice.

"April!" I yelped. "This is it."

"What?" She stared at me in confusion.

"This is the thing. I'd always lived in the future. This is exactly the issue. But now I get it. I finally get it!" I clapped. "I'd been like McNulty!"

"What?" She rolled her eyes. "Don't tell me you're running around womanizing."

"No, that's not what I meant. But it's like I've been always jumping ahead and worrying, always on the next thing. Like my job, or you leaving, and never living in the present. Never actually living my life."

"I see." April raised her eyebrows. "So, you're a yogi now?"

"What?"

"This is what they teach in yoga. To live in the present."

"For real?"

"Yep." April nodded.

"So, like even my stepdad, I was always so focused on settling the score with him. But that was always in the future. I was never actually living, only waiting for him to be punished."

"I never knew you were so serious about it." April narrowed her eyes. "The whole revenge thing."

I shrugged. What could I say? I couldn't exactly admit to April I'd been planning a murder, could I?

"Listen, you wanna finish watching this another time?" she asked, turning back to the screen.

"Umm, I guess," I started to say, and at that moment, the phone rang. It was Vlada. I was about to let it go to voicemail, when April asked, "Aren't you going to answer?"

"I wasn't going to. Kinda wanna hang out with you."

"But maybe it's something serious?" April knew about the role Vlada played in my life. "She never calls you, right?"

"Yeah, you got a point," I said, and answered the call; right away, Vlada's low voice boomed into the receiver.

"Rodion, hi, I wanted to call you right away!" She took a deep breath. "I was trying to reach your brother, but Sergei isn't answering. I wanted to tell you myself, I just heard from Zhanna."

Vlada paused for effect. She and Zhanna were still best friends, still saw each other regularly, only without Mama.

"And Zhanna might also call you, but I wanted you to hear it from me."

"Yes," I said, frowning. I wondered what was so important that the two of them needed to share the news together.

"What is it?" April asked, and Vlada must have heard her voice, because she said, "Is that April? Tell her I said hello. Please come over together soon."

"Vlada says hi," I repeated obediently.

"Please tell Vlada I said hello!" April said, and I was about to hand April the phone when I heard Vlada's voice.

"Rodion, Philip is dead. He died in a car accident. A Ryder truck. Killed on the spot, right on Forward Avenue." The room spun. "A hit-and-run. They never caught the driver. Philip was going over to see his mother."

Shivers ran down my spine and my hands felt ice cold.

"Did you hear what I said? Dead," Vlada repeated. "If you live like a dog, you will die like a dog!" she added in Russian. It was a Russian proverb, one of her favorites. "It's in the news. I'll send you the link. I just have to figure out how to put it in a text message." There was a beeping noise, and the phone went dead.

"Rodion, are you okay?" April asked.

"Yes." I nodded and felt the phone slip from my hands.

CHAPTER 40
THE CURE

When I came to, I was on the couch in my living room. There was a sharp odor, acrid and strong, and I sneezed and opened my eyes. McNulty's face was frozen on the screen, just the way April and I had left it when Vlada called. I moved my hand and felt something cold on my forehead. Lifting my arm to remove it, I felt a wet towel, but strong hands stopped me and a low voice said, "Rodion, please, don't get up. A few more minutes. I'm just going to make you a cup of tea."

Vlada materialized in front of me, her eyes inspecting me for damage. I must have looked fine, because a moment later, she turned to her left and said, "You see, April, I told you it would work. Remember, pepper works in case you don't have anything else available." Vlada disappeared into the kitchen, and I heard the clanking of dishes.

"Rodion." April came into view and sat down next to me on the couch, taking me by the hand.

"What happened?" Disobeying Vlada's orders, I pulled off the wet cloth from my forehead and sat up. "Did I pass out?"

"Yeah." April cleared her throat. "Right after Vlada called with the news. Then she called you right back, so I picked up." April averted her eyes. "And I told her what had happened, so she came right over."

"Oh, wow." I shifted in my seat, adjusting slightly. "How long was I out for?"

"Oh, not long." April shrugged. "But it was pretty scary."

I nodded, though I didn't feel scared one bit.

"Wait, is it true? Phil is dead?" I remembered the news Vlada had delivered. April nodded.

"A car accident?" My mouth gaped open.

"Yes, well, Vlada said it was a hit-and-run." April frowned. "Vlada is very worried about you," she added, and looked to the kitchen, and we heard the teakettle whistle, as if on cue.

"April, wait, was he killed by a truck? A Ryder truck?" I fidgeted.

"She didn't say."

"Are you sure? I think she said it was a Ryder truck," I yelped. "April, I saw it in my dream. When I was at your aunt's!" I was nearly screaming now. "It was in my dream. I saw it happen!" I would not tell April about the other details, such as seeing my own death, or that I'd been planning Phil's murder in my dream, but this was bad enough.

"You actually saw it? Like you predicted his death?" April stared at me, and I gulped.

"Yes."

"She brought this over. Not that I can read it."

April handed me a folded newspaper. It was a copy of the *New Russian Word*, Vlada's favorite. She still subscribed to the weekly print edition and read it diligently, cover to cover, keeping old newspapers stacked in her living room and reusing them to wrap gifts.

"I think this is it." April unfolded the paper, and I saw the obituary for my stepfather, a huge photo of him in a suit and tie. It must have been recent, for he looked older, and nearly completely bald. The photo had a black thick outline, and I read the text, slowly putting the Russian words together.

> *Gone too soon. Philip Begunov was killed in a tragic accident. A talented scientist, Philip moved to the United States in 1990 and launched a successful career in his new hometown, Pittsburgh, PA. He is survived by his mother, Oxana Begunova, his loving wife, Marina, and his son, Denis.*

There wasn't one mention of me or Sergei, and I swallowed hard. Nothing about being "preceded in death" by Mama. I guess no one mentioned ex-wives in an obituary? The rejection still cut like a knife, a reminder of how we had been discarded from Phil's life. But there wasn't the same sense of urgency as I felt before. No anger rose in me, and I felt no glee over my enemy's death. I stared at the newspaper and, as the realization sunk in, I said to April, "You know, I don't really feel good about it."

"Why would you feel good about it?" April opened her eyes wide.

"Well, because of what he'd done," I started to say, but my words felt hollow. April watched me expectantly, and I added, more out of habit, "Like, don't you want the bad guys to pay?"

"I guess so. But that means you still care. The best thing is not to care."

"How do I do that?"

"You forgive."

"Did Mike tell you to say that?" I gulped.

"No." April shook her head. "But it makes sense, doesn't it?" She smiled at me, and my heart melted. "Rodion, look at this." April pointed at the dates. "It looks like he was killed on your birthday."

My eyes came into focus, and I noticed the numbers above Phil's photo.

July 13, 1952 — August 8, 2008.

"Weird." I stared at the newspaper in disbelief.

"It is, right?"

"Yes." I nodded. "But in my dream, he actually died on Mother's Day. Also strange."

I could clearly see my vision now, stalking Phil at Trader Joe's, lying in wait at the construction site, and then the Ryder truck appearing out of nowhere. Crushing my nemesis, my double behind the wheel. Another detail I wouldn't be sharing with April.

"Oh. Mother's Day. I'm sorry, Rodion, I know that guy really messed you guys up."

"Yes." I swallowed hard. That was one way of putting it.

"So, maybe there is a way for you to move on with your life now?"

"To move on? How?"

"I mean, the guy's gone, right? So, there isn't much you can do. So, maybe try to forgive him?"

"But April, I saw it. I actually saw what had happened to him."

"Aunt Molly did mention you had a strong channel. And she also said some of the stuff might come true, and some might not."

"You mean that stuff about a movie script?"

"Yeah. I guess this is one script that was actually made into a movie."

The knife! I remembered it that very second and ran over to the shelf, where Sergei and I kept it behind the urn with Mama's remains. But the urn wasn't there. Neither was the knife. Instead, there were several books: The two-volume Russian edition of *The Count of Monte Cristo* we had brought with us from Moscow, the English one I'd gotten, and a book I didn't recognize. It was a beautiful hard-cover edition of *Crime and Punishment* by Dostoyevsky, with sprayed edges. I opened the book and stared at it, wide-eyed.

"Did you finally decide to read it?" April asked, walking over to me.

"*Crime and Punishment*?" I mumbled, flipping through the book.

"Yes! You've had all summer to read it." April shook her head in mock indignation. "I got it for you as your graduation gift."

"You got me this?"

"Yep. And you got me my necklace. Which I absolutely love." She produced a silver chain and two hearts intertwined.

"Oh, yeah."

"Don't you remember?" April gave me a curious stare.

I was about to respond, but Vlada came in, carrying a huge mug of tea, steam rising. The smell coming from it did not bode well for me. It must have been one of Vlada's herbal recipes. Vlada believed that for a cure to work, it had to make you suffer. A tea had to be scalding hot, bitter, and strong, and an ointment had to burn. "Otherwise, you don't know if it's working!" she would add proudly, administering her treatments.

"Rodion, sweetheart, here, this will make you feel better." She handed me the mug, a look of pride on her face. "It's a dandelion and ginger infusion."

"I didn't know you can make dandelion tea," April said, her voice full of admiration.

"Absolutely. I'll give you the recipe. It's an amazing treatment for just about anything. Better than all your fancy organic recipes." Vlada's eyes lit up. "Here, Rodion, please drink the whole thing."

"Thank you." I accepted the mug and nearly dropped it, because it was so hot. But Vlada watched me intently, and I forced myself to take a sip. Refusing her would be the gravest offense.

"So, this is it," Vlada said, pointing to the newspaper.

"Zhanna heard it from one of her clients. The whole community is talking about it. It happened right on Forward Avenue, right in front of his mother's building. No witnesses. A hit-and-run."

"Was he hit by a Ryder truck?" I asked, gulping.

"A Ryder truck? Did I say that?" Vlada opened her eyes wide.

"Yes, on the phone." I nodded vigorously.

"Oh, maybe. Zhanna said something about it being a larger car. That's what the police think. I guess someone saw a truck. It's that awful construction site, has been going on for years now. That place is such an eyesore. But at this point, it doesn't really matter, does it?" Vlada sighed. "Just to think, things could have turned out differently for all of us," she added, and I didn't clarify what she'd meant.

"Yes." I noticed April looking from me to Vlada with concern.

"I guess you shouldn't speak ill of the dead." Vlada scanned the room, as if to make sure no one but us was listening. "But I'm not going to feel sorry for him. Not after what he did to poor Lydia." Vlada crossed herself, right to left, the Orthodox way. "And to you and your brother," she added after a pause, looking over at me.

I took another sip of the tea. It was bitter and my eyes watered. It might have been the tears, but I blinked them away. I wasn't about to cry in front of April again. Once was enough.

I took a deep breath and looked at Vlada.

"It's probably not the right thing to say, but things worked out, didn't they?" I said.

"What do you mean?" Vlada raised her eyebrows.

"I mean, Sergei and me, we got to come and live with you. So, in a way, Phil brought us together."

I'd never openly thanked Vlada for being there for us all of these years, for supporting us, for raising us, for welcoming two orphans into her family. It felt good to do so. The opened newspaper with Phil's photograph stared at me, and I folded it, disappearing him from view.

"Rodion, I am going to cry." Vlada was now the one wiping tears away. "What a good boy you are. And April. The two of you. Such wonderful children."

"We're not children," I protested.

"Oh, of course you are. So young. Thank you, Rodion. I love you." Vlada gave me a huge bear hug.

CHAPTER 41
PIZZA PARTY

After April and Vlada left for the evening, I tried to clear my head. I had to have a break from all the emotions, from the drama, from guessing whether I was psychic or whether I just had weird dreams. There was one thing I knew that could make me feel better immediately. Stewart.

I popped in the cartridge and started playing. It was the old Stewart, the game I grew up playing. The fox's sly face appeared on the screen, calling me along, the red spiky hair bobbing as he ran. Like in the old days, Stewart winked at me and spoke to me. Nothing else mattered. I was clearing levels, moving with the cute fox, running beside him, winning.

Hey, hey, hey, a life. A life, Jimmy. You know what it is? It's what happens while you're waiting for moments that never come.

I heard Lester's voice in my head.

Yeah, I got it, I thought, and kept on playing. I wasn't waiting. I wouldn't be making the same mistake McNulty had made. I was living in the moment. Stewart and I were both in the present, living it up and gearing up for the next level. And the level after that.

I completely lost track of time when the noise of a motor running outside jerked me back to reality. A car door slammed shut. There were voices. The sound of footsteps approaching. I tensed, but then recognized Sergei. A moment later, the front door opened, and my brother appeared on the doorstep.

"Hey, bro, you're still up. We brought pizza." Before I had a chance to ask who was "we," Tammy popped into view.

"Hey, Tammy." I got up and put my console to the side.

"Hi! We just had a double date," Tammy said proudly, throwing an adoring look at Sergei.

"Come in, guys," she called to someone, and at that moment I froze. Kate walked inside. The very Kate from The Lab, with the blonde bob haircut, small blue eyes, her button nose. The arched eyebrows gave her face a look of perpetual condescension.

"Hi, I'm Kate," she said, extending her hand to me. "You look familiar. Have we met before?"

"Hi, I'm Rodion, Sergei's little brother." I cleared my throat, trying to sound casual, while doing my best to guess whether we'd met with this Kate before.

"I've heard so much about you," Kate said. Her face did not reveal a trace of recognition. "Sergei won't shut up about you."

"How do you guys know each other?"

"Tammy and I are best friends." Kate said. *Or maybe I'd seen Kate before?* I gulped.

"Yes, we are!" Tammy let out a giggle.

"Oh. Okay."

"And I'm Ben." A guy popped into view. It was no other than Ben from my vision. He was of average height, with red freckles spread thick on his face. Ben was dressed in a T-shirt with the Carnegie Mellon logo. He extended his hand and gave me a firm handshake. "You look familiar." Ben blinked. "Do you go to my gym, by any chance? Over in Shadyside?"

"No." I shook my head.

"Ben, no one needs to hear about your gym. Come on!" Kate threw her hands up in frustration. Her dismissive reaction was exactly like what I'd seen in my vision.

"Just like no one cares about your yoga studio."

The real Ben and Kate interacted much like the two of them did in my vision. Bickering. *How is that possible?* I did my best to avoid openly gawking at them in an attempt to compare reality with what I'd seen.

"We're just gonna have some pizza and head out," Kate said, taking a seat at the table.

"No, Kate, we might wanna hang out after." Ben frowned.

"Alright, guys, come on," Tammy said, appearing from the kitchen, carrying a roll of paper towels. "Let's eat. Wanna join us, Rodion?"

"Thank you, yes." I nodded, taking in the room. Kate and Ben, Tammy and Sergei. And me, next to them. Just a regular kid who may have traveled into the future and channeled a death.

I took a seat next to Sergei.

"Did you hear about Phil?" I asked my brother, keeping my voice low as I served myself a slice of pizza.

"If you live like a dog, you will die like a dog." Sergei noted, quoting Vlada in Russian as he bit into his slice. "Vlada left me a message."

"What are you guys talking about?" Tammy asked from across the table. Though she rarely spoke Russian, she understood it. "Who died?"

The whole table suddenly fell silent. Three pairs of eyes were watching Sergei and me intently. I noticed how Kate squinted at me, and I may have imagined it, but I saw a flash of recognition in her eyes. Ben's mouth hung open, a slice of pizza frozen in his hand.

"Just someone we used to know." Sergei shrugged and went back to chewing. "You know how the Russian community is all about gossip."

"Oh, yeah." I felt Tammy's eyes zeroing in on me, as if to verify this information, and I made sure my expression was inscrutable.

"I didn't know the Russians were into gossip." Kate turned to Tammy.

"Me neither. I've been here since childhood." Tammy giggled.

"I think you'd fit right in with those gossipy Russians," Ben sneered at Kate. "All you do is gossip."

"Ben!" Kate said something in protest, and Tammy rushed to her friend's defense as more bickering ensued.

"Hey, Sergei, what happened to Mama's urn?" I asked my brother, grateful that my voice was being drowned out by the loud chatter on the other side of the table.

"Auntie Lena took it with her to Moscow," Sergei noted casually.

"Wait, Auntie Lena was here?"

"Yeah, she came the year after Mama died. Remember?"

"I don't remember," I gulped, turning at my brother. Sergei wiped a crumb of pizza off his chin.

"Well, I guess you were only nine. And you spent all your time with that console at Vlada's."

"So, Auntie Lena was here?"

"Yeah, she couldn't come right away. Because of the crisis of 1998, Auntie Lena had lost a lot of money, so needed to save up, but then she came to see us as soon as she could."

My brother continued speaking, gesticulating, as I sat, racking my brain for a memory, for something to help me recall this visit. *And Mama died in 1998.* I remembered a part of my vision at Molly's. *The crisis of 1998. That's how I knew about it.* It was as if pieces of a puzzle were ready to come together. Sergei had stopped speaking, and I realized he was staring at me, expecting an answer.

"So, there was a crisis in Russia?" I said, to keep the conversation going.

"Yes, it was very bad. The place was a mess. Auntie Lena kept telling us she thought it was a good thing we'd left when we did. She and Vlada spoke about it for hours at a time."

"For real?"

"Yes, they had a theory of whether Mama would have been better off in Moscow and whether she'd done the right thing to have moved."

"What?" I nearly jumped. "Are you serious? Why didn't you tell me about it?"

"What's there to tell? They just kept going in circles, but in the end, they decided you and I were better off in America, regardless. And that Mama would have had a really hard time back in Moscow."

"That's insane. So, Phil wasn't to blame for her death?" I mumbled.

"No idea." Sergei shrugged. "It might have been to convince me to stay in Pittsburgh. I wanted to go with Auntie Lena, remember? To go back to Moscow. But we'd need to renew our passports. It was such a hassle." Sergei pushed his plate to the side and wiped his face with a paper towel.

I had no recollection of this ever happening. *Was this a script that had been made into a movie, but I had forgotten about it? Or had I rewritten my past?*

"But I don't remember any of this."

"That's trauma," Sergei said casually. "I just started seeing this therapist, and that's what she tells me."

"You're seeing a therapist?" Another piece of the puzzle clicked into place.

"Yep." He nodded. "You might want to, as well. Tammy convinced me to do it."

Sergei looked over at his girlfriend, and I followed his gaze. The dynamic on the other side of the table changed, as Tammy and Kate were now engaged in a lively conversation, while Ben stared quietly at his phone.

"So, I've learned our brain blocks certain things, especially if the events are traumatic. It's something we do to preserve ourselves, a survival mechanism. And sometimes going back to remember things like that is not even that healthy." Sergei gave me a pointed stare.

"I see. So, how do I even know things were real?" I swallowed hard.

"I dunno, Rodion. How do you know if things are real?" Sergei chuckled.

"But what if you remember something different? Like I remember Mama's urn sitting on the shelf and you're saying Auntie Lena took it with her." I fidgeted in my seat.

"No idea. But Auntie Lena definitely took the urn with her. She said she could figure out a way to bury it in our family plot. Knew some guy who did gravestone design, and he had connections."

"We have a family plot?"

"Yes, what do you think? We just came from nowhere?" Sergei sighed. "I guess you were so young when we left," he immediately corrected himself.

"And the knife?"

"What knife?"

"The one with my name on it. Remember the one from our grandfather?" I tried to keep my voice from trembling. The special knife dedicated to me, the knife passed on from my heroic grandfather to me, couldn't just disappear. Was it also somewhere in Moscow? Had I dreamed up its existence?

"No idea." Sergei shrugged. "I think when we moved to Vlada's, it might have gotten lost."

"But I remember seeing it." I threw my hands up in protest. "Was it not real at all?"

"Sorry, bro. Why are you talking about this now? Is it because of Phil's death?"

"I guess so."

"Forget about that, dude. Seriously." Sergei shook his head. "Life goes on." Sergei winked at me.

CHAPTER 42
THE LAB

Over the next few days, after learning about Phil's death, I pondered my future. Now that my revenge plot against Phil had lost its purpose, I had no life goals left. It was as if a rug had been pulled out from under me. For the first time since graduation, I thought about what to do with my life. Despite April's promise, I didn't believe the job at The Lab would materialize. *And what if The Lab was as creepy as I'd seen in my vision?* The idea was unsettling, to say the least.

Absorbed in these thoughts, I planted myself in front of my console and played Stewart. The old game was the only thing that made me feel in charge of my life, and I clutched the controller in my hands, clicking away. Another disturbing idea was my conversation with Sergei about trauma. Hard as I tried to remember Auntie Lena's visit, to recapture a part of my memory, I failed. The idea of going into therapy to dig into those hidden parts of my brain was too frightening, and I brushed it away. Remembering Lester Holmes and his instructions to McNulty, I focused on Stewart instead.

My phone pinged and April's text popped up on the screen, snapping me back to reality.

Hey, Rodion, want to come help me pack?

Yes, I'll be right over

I responded, and got ready.

The familiar walk to April's house calmed me, and by the time I got there, I was in a good mood. I found April sitting in the middle of her room, surrounded by piles of clothes, a stack of boxes to the side. A suitcase was laid out, splayed open, right next to her bed.

"Hi!" She jumped up and gave me a kiss.

"Hey, what's going on?"

"I'm just having a hard time getting everything ready. I didn't know packing would be so hard. I told my mom I don't need any help, and now I'm kinda stuck." April threw her hands up in frustration. "And this suitcase, we decided I'll only take one. There's no space in the dorm room." April leaned over the suitcase and tried to stuff the clothes inside, pulling at the zipper.

Suddenly, I had a flashback to the days right before our departure for America, to the apartment in Moscow, to Mama opening and closing suitcases. I was transported back to our apartment and saw myself in the dirty kitchen, waiting for my life to change forever. Willing the vision to go away, I plopped on the bed and clasped my head.

"Are you alright?" April's mouth gaped open as she stared at me.

I was about to lie, as I usually did in moments like this. But this time, something in me compelled me to do otherwise, and, as April continued to look at me, I squeezed out, "Actually, not really."

April blinked fast and sat down on the bed next to me.

"Tell me, what's going on? I was worried about you after, you know, the newspaper and Vlada."

"Oh, yeah." I averted my eyes. Speaking about feelings

and putting things together was incredibly difficult. My voice felt hoarse. "I just remembered my mom, that's all."

"I am sorry, Rodion." April took my hand. "If you ever want to talk, I'm here for you, okay?"

"Okay." I nodded.

I was about to say something else, but there was a knock on the door, and April's mom walked in. Her hair was pulled back in a ponytail, and she looked very young.

"Hi, Rodion, great to see you." Mrs. McPherson smiled at me.

"Hello, Mrs. McPherson."

"Maybe you can talk some sense into April. She refuses to have me help her, and we're leaving the day after tomorrow."

"Of course." I nodded.

"Mom!" April protested. "I got it."

"I can see that." April's mother shook her head. "By the way, Rodion," Mrs. McPherson said, turning to me, "I'd love for you to come to Philadelphia to drop April off."

"Really?" I opened my eyes wide.

"Yes. I think it would be fantastic. Chuck was just invited last minute to attend a conference in London and so it's just me and April."

"Absolutely. I'll be able to come and help," I perked up.

"Thank you, Rodion. April is so lucky to have you. And I hear you'll be working at Chuck's Lab. That's absolutely fantastic. It's such a wonderful opportunity."

"Yes. I am really looking forward to it." I fidgeted and stared at my feet. *The Lab is going to happen!* flashed in my mind.

———

The offer from The Lab didn't come in a fancy package, and wasn't delivered by DHL, like in my dream. It arrived as a simple letter, my address handwritten on an envelope.

The offer was generous, but not over-the-top. Sergei reassured me it was reasonable and commensurate with my qualifications (none) and level of education (high school).

"But I'm supposed to be doing secret research!" I insisted. In my head, I was already negotiating a higher salary.

"I don't know where you get these ideas. I'm sure April's dad is just being nice, offering you a job. You should be grateful."

"I am grateful. But I wish I got paid more money." I remembered my dream, the incredible salary, the savings. *Why couldn't that be true? Was it a script that would never be turned into a movie?*

"So, just wait and see how things go."

Several days later, the Tuesday after Labor Day, I headed to The Lab, my stomach in knots from anticipation of what The Lab would bring in real life. I woke up early and walked through Schenley Park, just as I had done in my dream. Only this time, I crossed Flagstaff Hill, pausing to take in the view of Downtown Pittsburgh. Immediately, I thought of April, of making love to her there, and my heart ached at the memory.

Half expecting The Lab to be in a mansion on Forbes Avenue, I stopped several times to verify the address, until I located the right building. The real-life lab was on Carnegie Mellon University campus in a five-story gray building called Hanover Hall. Mustering the courage to enter, I circled the block several times, then planted myself at a bench in front of Hanover Hall, observing people going in and out. I checked my watch. I was still fifteen minutes early, but Sergei told me I should come ahead of time on my first day.

I guess Ben and Kate won't be there, I thought, entering the building. I took in the tall ceilings, the massive steps, and the bars on the bay windows. Steeling myself, I followed the instructions in the letter and located room number 135. It was on the first floor, the frosted glass door closed. Stopping right outside, my hands felt like icicles. The expectation of doom, of AI taking over my brain, of Ryder popping out and manip-ulating my mind, was so strong that I stepped back. *It's not too late. I can leave*, I thought. The hall was empty and I gulped, pondering what to do next. If I fled, I would cave into fear, but I would preserve myself. But I would miss out on an opportunity of a lifetime, and not showing up on my first day of work would undoubtedly compromise my relationship with April's parents. Not to mention April herself.

"There you are, Rodion!" I heard, and felt a firm grip on my shoulder. Chuck McPherson materialized right beside me. "Welcome! You're early!" He sounded pleased.

"Hello, Mr. McPherson," I croaked.

"Please, call me Chuck. Come in, come in. Let me show you around. Introduce you to everyone." Chuck opened the door, and we entered.

Taking in the room, I followed Chuck to his desk, which stood in the corner of the large, open space, right next to a bookshelf bursting with folders and papers. Ten workstations were arranged in the middle of The Lab in two rows, with large computer screens positioned next to each other.

It was completely unlike the creepy lab, and did not look like a place where someone would lock me in a basement, feed me sandwiches, and conduct experiments that would require mental evaluations and oxygenation training. Where AI would overtake my brain and manipulate me into making bad decisions.

"Thanks for helping Elizabeth to drop April off. This job is so demanding, and I hate not being around much. But having you there really helps," Chuck said, moving a stack of papers to the side. "Here, have a seat." He pointed to a chair right next to his desk. "Now, did April tell you anything about the work that we do here?" He scratched his chin, then added after a pause, "Actually, I suppose April doesn't know that much."

"No." I shook my head.

"So, let me tell you then. Have you heard of this pioneering technology? It's called 'a digital double.'" April's father rubbed his hands as his eyes sparkled. "It's ground-breaking."

"Like a replica?" I unclenched my jaw, as the tension I'd been feeling since that morning had dissolved. April's father was openly discussing The Lab with me, which meant that whatever experiments were going to take place there involving me would not be dark and dangerous.

"Yes, exactly. Is there a movie out there with this stuff or something? There's always stuff in Hollywood that, I swear, predicts the future."

"No, I just guessed," I said, doing my best to stay calm. I couldn't wait to hear more about this project and compare it with what I'd seen in my vision. *Was Aunt Molly right? Did I really have a 'strong channel' and could predict stuff?*

"Well, that's one good guess! Because, Rodion, we're going to be testing your digital double. A replica of you that will make decisions in a virtual world. And then using real-world data to make it happen. The digital double will be your exact replica, a copy of yourself, a digital doppelganger, so that whatever the double does can be accurate and reflect perfectly how you would operate in the real world." Chuck's voice trailed off, and he stared into the distance. "One day, we're gonna use this technology to do incredible things, Rodion. We're going to go to Mars. Heal people. Technology and real life will work together seamlessly."

"Good morning, Chuck," I heard a throaty voice coming from behind me. I recognized it right away. The last time I'd heard it, it threatened to erase my memory.

"You must be Rodion. I'm Sarah." A woman wearing enormous high-heeled orange platform boots appeared right next to me. Her hair lay in thick curls on her shoulders. I stood up to shake her hand, scanning her face for signs of recognition. But her expression was neutral.

Please don't be a shrink. Please don't be a shrink.

"Sarah is our admin," Chuck said. "Keeps me on the straight and narrow."

"Not just you!" Sarah flipped her hair back. "Speaking of which, did you happen to give him the NDA?"

"No." Chuck frowned. "I forgot."

"No biggie." Sarah produced a clipboard with a paper on it. "I need you to sign right here. And here." She tapped one of her manicured fingers twice on the page and handed the clipboard to me. "We do top secret research here, Rodion," she said, as she watched me read over the paper. "Need to protect ourselves from a potential liability."

"Yeah. It's kinda like *Fight Club*." Chuck turned to me. "Have you ever seen the movie?"

I nodded. I knew where this was going.

"Remember rule number one of Fight Club?" He chuckled, watching intently as I signed my name on the NDA.

"You DO NOT talk about Fight Club?" I said with enthusiasm. I wanted Chuck to like me.

"Exactly."

CHAPTER 43
THE LAB

On my way home that evening, I called April and did the exact opposite of what I'd seen myself do in my vision. I told her everything about The Lab and the digital double I'd soon be testing.

"Rodion, it sounds really cool," she said, once I mentioned the technology to her.

"Yes, but also, I signed an NDA." I cleared my throat. "What if they make me do something weird?" I was walking on a busy stretch of Forbes Avenue, approaching Murray, and lowered my voice, aware of the passersby who could over-hear the conversation.

"I think it's just so the technology isn't stolen."

"Oh, yeah, the technology…" My voice trailed off as I considered the consequences of April's words. In my dream, I'd been so focused on my personal safety I did not consider the other side of what The Lab was doing.

"Yeah, my dad always says it's a big risk. That's why he was very excited to have someone he could trust join the team."

"You mean me?"

"Yes, I mean you." She let out a giggle and my heart melted. "Love you."

"Love you, too."

I turned onto Murray Avenue and, as I looked up, the green background and the white cursive letters of the bookstore caught my eye. I'd been to it lots of times, mostly to warm up on the way home from April's, since I never had the money to buy anything.

But this time, knowing I'd be getting paid soon, I walked in with a different attitude. *I'll browse and pick something out and get it once I get paid,* I decided, heading straight to the second floor, to the Fiction section. I stopped at the tables featuring New Releases, flipped through a few covers, and then walked straight to Dumas, locating *The Count of Monte Cristo.*

As I pulled the tome out, I saw his face. It was the image of the Count from my vision, more akin to a nightmare. A wide-brimmed hat concealed his smirking face almost entirely. My hands shook as I grabbed the book and walked to an armchair. I'd read the novel so many times before, and yet I felt panicked, as if I expected something new to happen. Right away, I skipped to the part of the Count's revenge. The part that had captivated me in the past. As I read the familiar paragraphs, I felt a strange sense of nausea. The Count's actions appeared petty at best. I saw him in a new light. Cruel and unforgiving. My hero was nothing like I remembered him, had no good qualities, and I wondered whether I wanted him to be my hero at all. *Not the Count!*

I swallowed hard, abruptly rose, and walked back to the shelf to put the book back.

"Excuse me, may I help you?" I turned around and saw a girl. She had milky white skin, and her bright-red hair was cut in a diagonal fashion. She was wearing a tight white T-shirt that accentuated her prominent bust, and, as I averted my eyes trying not to stare, I glimpsed her silver name tag. It read *Dawn*.

"No, thank you." I shook my head, feeling my face flush with embarrassment.

"If you've never read it, you should." Dawn fixed her gaze on me.

"What?" My palms felt sweaty.

"*The Count of Monte Cristo*. It's a great book."

"Oh, yeah, thanks, I've read it before."

"Well, if you're looking for a gift, I can make a few recommendations."

Dawn walked up closer. *This isn't happening! She can't be real.* I clenched my fists, digging my nails into my palms to keep myself from fainting.

"Okay," I croaked, hating myself for being too weak to end the conversation and walk away.

"Who is the gift for?" Dawn licked her lips, and I swallowed hard, feeling myself being drawn to her. "Is it for your girlfriend?" She opened her eyes wide, as if challenging me.

"No." I shook my head. "It's for me."

"So, you aren't together anymore?" Dawn batted her eyelashes. "You and that chick with long hair?"

"Wait, what? Have we met?" Something in me snapped. Raising my eyebrows, I put my hands in my pockets.

"You went to Allderdice, right?"

"You went to my high school?"

"I didn't realize I was so easy to forget." Dawn rolled her eyes. "Whatever."

"I am sorry," I mumbled, averting my eyes.

"It's alright. My hair was jet-black then. We sat next to each other in Health and talked about The Doors."

The memory came back to me. The crowded classroom. A girl asking me about Jim Morrison, commenting on my T-shirt.

"I remember you." I jumped. "I do! Yes, I remember now. But that was like, a long time ago."

"I dropped out my junior year." Dawn shrugged. "Figured there was no point."

She let out a deep breath and scratched her shoulder. I noticed the fox tattoo snaking down her neck. The lower part of it was faint. Following my gaze, Dawn said, "I'm getting it removed. I just gotta save up to do it."

She hadn't been some mythical creature, a phantom of my imagination, haunting me. My mind hadn't conjured her from memories buried deep in my subconscious. Dawn was a real person I'd met before. Whatever fascination and attraction I felt to Dawn disappeared.

Once at home, I planted myself in front of the console and was about to start the game when I remembered Dawn's relationship to Sarah Donato in my dream. *I wonder if they're related in real life? But I guess it doesn't really matter*, I thought, staring at Stewart, who was frozen on the screen. I couldn't be sure, but I thought I saw him turn to me and wink.

————

It took me a few weeks, but by the end of September, I no longer hesitated before entering The Lab. The vision, the creepy Dr. Donato, the premonitions I'd experienced while at Aunt Molly's, slowly faded into the background.

I was almost normal, operating in the real world. As normal as I could be as a high school graduate who was testing groundbreaking AI technology, that is. I'd stopped comparing the vision to reality.

The high-tech part of The Lab was easy to forget, at least initially. My job turned out to involve a lot of sitting around and waiting for the coders to program the next step and get it ready for testing, which was when I came in. The digital double wasn't yet ready, and I tested small parts of the program, each time wondering whether I would get to meet my replica and feeling relieved when I didn't.

Chuck McPherson was rarely there. After giving me the orientation on my first day, Chuck disappeared and didn't come back until mid-September. And when he came back, he rarely spent time in The Lab. He would run in first thing in the morning, greet everyone, then go over his schedule with Sarah Donato, and rush off to one meeting after another. I assumed he paid little attention to what was happening with me.

The coders were all grad students, guys in their late twenties. They all knew each other, some of them were roommates, and they kept strange hours. It wasn't unusual for me to find one or two of them first thing in the morning, surrounded by crumpled bags of potato chips, candy wrappers, crushed cans of Red Bull, and empty cups of coffee as they stretched and funneled out of The Lab after pulling an all-nighter. If they didn't leave before Sarah Donato appeared at 9am, she would chastise them for making a mess.

"Now I've had it," she'd say, hands on her hips, standing in the middle of The Lab, with a look of a general disappointed in her army. "Please pick up the trash on your way out." She'd raise her eyebrows and follow the coders with her eyes until they left.

"Yes, Mrs. Donato." The culprit would give her a side-eye but obey. "Sorry, Mrs. Donato."

These guys mostly ignored me, calling me only when they needed me, and I didn't mind. All in all, I tested at most for an hour a day, and the rest of the time waited around, growing increasingly bored. I'd watch the coders program, trying to understand what they did. I remembered the Count, the source code, and wished in real life it was so easy and I could magically learn programming.

One day, when I was standing behind one of the coders, observing, trying to piece together what he was doing, I heard a rustling noise and found Chuck McPherson next to me. It was one of the rare occasions when he was in town and not in one of his meetings.

"Rodion, let's talk."

"Of course," I mumbled, following him to his desk. I expected Chuck to offer me a seat, but he pulled on his jacket and led me to the door.

"Let's go for a walk," he said, as we walked out of Hanover Hall. "Rodion, I've been thinking about your situation."

"My situation?" I felt a knot form in my stomach. "I didn't know I had a situation," I wanted to say, but stopped myself.

"Yes. This job, The Lab, what you're doing, it's a great opportunity, but you should also think about your future. I've seen you watch the coders, and I can see you're eager to learn."

"I'm just curious," I gulped, stunned to find out Chuck had been paying attention to me.

"Exactly. Where do you see yourself in five years, Rodion?" Chuck stopped walking, and I almost stepped on his toes.

"Five years? That's a long time." I scratched my head.

"It might seem that way to you now. But it's really not. As you get older, time moves faster. Fact of life." He patted me on the back. "You don't want life to pass you by, Rodion. And I'm speaking to you this way because I have a vested interest in your future. You get that, right?"

I knew he meant my relationship with April, but couldn't force myself to nod. Facing this topic head-on had caught me completely off guard.

"I would like you to succeed in life, Rodion," Chuck continued. "If you and April are to have a future together, and it seems like things are moving in that direction for you two."

My face was crimson now, and I looked away, unable to speak.

"You're young, sure, but Elizabeth and I also met when we were young. Our freshman year in college." He paused and I stood, waiting for him to continue. "Now, where were we?"

Chuck started walking again, and I followed him, keeping at a polite distance, grateful he had asked a simple question.

"You were speaking about my future," I responded.

"Yes, your future. I wanted to suggest that you look into applying to colleges."

"Colleges?" I gasped. "But what about my job?"

"You can work part time if you get into college. Actually, what am I saying? Not IF you get in. WHEN you get in. I've seen your high school diploma, you got good grades."

"But why would I go to college? I can just work at The Lab!" I threw my hands up. I'd gotten two pay checks so far, and was just getting used to having money. I'd been able to help Sergei with rent and even started saving for a car. Going to college would destroy that, deprive me of my income.

"Rodion, we're testing software. And what happens once we finish testing it and roll it out?"

"But Bill Gates never went to college!" I protested. "And neither did Steve Jobs!" The names of the two technology giants were the first ones that popped into my head.

"Very true, but Sergey Brin went to college. And so did Larry Page."

"I don't think I can pay for college," I added after a pause. I knew how much my brother had struggled and the loans he'd taken to put himself through college and law school, and didn't want to repeat the experience.

"The Lab can sponsor you," Chuck said softly.

We walked in silence for a few minutes, moving to the far side of campus, the one that bordered Forbes Avenue. I noticed the outlines of the mansion that housed The Lab I'd seen in my vision.

"Let's go in here, Rodion." Chuck led me into a building, and I realized it was the Admissions office. "College can open doors for you. I think you can achieve great things in life, but you need to apply yourself," he said, guiding me to a stack of glossy brochures. "Now, read this and let me know what you think." He handed me one of them. "It contains all the deadlines and what you need to do."

"Thank you."

"Now is the time to take the SATs. I suggest you think about what I've said. I would be happy to provide you with a letter of recommendation," he added after a pause. "And before you know it, you'll be the one inventing pioneering technology and not just testing it."

"I never thought of that." I stared at Chuck.

"There you go. Now you've got some food for thought."

We walked back to The Lab in silence. I held the brochure in my hands, feeling its glossy cover with my fingers.

CHAPTER 44
THE DOUBLE

n late December, I came to The Lab to find the whole team in place. It was the last day before winter break, and The Lab would close for two weeks, along with the rest of the university campus. April was coming home later that day, and my mind was on seeing her again and being together without interruption for over two weeks. April and I had agreed that we'd go see Aunt Molly right after Christmas, and looked forward to the trip, eager to check in with her and Mike to keep my promise.

The Lab was abuzz, with all the coders assembled in the middle of the room, crowding together. Chuck McPherson and Sarah Donato stood next to each other, and Sarah was showing him something on her clipboard.

"Today is the day, Rodion," Chuck turned to me. "Are you ready?"

I nodded. I'd been waiting for the unveiling of my digital double with some trepidation, and now the day had come.

"Have a seat." Chuck pointed to my workstation, and I sat down at my desk. The crowd of coders shifted and now hovered over me, all chattering in excitement.

I squeezed into my chair and put on the headphones. As

soon as I moved the mouse, the screen flashed and for a second, I felt as if I were about to be transported to the basement of the mansion on Forbes Avenue.

I half expected the Count to appear on the screen, but instead, I saw my face looking back at me. It was Ryder. My digital double. The exact replica of me was right there. It was an out-of-body experience. I'd been split into two parts; I'd been duplicated and while I sat on the chair, mouse in hand, another me was moving on the screen, about to jump into action. The feeling was just like what I'd experienced during my vision. I gasped and fought the urge to rip my headphones off and run out of The Lab.

"Aha! Would you look at that?" Chuck exclaimed. "The resemblance is stunning. Good job, guys!"

"This is incredible. They look exactly alike!" Sarah Donato chimed in.

"Creepy, isn't it?" one of the coders added.

I stared at my double, unable to move. My hand hovered over the mouse, but my fingers were frozen, gripping it in terror. I tried to speak, but no sound came. Ryder was real. He was back and was about to take over. I knew it in my gut, and that realization made my blood run cold. Feeling as if one wrong move could lead to disaster, I didn't dare shift the mouse and sat, staring at the screen.

"So, team, right after we come back from winter break," Chuck said, "we'll go to the next phase of testing."

"Can't we start the testing today?" one coder asked, and another one chimed in, and I sensed disaster was imminent.

"Yes, let's see what he can do!"

"Alright, I don't see why not," Chuck said after a pause. "Go ahead, Rodion."

My hands trembled. I didn't dare disobey Chuck, and I clicked the mouse, closing my eyes so I wouldn't see the nightmare that was about to come to life. Immediately, the image of Ryder crushing my stepfather flashed in front of my eyes. Ryder was behind the wheel of a truck, the hood pulled over his face. The next moment, Ryder popped out of the screen and was now sitting next to me, rubbing his hands. He was speaking to me directly, and time stood still. Chuck, Sarah, the coders, all disappeared, and I was left to confront my double on my own.

"Remember me? I am Ryder. I exist. You've made me happen!" The double guffawed, and I pushed my chair back to get away. "It's too late, Rodion. It's just a matter of time before I take over and you disappear. I am stronger than you. I've learned from you, observing you. And you let me," Ryder spoke, inching closer and closer, while I trembled in fear. He smirked and his face was right next to mine now, about to swallow me alive.

He crept over and continued, "How about it, Rodion? How about revenge?" He winked at me expectantly. "And Dawn? You know you've wondered about her. You know you want her."

My mouth was dry. I opened my mouth to speak, but no sound came.

"Yes, Rodion, just say yes. That's all it takes. Just let me take over. It'll be so easy." Ryder's tone changed, and he spoke softly, his manner courteous. "Aren't you tired, Rodion? Let's have fun together. Just say yes."

His hands reached for my throat and he clasped them around my neck, cutting off my air supply. His grip was firm, and I gasped for breath. I jerked my head back and moved to push his hands off, and felt the string of the bear claw necklace.

"Go away!" I screamed. "You're not me!" Clutching the necklace, I opened my eyes and saw the room. I was still in my chair, colleagues crowding over me. The expressions on their faces were friendly, kind, expectant. The image on the screen was still frozen, and I realized I hadn't yet started the digital double testing.

"Go ahead, Rodion, start the program," Chuck said; then, furrowing his brow, asked, "Are you alright?"

"Here, have a drink of water." Sarah handed me a glass.

"He must be creeped out. That thing looks just like him," one coder said. "It is kinda weird."

"Yes, totally weird," another voice chimed in.

"Ryder," I mumbled, my lips barely obeying me.

"Who is Ryder?" Chuck asked, frowning.

I pointed at the screen.

"You named him that?" Chuck gave me a curious look.

"Yeah." I nodded, fumbling for the necklace and tucking it back into my hoodie.

"But doesn't that sound too much like your own name? Why don't we pick something else?" Chuck suggested.

"Good idea, then it won't be as creepy," the coder standing right next to me said.

"What about Twinnie?" Sarah Donato tilted her head up at Chuck, looking like a curious bird.

"Or Doubby?" someone proposed.

"We don't have to name it now," Chuck said. "Let's just proceed."

"What about Artie?" The name popped into my head on its own, and I spoke before I even knew what I was going to say. But once I said it out loud, I knew it was perfect.

"Artie? Yes!" Chuck nodded. "I like that!"

"Is that short for Artificial Intelligence?" Sarah Donato glanced at me with surprise. "That's quite clever."

"I guess, yeah."

"Artie! Artie!" the coders cheered. I looked at the screen.

Staring back at me was an image of my double. *Artie*, I mouthed, expecting to shrivel in terror, but instead, the only emotion I felt was curiosity.

I sat up straight, hovered the mouse over his pixelated face, and clicked start.

EPILOGUE
08/08/26

heard muffled voices coming from downstairs. It was time. I would act surprised, just like April had instructed me to do. I fumbled, feeling for the bear claw necklace, and tucked it into my hoodie, and glanced over at the engraving of my favorite quote from *The Wire*. April had gotten it for me for Christmas 2008, and I'd kept it on my desk ever since.

Hey, hey, hey, a life. A life, Jimmy. You know what it is? It's what happens while you're waiting for moments that never come.

I shut down the laptop, relieved to finally be done with the video. It was hard to see myself on the screen, but it needed to be done. The PR team had just sent over the clip of the commercial with me as its star. They insisted I be in it and assured me I was the best marketing tool for the company.

"Twin Tech is there for you," I was saying in the video. I was wearing an outfit that was supposed to make me look more credible as a "tech CEO," fancy black jeans, a designer turtleneck that cost as much as a rocket ship, and outrageously overpriced white sneakers. In real life, I preferred to dress much more simply, but the PR team insisted I needed to project wealth to sell the product.

"Hello, I am Rodion Likharev, CEO of Twin Tech. Our pioneering digital double technology will turn your world around," I was saying, doing my best to look relatable and reliable at the same time. "When I first started testing the digital double technology, I was just eighteen years old."

The screen now showed the younger version of me, dressed in jeans and a hoodie, staring at an image of a virtual me with an expression of what was supposed to be awe and curiosity, but, in my opinion, made the younger me look incredibly dull. I shook my head and sighed. I would need to provide my comments to the PR team, but this could wait. "Now, nearly two decades later, I can reassure you no one in the world understands the capabilities of the digital double technology better than me. Having dedicated most of my life to testing AI to perfect this tool, my company is there for you when you need it." The image turned to the present-day me, and I nodded in satisfaction. *At least they got this part right.* I paused the video, rose from the couch, and opened the office door.

"Shh," I heard. "He's coming."

I smiled. I loved my team. They were the best. My coach had asked me once, in the early days, soon after I'd taken over managing The Lab, whom I wanted in my bus.

"What bus?" My coach and I always spoke on Skype. She refused to leave her farm and come see me in Pittsburgh, and considered any other technology to be suspect. Somehow, Skype had made the cut ages ago, and we stuck to it.

"Think of your team as a bus. You're the driver. Whom would you take to be on your bus?"

"A bus? That's a great way to look at it," I told Molly then.

I'd hired her to coach me ten years ago, and considered it

the best decision of my life. Well, the second-best decision of my life. The first one was marrying April.

So, when I put together my team, I applied the bus analogy. I was picking the right passengers for my bus. However simple, it worked, and I was able to select the best, most loyal and productive team. We worked like clockwork together.

Of course, there was a bit more to how I picked the passengers for my particular bus. Molly was the only one who knew about my visions and the ability to channel the future, and helped me sort through what I saw, creating my reality. I'd learned that my visions were more like metaphors. They weren't exact projections of the future, but had elements of it, subject to interpretation. And Molly helped me in interpreting them correctly. She also taught me not to be afraid of seeing things.

"Rodion, it's a gift. Truly. Use it for good, that's all I ask of you."

"Alright, Aunt Molly," I told her. I sometimes called her that, though more as a joke.

"Coach Molly. Please," she corrected me with a smile. "The key is how it makes you feel. If it's fear, you'll sink into negativity, and you know it won't end well. And if it's positivity, love, acceptance, you know you're on the right track."

"Sounds easy." I sighed.

"Being true to yourself should be easy," Molly noted. "I am proud of you, Rodion," she added, kind wrinkles forming around her eyes.

I descended the steps and saw a huge sign hanging over the door.

Happy Birthday, Rodion! it said. The sign was black and gold, The Lab's signature colors. We picked black and gold to honor the Pittsburgh sports tradition, to show the world where we came from. April was in charge of the design team, and I went along with whatever they did.

The rebranding happened right when we bought the mansion on Forbes Avenue.

It was a decision I didn't take lightly. Passing by this very space every day on my way to The Lab's original location in Hanover Hall, I remembered my first-ever vision and wondered why I'd seen the place in such detail. My question remained unanswered until one day, I saw the *For Sale* sign next to 5252 Forbes Avenue.

When I checked out the listing online, it was an exact match to what I'd seen in my vision, down to the layout, the entrance, even the white couches in the living room. The next day, April and I went to tour the property, accompanied by our real estate agent.

"Are you sure this is a good idea?" April kept asking on our way there. "To move The Lab into this space?"

"I just have a feeling about it. It's got everything going for it, the location, it's big enough, and we'll own the place," I repeated over and over again, while in my mind I ran through different scenarios of how this idea could fail miserably.

But in the end, it was April who insisted we buy the place. She fell in love with the property the second we stepped inside, and after that, I had no doubt we were making the right choice. We'd moved The Lab into the mansion on Forbes Avenue and it became our corporate headquarters.

"Happy Birthday, Rodion!" my team cheered, as I walked down the steps.

"Happy Birthday, Boss!"

"Happy Birthday! Happy Birthday to you!" they broke into a song.

I saw Chuck McPherson standing in the corner, smiling. Ever since passing on the management of The Lab to me, he'd been our advisor, appearing only once or twice a week. And then I noticed April. She stood in the middle, smiling, and right next to her was a cart with a cake. I knew right away what it was. The cake Mama used to bake me. My heart leaped.

"We ordered you a honey cake. The Russian recipe, just the way you like it," April whispered into my ear. "Happy Birthday. Make a wish."

And I did.

The End

Thank you for reading 'I, Rodion'. If you enjoyed it, I would love your honest review on Amazon and Goodreads. Why am I asking for reviews? For an indie author like myself, each review means I can get more books to other readers who enjoy stories written in the magical realism style. This is why every single review means a huge amount to me.

Thank you for your support. And above all, happy reading.

ABOUT THE AUTHOR

Alexandra Pugachevsky has always believed that magical elements exist in all aspects of our lives and reality is multi-dimensional. She writes in the magical realism genre.

Having immigrated to the United States in her teens, Alexandra fell in love with the city of Pittsburgh, and has retained that love until now. She can't help but write about the Steel City.

Alexandra Pugachevsky holds a BA in International Relations and French from the University of Pennsylvania and a Master's in Foreign Service from Georgetown University.

An international development professional by day, Alexandra has made the Washington, DC Metropolitan area her home.

facebook.com/sashkina.author

instagram.com/sashkina_author

bookbub.com/authors/alexandra-pugachevsky

youtube.com/@sashkina

amazon.com/author/sashkina

EXCLUSIVE FREE BOOKS

YOUR FREE BOOKS ARE WAITING...

If you'd like to stay in touch, Download exclusive free stories when you subscribe to the newsletter.

———

Connect with the author
Website: sashkina.com
Email: sasha@sashkina.com